Frustration grew inside him.

She looked exactly as he remembered from eleven years ago. A little older, perhaps more mature, but the essence of Jenny remained the same.

Dark blond hair fluttered around her shoulders. Her burgundy wool sweater hid her curves from view. But Chase could still feel the imprint of her breasts on his bare chest. The taste of her kiss lingered, as did the passion.

He'd spent eleven years hating Jenny Davidson. Did, in fact, still hate her.

And he'd gladly sell his soul to the devil for an hour in her bed.

Dear Reader,

Welcome to Silhouette **Special Edition** . . . welcome to romance. Each month Silhouette **Special Edition** publishes six novels with you in mind—stories of love and life, tales that you can identify with . . . as well as dream about.

This month has some wonderful stories for you—after all, March comes in like a lion and goes out like a lamb! And in Lisa Jackson's new series, MAVERICKS, we meet three men who just won't be tamed! This month, don't miss *He's Just a Cowboy* by Lisa Jackson.

THAT SPECIAL WOMAN!, Silhouette **Special Edition**'s new series that salutes women, has a wonderful book this month from Patricia Coughlin. *The Awakening* is the tender story of Sara Marie McAllister—and her awakening to love when she meets bounty hunter John Flynn. It takes a very special man to win That Special Woman! And handsome Flynn is up for the challenge!

Rounding out this month are books from other favorite writers: Elizabeth Bevarly, Susan Mallery, Trisha Alexander and Carole Halston!

I hope that you enjoy this book, and all the stories to come! Have a wonderful March!

Sincerely,

Tara Gavin
Senior Editor
Silhouette Books

SUSAN MALLERY

MORE THAN FRIENDS

Silhouette®

SPECIAL EDITION®

Published by Silhouette Books New York

America's Publisher of Contemporary Romance

To Jolie—for the Mole Ride and the hand-wringing, the endless conversations about *Star Trek: TNG* and plot points. My love and thanks.

SILHOUETTE BOOKS
300 East 42nd St., New York, N.Y. 10017

MORE THAN FRIENDS

Copyright © 1993 by Susan W. Macias

ISBN: 0-373-09802-2

First Silhouette Books printing March 1993

Printed in the U.S.A.

Books by Susan Mallery

Silhouette Special Edition

SUSAN MALLERY

has always been an incurable romantic. Growing up, she spent long hours weaving complicated fantasies about dashing heroes and witty heroines. She was shocked to discover not everyone carried around this sort of magical world. Taking a chance, she gave up a promising career in accounting to devote herself to writing full-time. She lives in Southern California with her husband—"the most wonderful man in the world. You can ask my critique group." Susan also writes historical romances under the name Susan Macias.

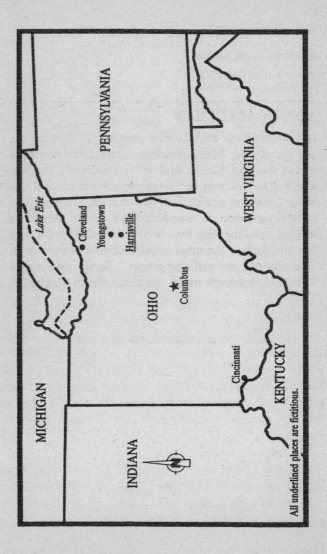

MICHIGAN

INDIANA

Lake Erie

• Cleveland
Youngstown • •
Harrisville

OHIO

★ Columbus

PENNSYLVANIA

WEST VIRGINIA

• Cincinnati

KENTUCKY

All underlined places are fictitious.

Prologue

"I think we should start seeing other people."

The words smashed into Chase Jackson like a blow from a steel rod. Air rushed from his lungs and an aching cold crept down his spine. But he didn't turn around.

Instead, he reached down and picked up a pebble. Running his fingers over the smooth surface, he forced his tense muscles to relax. He tossed the stone with a quick flick of his wrist and watched it skip twice across the sluggish, muddy river before it sank out of sight. Only then, when he was sure none of the pain would show, did he step back and face her.

"Is there someone else?"

The slight tremor at the end of the sentence was the only hint of his turmoil. His father would be proud of his control, he thought grimly. Not that they'd ever discuss this conversation. The elder Jackson didn't approve of his relationship with Jenny Davidson, but then neither did her family. Or the entire town for that matter.

"Well?" he asked. "Is there?"

"No."

She sat in the shade of a willow tree, her back pressed against the trunk. Long legs, slender and tan, were pulled up close to her chest. Was the action for protection? Her arms clasped her knees tighter to her body, her hands squeezing so hard he could see the white knuckles and taut tendons. But she never once raised her eyes to his. Fluffy blond curls hid her face from view.

He wanted to go to her and force her to take back what she'd said, demand that she make the horrible knot in his belly disappear, but something warned him his world would never be the same again.

"Then why, Jenny? What happened? Is your father making you do this?"

"No." Her chin came up in a familiar pose of stubborn pride and he could see her eyes. Tears darkened the irises to forest green. Mascara collected beneath her lower lids. "This has nothing to do with him. I th-thought..." Her voice cracked. "I thought it would be better—with your going away to college and all. You don't need to be involved with someone like me." She hiccuped and the tears flowed in earnest.

In two strides he was beside her, holding her close, murmuring words of understanding. But he didn't understand. Damn it, what was going on here? He loved Jenny and she loved him. Or so he'd thought until two minutes ago.

Her body felt warm and willing in his grasp. The familiar scent of her skin and hair, the quickening of her breathing, the way she curled up all trusting in his embrace, reminded him that time was limited. He was leaving in a couple of weeks. They had agreed to wait for each other; perhaps the time for waiting was over. He brushed the tears from her face.

"Is it because you're scared?" he asked, shifting her until she was lying on the cool grass. His right hand stroked her side from ribs to hip, moving slowly over the soft cotton of her tank top and shorts, closer to the swell of her breast. A smile tugged at his lips. "I'm scared too, kiddo. But we can muddle through together. People have been making love for centuries. How difficult can it be?"

"Chase." She whispered his name like a prayer, and touched his cheek and the line of his jaw. "I love you more than anything. I'll love you forever. But I can't—I can't see you again."

"Why?"

"Don't ask me that. Just accept it. Go on without me. It'll be better. You can find somebody else at college. Somebody who fits in with who you are."

"Don't give me that crap." He sprang to his feet and began to pace in the clearing. "My dad owns the steel mill and yours runs the union. So what? It's been that way our whole lives. Why should it suddenly matter now?"

"It just does."

Jenny had also risen. She stood next to the tree, her arms crossed protectively over her chest.

He moved closer. She stiffened but didn't pull away.

"You've been acting strange for a while now," he said, recalling what he'd thought were unrelated incidents from the past few weeks. "You kept saying nothing was wrong, but I know there's something you aren't telling me."

There had to be. There was no way Jenny had suddenly stopped caring about him. The knot in his stomach doubled in size. Dear God, Jenny was all he had.

Their eyes met. For several seconds he held his breath and watched the battle rage within her. Fear and need competed with an emotion he couldn't identify, but might have been labeled shame. When he was sure she was finally about to tell him the truth, she turned away.

"I want..." She paused. "Please take me home."

It was over. Jenny had been his best friend since they were kids and suddenly she was a stranger. A stranger who didn't give a damn about passionate promises of love and forever. He didn't say a word. He just pulled the keys from his jeans pocket and walked down the path, Jenny following.

The ride was accomplished in silence. He wanted to ask her again to explain what had happened—what had gone wrong. He wanted to plead with her, to beg her to say she still cared.

Instead, he said nothing. The Jackson pride he hated in his father swelled within him. It straightened his shoulders and ensured his eyes stayed dry.

When they reached Hamilton Crossing, the border of Harrisville, Ohio, he slowed the car. Even looking straight ahead, he could see Jenny biting down on her lower lip. *Say something,* he demanded silently. *Tell me this is all a bad joke.*

The powerful Camaro rumbled impatiently; a plane flew overhead.

Drawing in a breath, he pressed hard on the accelerator and they shot forward. All too soon the rural roads gave way to houses and cars. Four streets past the second signal, he turned left, then right.

Blue-collar workers living in blue-collar homes. Some of the houses were freshly painted, others run-down. They were small; well, smaller than the three-story mausoleum he lived in.

Chase and Jenny had never understood the fuss everybody made about their relationship. But now, with Jenny so withdrawn beside him, he saw the neighborhood with clearer vision. Men stopped working in their yards to watch him drive by. Children paused at play, and lace curtains were pulled away from kitchen windows.

The town hated him, almost as much as it hated his father. The people resented their dependence on Jackson Steel. The animosity hadn't bothered him before. He and Jenny had planned to leave—to start over and do something with their lives, something other than form endless sheets of steel.

Now all that had changed. He was going away to college and Jenny... Jenny wasn't going to wait.

He slowed the car, then pulled to a stop in front of a yellow clapboard house.

Fall was two weeks away, but old man Davidson was already hard at work, hanging storm shutters. When Chase cut the engine, Davidson paused in his task, then stopped altogether. After setting the shutter on the ground, he wiped his hands on his jeans and walked slowly toward the car.

Great, Chase thought as he stepped out and stood beside the hood. It wasn't enough that Jenny had dumped him. Now Davidson looked ready to take off the first two layers of his hide. Not that they'd ever gotten along. The mill owner's son and the president of the local union weren't likely to have a whole hell of a lot in common. Except Jenny.

"Afternoon, Mr. Davidson."

Davidson ignored him. He jerked open the passenger door. "Go inside, Jenny. Your mother's waiting for you."

"Daddy." She got out and touched his arm. "Are you all right?"

He offered her a slight smile that didn't reach his eyes. "Go inside," he repeated.

She paused, then looked at Chase. Emotions skittered across her face. "I love you. I'll always love you. I know it doesn't seem that way now—" She reached out her hand toward him but the car stood between them.

He took a step forward. She shook her head to stop him.

"I'll never forget you, Chase Jackson," she said, then turned and ran into the house.

He watched her go and sensed more than saw the older man move closer. Davidson wasn't tall, but he was beefy. The barrel chest strained the buttons of his red plaid flannel shirt. Well-worn jeans hung low on his hips, cradling the overhang of his beer belly. He might not be pretty, but he was fast and mean.

When Jenny's father stepped off the curb and onto the street, Chase fought the urge to back up.

"Is there a problem?" he asked, managing to keep the apprehension from his voice.

"You bet there is." The neutral tone of voice had given way to raw anger. Davidson kept coming, then stopped when he was less than a foot away. "You think because you're some rich brat you can just take what you want? I've got news for you, sonny. There are laws against people like you." The older man's blue eyes were cold and threatening. "And if the law won't help me, I've got lots of friends to make sure you pay."

Chase swallowed. "Mr. Davidson, I don't understand what..."

"See if you understand this, boy."

Without warning, he threw a fast right hook. Chase started to duck, but the heavy fist crashed into his cheek and jaw. It was like running face first into a stone wall.

Everything dimmed, and he slumped against the car. In the distance he could hear Davidson's harsh breathing and muttered curses. Blood dripped from Chase's nose and down the back of his throat.

Shaking his head to clear his vision, he pressed against the hood and straightened. Red-hot pain throbbed in time with his heartbeat. He probed his rapidly swelling cheek. He could taste blood. Three teeth were loose and his nose felt broken.

"I'd kill you if I could," Davidson said as he flexed his bruised knuckles. "But with the local judge being a good friend of your father's..." Hatred clouded his eyes and hardened his expression. "Remember what I said about my friends. If any of us see you around here again, you'll regret it. You hear that, boy? I've got my shotgun primed and ready."

Chase wiped his face with the back of his sleeve. "I got it, all right." He opened the front door of his car, then hesitated. "But you mind telling me what you think I did?"

For a moment he thought the older man might make good on his threat to kill him. Rage mottled his skin and the veins in his neck and forehead bulged. "You cocky SOB" he growled. "She trusted you. I never liked you sniffing around my baby, but she claimed you were just friends. With friends like you, a man needs to be checking his back for a knife."

Chase shook his head again. The blow must have affected him more than he thought. "I don't..."

"You bastard! She's pregnant!"

Chase caught his breath in surprise, then groaned as pain shot through his jaw. But it was nothing compared with the tearing he felt inside. Pregnant? Jenny?

"Wait a minute," he ground out. "I never... That is, we didn't... Who—"

"You've got a helluva nerve asking who." Davidson moved closer. "Clear out—before I lose what's left of my temper."

Chase glanced at the house, but Jenny's bedroom window was empty. Slowly, fighting back the throbbing in his face and his gut, he stepped into the car and started the engine.

The water in the basin was bright red. Chase washed the rest of the blood from his cheeks and mouth, then pressed a towel against his nose. He could go to the family doctor, but then his father would find out. He'd rather patch himself up than have to answer any questions.

Jenny, why?

The bedroom door opened with a bang.

"This time you've gone too far."

Perfect, he thought, turning toward the man in the doorway and straightening up. News traveled fast in a small town.

"Davidson called you," he said as he tossed the towel on the counter and slipped off his shirt.

"Do you have any idea how it feels to get that sort of information about your own son?"

"No, sir." Chase stared directly in front of him while he spoke. The older man paced the room.

His father was six feet tall. Despite his fifty years, he stood straight, as though his spine were made of the steel produced in the mill on the other side of town. Dark hair streaked with white swept off his forehead. Eyes, once blue, had faded to an ice-cold gray.

"What were you thinking of?" he demanded. "Didn't you even stop to consider the fact that I'm heading into negotiations with the union? If you were going to knock up some tramp, did it have to be the union president's daughter?"

Chase dropped his bloodied shirt into the trash and pulled a fresh one out of the drawer. Everyone told him he was a perfect replica of his father, when the old man had been eighteen. But that was only on the outside. Inside, they weren't anything alike. For as long as he could remember, they'd fought. His only goal in life had been to make his father proud of him; his father's only goal had been to produce another Jackson to run the family business. They'd both failed miserably.

A trickle of blood began at the corner of his mouth, but Chase didn't bother to wipe it away. He hadn't known it was possible to hurt more, but he did. She'd betrayed him. "Did it ever occur to you that I'm not the one who got Jenny Davidson pregnant?"

His father sighed. "Haven't I taught you anything? A man faces the consequences of his actions." He stuck his hands into his pants pockets. "Davidson and I won't allow a marriage between you two. She'll go away until it's born and then a suitable home will be found for it. But you…" His father fixed him with a cold stare. "You won't be going to college this year. You'll stay right here, working at the mill. Your paycheck will help defray the cost of Jenny's expenses. Next September, you'll leave for university, having, I hope, learned your lesson."

Long after his father had left the room, Chase stared at the closed door. Silence filled the house. If his mother were still alive… But she wasn't. It was him and the old man.

He didn't even have Jenny anymore. If he ever had. The girl he knew would never have betrayed him this way.

Nobody listened, he thought as he paced the room. He could explain for the next fifty years, but no one would listen and no one would believe him. Only Jenny knew the truth and she sure as hell wasn't telling it.

He stopped in front of the picture on his nightstand. Green eyes gazed into his as laughter teased her lips. See other people. Yeah, right. Only she'd started months ago. No wonder she'd been acting strange these past few weeks. He'd been a fool. Worse. He'd been had.

"Why did you tell them it was mine?" he whispered to the picture. "Why did you lie?"

All these years he'd been treating her like some princess and she'd been fooling around with some other guy. He picked up the picture and stared at it a moment, then threw it across the room. The glass in the frame shattered and fell to the ground.

Chase brushed his sleeve across his eyes. He was eighteen—too damn old to cry. He walked to the closet. At the bottom was a duffel bag. In a matter of minutes, he'd shoved some clothes into the bag and tied it shut. The only personal item he took was a snapshot of his mother.

It was almost dark when he tossed the bag into the trunk of his car. There was three hundred dollars in his pocket, taken from the household emergency fund. He figured his stereo and TV, paid for out of his summer earnings at the mill, would make the exchange even. Without looking back, he shifted into first gear and moved down the driveway.

By the time he hit the interstate, the aspirin he'd taken earlier was beginning to ease the throbbing in his face. As he joined the westbound traffic, he realized his father had never asked about his injuries or offered to get the doctor to take a look.

The hell with 'em, he thought as he flipped on his headlights. There was nothing for him in Harrisville. He'd never come back. Not until Jenny was gone and the old man was dead.

The fullness and joy of a theater have not been experienced. In this way, even for and to Harrisville. His wife killed himself don't stop stop and has he or was dead.

Chapter One

"Plane arrives at five. Stop. Don't bother to meet me. Stop. I'll rent a car and drive to the mill. Stop."

Jenny Davidson read the telegram for the hundredth time. The message didn't get any longer or more personal. It had been eleven years since Chase Jackson had driven out of Harrisville and out of her life. Eleven years of silence. Eleven years of wondering if he'd ever return.

He hadn't. In the end, she'd been forced to call him home.

She folded the piece of paper and tucked it in the corner of her desk blotter, then picked up a pencil and stared at the report in front of her. The quarterly tax returns were due. She had to review the forms, verify the figures and write out the checks. The task was as familiar as making her bed. So why did the numbers dance unintelligibly before her eyes? Damn. He still got to her.

Jenny tossed her pencil on the desk and leaned back in her chair. The office was quiet. The clerical staff left at four-thirty and it was already after six. In the distance, she could hear the rumble of the steel mill.

If she turned and looked out the window behind her, she'd see the main building of Jackson Steel lit up like a Christmas tree. The great cavernous structure, where iron ore was turned into endless sheets and pipes of steel, hissed and smoked with a life of its own. The late shift would be breaking for lunch in the next couple of hours. The sounds of the workers calling to one another would drift up into her office. But she'd be long gone. The trip from the airport to the mill was about an hour. Adding the time for Chase to grab his luggage and rent a car, he was due soon. She'd tell him what he needed to know, then send him on his way. He was her boss's son, nothing more.

Right, Jenny thought, pulling open the bottom drawer of her desk and dragging out her purse. *And I'm the Queen of England.*

A few quick strokes of a brush brought her shoulder-length hair into order. She reached for a tube of lipstick, then hesitated. She didn't want him to think his return concerned her in any way.

Get a life, Jenny, she told herself silently. The man had come back because his father was sick in the hospital. If Chase had ever cared about her, he wouldn't have disappeared without a word all those years ago.

Swearing softly, she opened her compact and applied the lipstick. Who cared whether or not he thought she'd gone to any trouble? With Chase Jackson back in town, she was going to need all the confidence she could get. The soft pink color slid smoothly over her trembling mouth. She was as nervous as a cat in a room full of rocking chairs.

After stuffing her purse back into the drawer, she picked up her pencil and pretended to work. The tick of the wall clock sounded overly loud in the still room.

Was he close? Had he passed Hamilton Crossing? Was his car pulling into the parking lot yet? What would he look like? Had he changed? Would she know him? Did he ever think of her... remember what they'd had... what they'd lost? Did he still blame her for something that had never been her fault?

"This is silly."

The sound of her voice startled her and she jumped in her seat. Jenny shook her head, then rose from her chair and walked over to the metal table against the far wall. A half-full coffeepot hissed slightly as she raised the glass container and poured the steaming liquid into her mug.

By conventional standards, her office wasn't large, but it suited her needs. She'd been offered something bigger when she'd been promoted to head bookkeeper, but had turned down the corner space. There was no point in having all that extra room, she thought as she stirred in a package of sweetener. She worked in a steel mill. Nobody got carpeting or drapes. They'd be destroyed in no time. The furniture was functional pressboard and metal, soot covered the windows. The concrete floors were washed down twice a week, the walls painted yearly.

She glanced down at her jeans and button-up shirt. Not exactly cover material for *Working Woman* magazine. But she couldn't wear silk and panty hose into the mill.

The sound of heavy feet in the hallway broke into her thoughts. Before her heart had a chance to leap into her throat, she recognized the even tread. She set her cup on the desk, then filled a second mug, adding a generous teaspoon of creamer and three lumps of sugar. As the large man entered her office, she held out the drink.

"Hi, Daddy. No. Chase isn't here yet."

The elder Davidson grunted, then took a long swallow of coffee. He grimaced. "See you're still using those fancy beans. Coffee out of a can's been good enough for me all my life."

"Yeah, yeah. Sell it somewhere else. If you didn't secretly like my coffee, you wouldn't make so many trips up here to drink it." She stepped back and perched on the corner of her desk.

"I don't know what you're talking about. Just checking up on my little girl." Frank Davidson winked, then walked to the window and stared out into the darkness. "There's talk of laying off half the shift."

"There's always talk. It doesn't mean anything."

"If the old man dies, it'll be more than talk."

Her father spoke without turning around, but she could hear the tension in his voice, see it in the stiffness of his shoulders and back.

All her life, she'd thought of her father as invincible. Hard, yes, but fair, and always there for his family and the union. But now... She glanced at the gray stealing the brown from his hair. He was almost sixty. Thanks to her mother's insistence that he start taking care of himself, the beer belly was almost gone, but new lines aged his face. Old man Jackson was only a few years older than her dad.

"When was the last time you went to the doctor?" she asked, her voice a tad sharper than she would have liked.

"Last month." He turned slowly and grinned. A familiar twinkle in his deep blue eyes chased away her fears. "I'm healthy as a horse and still strong enough to give my girls the whippings they need to stay in line."

"I'm really scared." Considering all four Davidson girls had been daredevils, the number of whippings throughout the years had been surprisingly low. She could only remember one she'd received. The circumstances weren't clear, but they'd had something to do with a badly hit softball and the big window in the front of the house. It hadn't even been her fault, she remembered. Chase had thrown it too hard and...

Chase. She sighed.

"That boy's always been trouble," her father said, reading her mind. "He's not even back and you're mooning over him like a lovesick puppy."

"Who's mooning? I was just thinking about..."

Her father stepped next to her and touched her face. "He's not right for you, Jenny. Never was. Our kind and his don't mix."

"Oh, Daddy. It's the nineties. Don't you think the whole class issue is a little outdated? Anyway, he doesn't own the mill."

"His father does. Same thing. You mark my words. Stay clear of that Jackson boy or he'll break your heart." He set his mug on her desk and kissed her cheek. "I couldn't bear to see that happen a second time." When he reached the doorway, he turned back. "Your mother's expecting you for dinner Sunday."

She rolled her eyes. "Yes, Daddy. I do remember some things, even without your prompting me."

"You're not too big—"

"To spank. So you keep threatening. Get out of here or you'll have to explain why *you're* late for dinner."

When the sound of his footsteps had faded, Jenny glanced at the clock. Chase was getting closer. She could feel it. The once-familiar room seemed to close in on her. Damn you, Chase Jackson. It had been eleven years. Why did he still have the power to affect her?

* * *

Chase eased the Bronco into neutral and let it slow to a stop. Up ahead was Hamilton Crossing. He was almost home.

No, he told himself firmly. Home was a ranch-style house on the outskirts of Phoenix. Home was an acre of desert with the ground still warm at midnight. Home was a perfect sunset against a mountain range—no smoke, no ash, no smell of steel. Harrisville wasn't home; it was the place he'd left behind a long time ago.

He rolled down the window and inhaled. The crisp night air carried with it the scent of autumn. In the darkness, he couldn't see the flaming colors of the changing leaves, but he could feel the promise of winter. Sometimes he missed the snow, but that was all. Nothing else in Harrisville called to him . . . ever. Except maybe Jenny.

Damn! He'd been back in town thirty seconds and already he was acting like some lovesick teenager. Hadn't he learned his lesson? Jenny Davidson had lied to him. She'd betrayed him, made a fool of him, then had him run out of town on a rail. He rubbed his jaw. No doubt she'd left years ago, taking her kid and the lucky father with her. He hated her and everything she stood for.

No. That wasn't true. He'd given up his hate a long time ago. Now he felt nothing. Nothing for any of them.

The sound of night creatures drifted to him. It was all returning, like a bad dream. He fought the urge to turn around and drive back to the airport—that wouldn't accomplish anything. The sooner he got to town, the sooner he could leave.

Shifting back into gear, he pressed his foot on the gas and eased onto the empty road. There wasn't much traffic at this end of town. The mill shifts would have already changed and no one else came this way.

He drove without thinking, slowing on the turns, accelerating on the straight patches until, without expecting it to be so short a trip, he pulled into the steel mill parking lot.

Nothing had changed. The screeches and groans as men forged steel from iron clamored around him. The air was heavy...hot. Up ahead, the mill itself loomed large in the black night. Artificial light illuminated the hungry mouth of the dragon. God, he hated this place. He didn't worry about dying. He'd been to hell and the devil lived inside a steel mill.

To the left of the mill, the two-story office building stood alone, like an abandoned child. Most of the offices were dark, but one, on the second floor, shone like a beacon. The telegram about his father had come from the mill office and the message had asked him to stop there on his way to the hospital. No doubt his father's secretary had stayed late to give him an update. Eleven years ago, Miss Barnes had been old and cranky. Seemed unlikely that time would have mellowed her spirit. Better not keep the lady waiting.

His long stride covered the ground from his car to the office building in four easy paces. The door opened silently. A light on the stairs beckoned.

The first step was easy, the second higher...harder...as though he were moving backward through time. Knowledge and wisdom and maturity dropped away, like winter layers on a sunny day, until he felt like a teenager again. He half expected to see his father's angry face, Jenny's laughing one.

Laughing. Yeah...laughing at *him*.

Long-suppressed memories crowded around, mocking his intent. "You can't go home again," Thomas Wolfe had claimed. Chase prayed he was right. There were a lot of places he wanted to be; none of them was Harrisville.

At the top of the stairs, he paused. Not to get his bearings, since there was only one room with a light, but to remind himself that he had changed. He didn't need anything or anyone from this town. He'd come back because they said his old man was dying.

His boots echoed down the long hall. How many times had he made this exact journey? A hundred? A thousand? There had been all the summers he'd worked in the mill, and before that, when his father had brought him to spend afternoons in his office. It should have seemed like another lifetime. It seemed like yesterday.

A scuffling noise caught his attention and he paused.

"Dad? Did you forget something? Do you want me to call Mom and tell her that . . ." A woman stepped into the hall and froze. "Chase?"

It couldn't be!

He'd been prepared for every ghost but one. Jenny. The bitter rage he'd nurtured, fought against and finally conquered, returned to engulf him. He wanted to hurt her the way he'd been hurt, lie as he'd been lied to, make her feel the gaping hole he'd carried inside for so long.

She stood so still, so silent. He wondered if he'd conjured her from some dark pocket of his soul. Moving closer, he reached out his hand, hoping that by touching her, he could make her disappear. But instead of nothingness, his fingers felt the warm smoothness of her cheek. Wide green eyes, the color of early spring grass, searched his face.

She was older; he could see it in the wariness of her expression. They'd grown up. And apart. There was a time when his touch would have caused her to step closer, to offer a hug and a smile. A promise. Now, she slid away; his arm dropped to his side. No doubt she felt guilty.

"I see you made it," she said, tucking her hands into the front pockets of her jeans.

"Yeah." Her heart-shaped face had lost the pudginess of youth, but none of the beauty. "I didn't expect to see you here. Miss Barnes . . ."

"Miss Barnes retired four years ago. Time has a way of changing things. Even in Harrisville. Why don't you come in and sit down for a moment?"

Nothing made any sense. He felt like a salmon swimming upstream. The anger was fading fast. He tried to hold on, to remember her betrayal, but he became lost in the reality of seeing Jenny again.

He didn't remember her voice being that calm or competent. Nor did he recall full breasts pushing against her shirt, or hips flaring out in her jeans. As she turned to lead the way, his eyes dropped to the gentle curve of her behind. Womanhood suited her.

He stepped across the threshold and into another world. Familiar blue purchase orders sat in a neat pile on her desk. Tax forms covered most of the remaining space. An old wooden chair was pushed back against the wall as though she'd risen in a hurry. Even the coffeepot was in the same place, on the same table. The only incongruity was the modern-looking computer on a stand by the far wall.

"This is your office?" he asked from his place by the door.

"Yes. I inherited it when Mr. Peters took a job in Pittsburgh. I've been the head bookkeeper about two years now."

"Wilson still the controller?"

"Of course."

She poured a cup of coffee and handed him the clean, unchipped mug. He stared at the black liquid, then at her.

She looked confused. "You didn't want anything in it, did you? I mean..."

"It's fine. I still take my coffee black."

As she walked to her own chair, she motioned for him to sit in the one across from her desk.

"How was your flight?" she asked politely.

He shrugged as she sat down. "Uneventful." The scent of her perfume whispered to him. The unfamiliar fragrance was mature, more sophisticated, seductive somehow. He wasn't sure he liked it.

"Great." Her gaze rested on him for a moment, then moved away. "It's been a long time."

"Yes. Your hair's different."

She touched the shoulder-length locks. The light blond had deepened to the color of gold, providing a more dramatic frame to her fragile beauty. "It got darker."

"I noticed."

She smiled tightly and sipped her coffee. Every movement was studied, as though she was nervous, too.

The past—the lie—vibrated between them. It loomed like a great beast they ignored with mundane greetings and falsely casual conversation. He wanted to ask her why, but that would mean it still mattered. It was old news, he reminded himself.

While part of him remembered every curve of her body, every laugh, every word, the rest of him watched from a safe distance. He mentally probed his heart and soul, checking the thickness of the scars.

Nothing. He felt nothing for her and the past. It had been over between them for a long time.

"How's my father?" he asked finally, acknowledging the reason for his visit.

He watched as discomfort gave way to sympathy. She leaned forward, lacing her fingers together. "Not well. The first heart attack was about four days ago. It was over the weekend, so I didn't find out right away. I sent the message as soon as I was told."

"You sent the telegram?"

She nodded.

"You didn't sign your name."

"I know." Her shoulders hunched down. "I was afraid you wouldn't come if you knew I was still here."

He started to ask why, then put the question on hold. It would be easy to get lost in the past with Jenny Davidson, but that wasn't why he was here. Besides, it wasn't as if their story had had a happy ending. He could taste the bitterness. So much for wounds that healed. He took a sip of coffee. "You said *first* heart attack. Was there a second?"

"Yesterday. It was—" she held his gaze, her green eyes offering him comfort "—much worse. I'm sorry, Chase. The doctors, well, you need to speak with them."

"They make their rounds in the morning?"

"Yes. Visiting hours are limited. I called the hospital a few minutes before you arrived. Your father just had a couple of tests and he's pretty out of it. They said you could see him in an hour or so."

"I got the first flight out I could."

He knew his voice sounded defensive and he wondered who he was trying to convince. After eleven years, it was going to take a lot more than one bedside visit to make up for lost time. Besides, the separation had been two ways. Twice a year he'd mailed his father a note, telling the old man he was fine. Not once had there been a reply.

"No one questions your loyalty," she said.

"Maybe I question it." He mumbled the words under his breath, not sure if she'd heard and wasn't really concerned one way or the other. "You think there's someone on the hospital staff I can talk to tonight?"

"The nurses are all very helpful. They might be able to answer some of your questions."

"He's at Harrisville General?"

"In Cardiac Care."

"How long until he's out of danger?"

"They've warned us there are two critical stages. Three and ten days. If he makes it past a week, he has a chance of pulling through."

"But they don't expect him to last a week?"

"I'm not sure." She ducked her head and the soft hair fell like a curtain, hiding her face from view. "I wish I had better news."

Not likely. He'd spoken to a doctor in Phoenix before he left and wasn't surprised at the prognosis.

Chase stood up and crossed the small room to the window. In the darkness, the glass reflected his own image and a distorted mirroring of the room behind him. He saw Jenny twist in her seat to study him. What was she thinking as she bit down on her bottom lip? Years ago the gesture had signaled worry, apprehension or the fact that she hadn't studied for her algebra test. Yet that girl had grown up. What was the woman like? Did she still tell lies? Were they just as believable, told now with sophistication instead of innocence?

"I've been to see him," she said softly.

"And?"

"They keep him sedated most of the time. I'm not sure he knew I was there."

Chase shrugged. "I gave up being angry at my father about four years ago. I finally realized it didn't accomplish anything. I always meant to come back." One hand clenched the window frame. "Never occurred to me it would be too late."

"It's not." She was at his side in a heartbeat. "The doctors are hopeful."

"It doesn't sound hopeful."

"I'm sorry." She glanced down. "Doctors don't know everything."

She placed her hand on his arm. The contact, brief, almost impersonal, seared through the cotton of his shirt, like liquid steel. The reaction startled him as much with its presence as with its intensity. He could feel himself weakening, forgetting the past and . . .

He turned so they were facing each other and took her hands in his, palm to palm, his thumbs rubbing her knuckles. Long, delicate fingers ended in short, straight nails. No red polish, no smooth, perfect skin. No rings. These were hands that worked for a living.

He glanced at her face, but she was staring at their joined flesh. Did she feel it, too? The connection? Had it lasted all this time? He'd come home to see his old man and lay some ghosts to rest. He'd never expected to find her here. He'd spent eleven years hating Jenny Davidson. There was no room for anything else in his life now.

Slowly, his thumbs found and traced old scars. There was a thin line on her right middle finger, a token from a run-in with a school yard fence. Turning her hands over, he studied the calluses from her gardening trowel, the bump from constantly writing with a mechanical pencil, the three thin burn scars that matched the ones on his hands. They'd learned together that newly rolled sheets of steel needed more than a few minutes to cool.

Her life-line stretched unbroken across her palm. Years before at a carnival, they'd had a reading done. The old crone, in her badly fitting wig and voluminous scarlet robes, had promised abundant love and good fortune. At the time, they'd assumed she'd meant with each other. No! *He'd* assumed. That had been the summer Jenny had betrayed him.

She stood close enough for him to see the faint shadow cast by her lashes. The freckles still skittered across her nose. There had been seventeen, years ago. Probably still were.

He curled his hands around hers and squeezed. She accepted the pressure, returning it, making it her own. No one else had known him as well as Jenny. Not his family nor his friends, nor the women who had shared his life. And what had she done with that knowledge?

"I've missed you, Chase," she said, without looking up.

"I bet you have." He released her hands and stepped back. "Must have been tough to find someone else so willing to play the fool."

She winced, as if he'd physically slapped her. Good. Now she knew what it felt like to be pushed away.

"Chase, I didn't—" She nodded. "Okay. I get it. Have it your way. Here." She opened her top desk drawer and pulled out an envelope. "I wasn't sure if you still had the keys to the big house. There's a set inside, along with the cardiologist's business card, and my home number." Handing him the package, she cleared her throat. "Not that you'd call, but just in case."

He took the envelope and stuffed it into his back pocket. "You're right. I won't. Wouldn't want to upset your old man."

"Old man?" She frowned. "I don't live at home."

He felt like smiling for the first time since he'd received the telegram. "I meant your husband."

"I'm not married." She closed the drawer and sat in her chair. "I live by the high school. A little red house on the corner. You can't miss it. I've enclosed the address, too, in case..." She shook her head. "Never mind. It seemed like a good idea at the time."

"Thanks. I guess I'll head over to the hospital."

"I should get home, as well. I've got some things to take care of." She looked up and offered a slight smile.

He recognized the hurt in her green eyes. The knot in his gut tightened. She was getting to him again, and there wasn't a thing he could do about it. Why, after all this time, did she still have the power? Why couldn't he keep focused on what she'd done to him?

To top it all off, she hadn't said a word. Not one damn word. He scanned her desk, but didn't see a picture there. Nor were there any on the bare walls. No photos or proudly displayed sketches made by a—he did some quick figuring—ten-year-old child. Did she think he'd forgotten?

She turned off the coffeepot and walked to the doorway. "Ready to go?"

"Sure." He followed her down the hall and stairs, to the entrance of the office building. After she'd secured the lock, they moved toward her car. The gravel crunched under their steps. His rented four-wheel truck looked new and large compared with her five-year-old compact.

Jenny opened the door and tossed her purse onto the front seat. "I hope your dad's awake enough to talk to you," she said.

There was something familiar about the way she leaned against her car and looked up at him. How many nights had been spent like this, wanting to stay, yet having to leave? When they'd been younger, the time had been filled with last-minute whispers, as though the excitement of their conversation couldn't possibly keep until morning. Later, it had been digs and laughs about boys and girls and dating and school. Those last few months, the precious minutes had consisted of awkward, avoided glances and tender kisses that had flared into a passion so all-encompassing, it frightened them into their goodbyes several minutes before her curfew.

But only once before had he stood beside Jenny Davidson and felt the cold twist of anger clawing at his gut.

"That's it?" he asked, finally. A better man than he would have let it go. But if he had been a better man, he wouldn't have spent his life disappointing his father.

"I don't understand." Her fingers, pale in the faint light, clutched the frame of her car door. "Do you need something else?"

"Don't you think I deserve to know how my kid's doing?"

Chapter Two

Jenny took a deep breath and let it out slowly. Part of her had hoped Chase wouldn't bring up the baby, at least not so soon. There were other things she wanted to discuss instead. But, looking at the situation from his point of view, she couldn't blame him for asking. After all, her father had threatened him with God knows what and practically forced him out of town.

Still, would a reprieve have been so bad? Memories from those days flashed into her mind. Despite the years that had drifted by, the past still had the power to upset her. She'd only ever really lied to Chase once. It had been one time too many.

She slammed the door shut, then turned her back to the car. After placing her hands on the cool metal, she pushed until she was sitting on the hood, then wiggled to get comfy. "You might want to join me," she said, patting the space beside her.

"I'll stand." With that, he folded his arms across his chest.

Hadn't someone once said that confession was good for the soul? Jenny had the feeling that instead of feeling better, her admission was going to make her feel like living slime. The urge to walk around the truth was strong, but that wasn't her style. She'd just say it and let Chase react as he would. Not the whole truth, she conceded to herself. There were some things better left unsaid. Not secrets, just details that were irrelevant now and would only cloud his view of the picture.

He was already angry; she could feel it threatening them both. More important, he was hurt. For eleven years she'd missed him, longed for him, imagined their joyful reconciliation. He'd spent the same time despising her. Even so, she wouldn't add to his pain. That would be her gift, however unappreciated.

"I never told anyone you were the father."

"Oh?"

Chase stood less than three feet away. When he shifted his stance, she heard the crunch of the gravel underfoot. Funny how with all the noise from the mill she could tune in to the little things. Like the sound of his carefully controlled breathing. So much had stayed the same, she thought. The proud tilt of his head, the chin raised defiantly, just as she remembered. The way he balanced his weight evenly on both feet, almost like a sailor. More than anything, Chase had disliked being caught off guard.

"I guess your father accused me out of habit." He took a step closer, then stared up at the stars.

He sounded so bitter. Not that she blamed him. Still, she had held on to the thread of hope that he would guess what had really happened and come back for her. A foolish idea, her support group would have told her. Just because you love someone, it doesn't mean he can read your mind.

"At first, I refused to say who I'd, ah, been with," she said, surprised it was still difficult to tell the story. She should have been over it by now. "I was humiliated by the whole thing. I was afraid of your finding out. Of word getting around town and my being labeled a tramp. Dad assumed I was protecting you. Before I gathered the courage to tell the truth, you'd left town."

Chase cursed softly. The succinct word made her flinch. Not that she hadn't heard it before. One couldn't work at a steel mill for nine years without hearing colorful language, but the pain in his voice came from the heart.

"I'm sorry," she whispered. "I never meant for any of this to happen."

"You should have thought about that before you slept with the guy. My God, you were seventeen years old. We were kids."

"You sound angry."

"Of course I'm angry. I thought we were waiting for each other. Dammit, Jenny, you betrayed me."

She would have sold her soul to be able to see the expression on his face. But the darkness that hid her blush from his probing eyes also concealed his pain. Only his words hinted at the echoes of a young man's anguish.

"I never meant to." Guilt flashed briefly, but she pushed it away. It wasn't her fault. It had never been her fault. In a way, they'd both been betrayed.

He exhaled slowly. "Who was this guy? Kevin Denny? Was it Kevin?"

"It wasn't Kevin." She sighed. "It was...nobody."

"A virile nobody." He took the last step to the car and leaned against the front fender. "Not that it matters, but

I wish you'd told me. We were best friends, until that last day."

His voice. She could handle the other changes. He'd grown tall, filled out in the chest and shoulders. Hard muscles rippled with each movement of his tall, lean body. In the dim light, he looked like a statue brought to life. She'd expected the boy to turn into a man, but in her mind, she'd assumed he would sound the same.

She'd been wrong. The deep tones had mellowed. It was like comparing iron ore to finely tempered steel. Both were strong, but the former rusted and crumbled away. The latter, forged by fire, lingered, supported, glowed in the light. It could be molded and bent, but never broken. His words surrounded her, gave her hope, raised her spirits, opened doors to a past she'd long thought lost. He would survive this encounter, she thought, reaching a hand out toward his arm. He was the steel, she the iron ore. When he was gone, she would crumble away. She dropped her hand to her lap.

"The guy skipped out on you?"

"In a manner of speaking."

"I can't say you didn't get what was coming."

The verbal blow landed squarely on her stomach. Air rushed from her lungs and left her gasping.

"I don't deserve that."

"Really? I'd say you deserve a hell of a lot more." Chase paced in front of the car. "When I left that day—" He spun to face her. "I believed in you. Trusted everything you said. You *lied*. My father expected me to give up college and support you. And I hadn't even had the pleasure of screwing the lovely Jenny Davidson."

Anger flashed. She started to slide down from the hood. "I'm leaving."

"No!" His hand clamped on her arm and held her in place. "Not until you tell me why."

Even after all this time, the memory of what had really happened was difficult to deal with. Telling the tale would bring it all back. The smell of whiskey, the tearing of her dress, the tears of shame. Her first time hadn't been like she'd thought it would be, but then her first time hadn't been with Chase. She shook off the feelings and concentrated on the facts.

"Do you remember the carnival?" she asked. "Not the high school one we have every fall, but the big one that comes through town in July?"

"What does that have to do with anything?"

She touched his hand; he instantly released her. "Everything. Do you remember?"

"Of course." He glanced at her. "How could I forget? It was my first hangover. I believe I have you to thank for that."

She smiled sadly, remembering their innocence. How easily it had been stolen from them. "You're right. We were both bored. It was hot and humid and the pool was closed for a few days." The past drifted back, overlapping the present until she forgot to be afraid.

"You dared me to steal liquor from my father's study," he said.

"Only you would take Napoleon brandy."

"I always treated you to the best. God, I was a fool."

With a fluid motion that threatened to take her breath away, he settled onto the hood beside her. Their shoulders brushed. The feeling was so familiar, it was all she could do to keep from throwing herself into his arms. But Chase hadn't come back to see her. He'd never called or written. He only remembered the end—when he thought she'd betrayed him. Now he was determined to punish her for her crimes.

"After we polished off the bottle, you passed out," she said.

He shook his head. "All I remember is waking up in the middle of the parking lot and feeling like a thousand mill workers were hammering inside my head."

"Being a lady, I was much more genteel in my imbibing."

"Genteel, my ass. If memory serves, you liked acting big and carrying around a drink, but the taste made you gag."

"That, too." Her smile faded. "There I was with a curfew but no ride home. You had the Camaro, and I couldn't drive a stick shift. I tried calling the house and asking one of my sisters to pick me up, but Dad answered the phone. No way I could have told him what had happened. I started walking home. About a mile down the road, one of the carny workers picked me up."

"The blond guy with the mustache?"

"How'd you know?"

Chase frowned. "You'd been flirting with him all week. I was jealous as hell." His tone was reluctant, as if he regretted admitting the weakness.

Jenny bit her lower lip. "I think that was why I did it. Testing budding female wiles and all that. Stupid really. He drove me home, but I didn't get out of the car right away and . . ." She swallowed against the rising tide of the past. Stay strong, she told herself. It's over. "One thing led to another. I never meant to . . . well, you know. But it happened."

Could he see it was only half the truth? Would that even matter to him anymore?

"That's it?" he asked. "Some guy in the back seat of a car? I expected more of you, but then that's always been my problem."

He hadn't forgiven her. She'd known the risk she'd taken not saying anything all those years ago. She'd chosen to keep silent then. Nothing had changed. She was still choosing to keep silent, but this time it was for reasons of compassion rather than fear or shame. Perhaps when his father was better, she'd tell Chase the whole story. For now, she'd handle it the way she always had: one day at a time with the understanding that it had never been her fault.

"Why didn't you tell me?" he asked, his voice barely a whisper.

"I was ashamed."

"Instead, you let me run off."

"I didn't know you were leaving until long after you were gone. I tried to find you." She paused, remembering the long lonely days when there was no one to talk to but her family. When she'd been unable to look in the mirror without seeing the shame in her own eyes. "After a while I gave up trying. And then, it didn't seem to matter so much."

"And the baby?"

Even after eleven years, it still hurt to talk about her child. Mustering all her courage, she spoke with false casualness. "It's ironic. Just when I'd gotten used to the idea of being a mother, I lost my baby."

She slipped down to the ground. Tilting her watch toward the light by the mill, she squinted. "You'll be right on time to see your father at the hospital. The night nurses will have just come on duty, so you'll be able to get an update."

She wanted to say something else, redeem herself in his eyes. But it didn't matter anymore. She'd lost him the day she'd chosen to withhold the truth. All the wishing in the world wouldn't bring him back.

He started toward his truck. When he was about six paces away, he turned back. "Why did you think I wouldn't answer the telegram if I'd known you'd sent it?"

As soon as she'd told him why she hadn't signed her name, she'd known this question was coming. Her mind had offered a dozen different responses, none of them the truth. The instinct to protect herself, to be flippant and worldly, was strong. But her affection for Chase, the memory of the love they'd once shared, was stronger. She opened her car door. "Because in all this time, you've never forgiven me. And you've never once tried to get in touch with me."

There. She'd said it.

"Jenny, I..."

She could feel his confusion. "It's okay, Chase. It was all over a long time ago. We've grown up. Go see your father."

Chase stepped into the vehicle, but waited until Jenny had pulled out before starting his engine. The taillights of her car provided twin beacons out of the parking lot. Slowly, he followed her toward Hamilton Crossing. At the boundary of Harrisville, she turned right.

He paused for several seconds. He could follow her home, force her to tell him the secrets he sensed behind her casual confession about the past, but the first order of business had to be his father. Only after he'd seen the old man, found out how long he'd be in the hospital, taken care of business, would he be able to think about Jenny Davidson.

Yet as he drove, her words came back to haunt him. The darkness of the night hid the pain in her face when she said he'd never tried to get in touch with her.

He reminded himself that, after what she'd done to him, she deserved whatever she had coming. But that didn't make him care any less. Damn. Despite the thousands of miles that had been between them, despite the years that had passed and the very separate lives they'd lived, the connection was as strong as ever. Since childhood, they'd shared thoughts and emotions, almost as if they were two halves of the same being. He'd never expected that to have remained intact. Jenny was right—if he'd known she'd still be here, he might not have returned at all.

Crossing the main street of Harrisville, he turned toward the hospital. She'd been right in not signing the telegram and he hadn't known it until this second. Damn her. Damn them both.

After parking, he walked up to the wide double doors of Harrisville General. Hunched against the invisible weight of obligation, he wondered how he would make it through the next few days. Nothing had changed with Jenny. He had a bad feeling that nothing had changed with his father, either. Why had he bothered coming back? This town had always resented him; he'd been a disappointment to the old man.

"Can I help you?" The young woman behind the information counter smiled.

"I'm looking for Cardiac Care. My father is a patient here."

"And he is?"

Chase's throat tightened and he realized how many years it had been since he'd spoken the name out loud. "Jackson. William Jackson."

The tall brunette's eyes widened and her gaze flickered over Chase's wrinkled shirt. "Oh. Mr. Jackson. Your father is on the second floor. He's been here for quite some time." The censure in her voice was unmistakable. He was sure he'd never met this woman, but in Harrisville, some things never changed. "Take that elevator up, then circle around it and go straight back. I think the doctor might still be in the building. I'll page and check."

"Thanks."

He walked to the elevator and pushed the call button. Around him, the bustle of workers provided a muffled din to an otherwise quiet atmosphere. He smelled the lingering scent of dinner almost buried under antiseptic.

The doors swished open, then shut as quietly when he pushed the button. What was he going to say? He'd walked out of his father's house and never looked back. Even though twice a year he'd sent tersely worded messages, there had been no answer in all that time.

His hands clenched at his sides. How much had his father changed? Would there be a woman, perhaps stepchildren, hovering at his bedside?

Chase exited on the second floor and headed for the Cardiac Care unit. Swinging double doors separated that section from the rest of the ward. There was an intercom on one side, with instructions to press the red button and speak to a nurse. He stared at the wall and thought about returning to his truck and driving until Harrisville was a lifetime away.

No. That was the easy way, the coward's way. What was it his father had always told him? A man faces the consequences of his actions. He pressed the button.

"Yes?" a disembodied voice asked.

"I'm here to see my father. William Jackson."

There was a pause, then, "Come in."

The doors pushed open easily. A half-dozen rooms stretched in a semicircle around a long nurses' station. He stood close to the exit, unsure which cubicle contained his father.

A petite nurse stepped from behind the counter. Her pale blue uniform confused him at first, but then he recognized the smile and flashing humor in her brown eyes. "Terry?"

She nodded. "It's been a long time, Chase. I was wondering if you'd come back."

There were probably only three people in the whole town who would be happy to see him. If Jenny was the first, then Terry counted as the second. He started to hold out his hand in greeting, but then he hesitated. The gesture was too formal. Before he and Jenny had realized they were more than friends, he and Terry had been an item. Jenny had been his first kiss—they'd taught each other that particular pleasure—but Terry had been his first girlfriend.

She solved his dilemma by stepping close and offering a hug. "How have you been? We missed you at the reunion last year. No one knew where to send the invitation."

He moved back and smiled when she pushed up her glasses in a familiar gesture. "It's a long way from here to Arizona," he said quietly. "I live outside of Phoenix."

She nodded. "I always knew you'd leave Harrisville behind. That's all you and Jenny talked about." She stopped talking suddenly and glanced up at him. Her mouth pulled into a straight line. "I'm sorry. I didn't mean to bring that up."

"Hey." He touched her chin. "It's okay. I've seen her at the mill. She's the one who sent for me."

Terry tucked her hands into the center pocket of her smock and nodded toward the second room from the end. "Your dad's in there. He's pretty sedated. There were some tests earlier and the medication helps him sleep. That's what he needs most, now. Rest and time.''

Chase studied her. "How bad is it?''

She shrugged, careful to keep her eyes averted. "Hard to say, exactly. The second heart attack... Gosh!" She swallowed and risked a glance. "You knew about that, didn't you?''

''Yes. Go on.''

"The second heart attack was much worse. We weren't sure he'd... But don't worry, Chase. Your father's a tough and determined man. There's every chance he'll pull through." Her voice was strong, but lacking conviction.

"Can I go in?" he asked.

"Sure.''

He walked toward the room, stopping when she touched his arm. "What?''

Her brown eyes studied him. "There's a lot of tubes and machines. It looks worse than it is. He probably won't wake up until tomorrow.''

"I want to see him.''

She nodded.

Chase walked past her and entered the room. Machines hovered over the bed, electronic guardians making sure his father remained in this world. He'd expected the array, but it was still shocking. To the left a metal stand supported an IV drip. A heart monitor screen showed the fragile beat with a fluctuating red line. To the right, a large beige machine, about half the size of a washer, fed tubes leading to his father's mouth.

''What is that?" he asked softly, pointing to the rectangular piece of equipment.

"The ventilator. It helps him breath. We should be able to take it out in a couple of days.''

Chase nodded, then frowned. "There's no sound.''

"I know. The new machines are very quiet. You can see his chest moving, though." She patted his shoulder. "I'll be at the station. Push the call button if you need anything."

"Thanks."

He wanted to ask her to stay with him, but knew there were other patients requiring her care. Besides, he had to face his father sooner or later. Ignoring the tightening in his chest, he forced himself to study the draped body on the bed.

Once-thick graying hair seemed to have thinned over the years. Individual strands lay limply over his scalp. His father's strong face retained the planes and hollows he saw in his own mirror every morning, but the skin itself was ashen. His eyes were closed, but Chase knew the irises would still be the color of steel. It was the only thing that had set them apart. His eyes were brown, like his mother's.

Lowering his gaze, he saw his father had lost weight. Arms, once strong and tan, had withered until the outline of the bones was clearly visible. Powerful hands had shrunk to claws, the tips of the fingers appeared faintly blue.

Despite his reading about heart attacks during his trip across country, despite Jenny's comments and Terry's warning, he felt as if the man on the bed was a stranger. It couldn't be *his* father. William Jackson wouldn't let his own body get away with this. He'd fight any illness, conquer it, stomp it into the ground.

Chase looked around and caught sight of a plastic chair in the corner. He carried it next to the bed and sat down.

"I'm here," he whispered. "It's Chase. Your son."

There was no response.

"Dad?"

Again silence.

Chase stared at the hand closest to him. He should touch his father—offer tangible comfort. They were family.

Sure, he thought bitterly. Warm and loving relatives. That was why his father had never bothered to write back, had never called. Who was he kidding? He was here out of obligation and when the obligation had been fulfilled, he'd leave.

Chase remembered the first couple of years on his own. Working summers at the mill hadn't prepared him for being eighteen and alone in a strange place. In his brief letters, he'd hinted at the fear and difficulty, hoping his father would unbend enough to call him home. The silence had hurt more than the accusations. In the end, he'd stopped caring and Harrisville had ceased to be home.

He leaned forward and picked up his father's hand. The skin felt clammy, like a wet fish. He held on loosely. "I came back," he said quietly. "I came back as soon as I heard."

The fingers he held moved slightly, as if in acknowlodg ment. "Yes," he said, a little louder. "You're going to get well. The mill needs you. You don't want the union running things, do you?" The hand went limp in his grasp, then slipped back to the bed.

"Dad?"

Chase wasn't sure how long he sat listening to the silence, watching the slow rise and fall of his father's chest. No doubt visits were limited, but Terry never asked him to leave. A few times, she tiptoed into the room to check the machines, then made notations on a chart. Minutes, or maybe hours later, she handed him a cup of coffee. He smiled his thanks.

He continued to watch over his father. Half-remembered times from the past crowded in on one another. He and the old man had never been close. Strangers living in the same house, sharing the same blood, the same name. Chase had wanted to be friends, but they were too alike to back down and give in and too different to see eye-to-eye. He'd wanted a regular dad—one he could play ball with, one who would teach him things: William Jackson had wanted a CEO-in-training. All that remained of the battles were empty memories and a sense of duty. Still, he'd never thought it would come to this. He'd always thought his father was made of steel, not flesh and blood. Steel didn't die.

After a while, the muscles in his neck and back stiffened. He rose to stretch. When he stepped out of the room, an attractive woman in a white coat walked toward him.

"You must be Chase Jackson," she said, holding out her hand. "I'm Barbara Martin, your father's cardiologist."

Chase shook her hand, impressed by her firm grip and competent smile. He glanced over at the clock above the nurses' station. It was after ten-thirty. "Pleased to meet you, Doctor. But isn't it a little late to be making rounds?"

She smiled. "I like to check on my patients before I head home. Usually I get here before this, but there were a couple of emergencies to take care of."

He studied her, taking in the sensible short hair and friendly expression. She wasn't from around here, and he relaxed slightly.

"Uh-oh," she said. "You're not going to make some statement about my being a woman, are you?"

"No." Chase felt his spirits lift. "I was going to say how young you look."

"In that case I won't stop you. And I certainly won't mention that I have a daughter who just graduated from high school. Let's have a seat."

She led him down the hall to an alcove off the nurses' station. A small desk filled the space, with a second chair on one side. "I'm sure you have a lot of questions," she said, sitting down and motioning for him to do the same. "Let me bring you up to date on his condition and then you can ask me what you'd like."

Quickly, she outlined his father's medical history and the severity of the heart attacks. "The second was what we would consider major. At this point, our main concern is to have him rest and regain his strength."

She paused expectantly. Chase wasn't sure what he was supposed to ask. Finally he blurted out the only question he could think of. "Is he going to die?"

Dr. Martin set her pen on the desk and laced her fingers together. "That really depends on your father. The fact that he's survived as long as he has is good news. Now we wait."

"For what?"

"For the chest pains to stop. For him to start breathing on his own."

"When do we know he's going to be okay?"

The question hung in the air. The doctor glanced at Chase, then away. "Let's just take it one day at a time. We're doing all we can." She offered a tight, sympathetic smile. "I wish I could say more."

"I understand." He rose with her and shook her hand. "You'll be back in the morning?"

"Yes. I make my rounds about eight thirty."

"I'll be here."

"Mr. Jackson—"

"Chase."

"Chase, you look tired. Why don't you get some rest? If you make it into the hospital for my rounds, great." She handed him her card. "If you don't, call my office and I'll give you the latest report. He's hung on this long, it's unlikely there will be any change in the next twenty-four hours."

He tucked the card into his wallet. "Thanks, Doc. I really appreciate your help."

"My pleasure. Hang in there." She walked over to the desk at the nurses' station and spoke briefly to Terry, then handed her the chart and left.

Terry joined him in the doorway of his father's room. "Are you staying?" she asked.

"I think I'll go home for a while, then come back in the morning."

"Okay. I've got the number at the house." Terry looked down. "If there's any change, I mean."

"Sure." He headed toward the double doors.

"Chase?"

He paused. "Yeah?"

"Are you going to be in town long?"

He tilted his head toward the private room. He wasn't here for old times' sake; he was here fulfilling his duty. "That all depends on him."

"I just wanted to say that Tom and I would love to see you, if you have time. Just for dinner or to talk." Her brown eyes filled with compassion.

He used his index finger to push up her glasses. "Tom? So you *did* marry the high school football captain."

"Of course," she said and smiled. "He was the second best-looking guy in school. And by senior year, the best-looking one only had eyes for Jenny Davidson. Oh!" She covered her mouth with her hand. "Sorry. I didn't mean to bring up bad memories."

"No problem. Jenny and I have made our peace." He gave her a quick kiss on the cheek, wondering if she could see through the lie. "I'll be back here tomorrow. Are you working then?"

"The night shift. Then I'm off for a couple of days, but I'll keep in touch."

"I'd like that. Bye." Chase glanced back at his father's room, then pushed through the double doors and out into the corridor.

Once outside, he stood breathing in the night air. The smells of the hospital seemed to linger on his clothes and he wanted nothing more than a hot shower and a clean bed. The keys to the house were tucked in the envelope Jenny had given him. At this hour, he could make the trip in less than ten minutes.

But it was fifteen minutes before he started the truck, and another fifteen of driving around aimlessly before he headed toward the big three-story structure at the end of Harrisville's small but elegant upperside. The ivy-covered gates stood open, but the dark house looked as unwelcoming as a haunted mansion.

He sat in his truck and looked around. Nothing had changed. The shrubs and hedges rose to the exact height he remembered. His father had always seen to it that an army of gardeners clipped away any signs of growth. Even the rosebushes flanking the path to the front door maintained their precise shape.

Pulling the envelope out of his jacket pocket, he fingered the keys inside, but didn't leave the truck. In his mind's eye, he could see the foyer, all black-and-white tiles and crystal chandelier, bigger than most houses on the other side of town. Upstairs, three doors down, was his bedroom. If he knew his father, it would have been left undisturbed. Cleaned regularly, of course, by the staff, but not converted to a den or study. Chase laughed, the harsh bark cutting through the still night. The house already had a den and a study and a library. What did one unused bedroom matter?

The country station on the truck's radio eased into another song about lost love and misspent youth. Chase stared at the dark windows and swore. He could handle being alone; it was the ghosts that made him uncomfortable.

Without considering the consequences, he shifted into reverse and backed out onto the street. Two miles later, he parked in front of Jenny's single-story red house. Light blazed out onto the lawn. The welcoming glow warmed the ice around his soul. He had no business being here. But the pull was stronger than the anger. It was as if the emotion had been washed away, leaving behind only the memory of what should have been.

He was courting danger. He was a fool. That was something else that hadn't changed. He'd always been a fool for Jenny.

Stuffing the car keys into his jeans pocket, he made his way to the door and knocked softly. Before he had a chance to lower his hand, she stood before him, staring up through the screen.

Her dark blond hair looked slightly ruffled, as though she'd been asleep. But she was dressed in jeans and a T-shirt. Bare feet peeked out below.

Chase suddenly realized it was almost midnight. Except for their recent conversation at the mill, he hadn't seen Jenny in eleven years. He couldn't show up on her doorstep this late.

"I don't belong here. And you should slam the door in my face."

"You're right on both accounts," she said, holding open the screen. "Come inside."

Chapter Three

"It's late." Chase stood beside the door and shifted his weight. "I'm not sure why I'm here."

"I am."

"Maybe you could explain it to me."

"There's nowhere else to go. Despite everything, we used to be friends."

He looked unconvinced. "If you say so."

"I do."

Jenny wondered if he felt as nervous as she did. Even in the brightly lit room, the night crowded around them, bringing together past and present, overlapping space and time. Were they really strangers or did traces of the teenage lovers remain?

Lovers? Now why had she thought of that particular word? It couldn't be because Chase filled up the small area of her living room until there was barely enough air left to breathe. They'd never been lovers. Their frantic embraces hadn't had time to progress past exploration before he'd been forced out of town.

"Chase." His name fell from her lips and lingered in the room.

They stood near each other. Close enough for her to feel the warmth from his body, smell the masculine scent that was uniquely his, see the tired shadows staining his tanned skin.

"I..." He swallowed. "I'd better go." But he made no move to leave.

"That would be best." He'd already proven he had the power to hurt her. His rage could destroy her life.

But she didn't want him to leave. Not like this. There were so many things still to be said. Despite his claims to the contrary, he was going to need some help getting through his father's illness. She wasn't sure why she felt she was the chosen one. Seeing him through this would be as foolish as sticking her head into the mouth of a very hungry, very angry lion. Maybe it was for old times' sake, or the forever they never had. Maybe it was because she knew his anger came from knowing only half the truth.

"We could call a truce," she said softly. "Just until your dad's out of danger." She didn't voice the other possibility.

"A truce?" He glanced over his shoulder at the door, then back at her. "All right."

The overhead light outlined the strong lines of his cheeks and jaw. Dark eyes, the color of midnight, stared down as if he were seeing her for the first time. The once-smooth black hair looked rumpled, as though he'd dragged his hands through the thick locks. Time had been good to him, changing the boy to a man.

She leaned forward slightly and stared. Something wasn't right. Something about his face that... "Did you break your nose?'' she asked, suddenly realizing a slight bump marred the once-perfect profile.

"Your father had the honor of doing that."

His firm, male mouth threatened a smile. One side turned up slightly, then relaxed into a straight line. Jenny breathed a sigh of relief. She hadn't seen Chase smile in so long, something told her that all the time in the world couldn't dilute its devastating effect.

"I'm sorry." Impulsively, she reached out to touch him. Her courage deserted her and she started to pull away.

"Dammit, Jenny. Don't look at me like that."

"Like what?"

"Come here." He tugged her into his embrace.

It was like coming home. Sure, the planes of his chest seemed harder, broader, more defined, and he'd grown a couple of inches, but the feel of his arms holding her so tightly their bodies began to blend into one was exactly as she remembered. His hands splayed across her back, one above the other. The last two fingers of the lower hand teased at the waistband of her jeans. The steady beat of his heart under her ear was as familiar as her own. She thought he sighed softly. Did he feel it, too?

Whispered phrases drifted to her. None of the words made sense, and she answered, using the same meaningless sounds, murmuring her need, the pain, how much she'd missed him.

Her arms slipped under the jacket he wore and pressed hard against his sides and back. The flannel shirt was soft and warm, retaining the heat and scent of his body.

Gradually she became aware that her breasts, free of the usual confines of a bra, were crushed against him. That the pressure had shifted from comforting to sensual. That they had stood holding each other for several minutes. That the rumblings weren't words of love but the complaints of an unfed stomach.

Reluctantly, she stepped back. "You're hungry. You should have said something."

Chase shrugged. "It's after midnight. I didn't expect you to even be up."

"I wasn't," she admitted. "I'd gone to bed around ten, but then I woke up about a half hour ago and I had this feeling . . ." She glanced at the floor. "I can't explain it."

He placed a hand under her chin and forced her to look at him. "You don't have to, Jenny. Not to me." His dark eyes gave nothing away and she wondered what had happened to the boy who had worn his heart on his sleeve.

"Come on," she said. "I'll fix you something light."

"I don't want to be any trouble."

"Will you stop it?" Jenny grabbed his arm and pulled him through her small living area into an equally tiny kitchen. "You've been at the hospital for hours. I bet you didn't bother to eat while you were there."

"Would you eat hospital food if you didn't have to?"

"No. Sit." She pushed him into an oak chair and placed her hands on her hips. "Have you eaten *anything* today?"

"Some sort of meat substance on the plane. And the honey-roasted nuts. They're my favorite."

Arched brows rose and fell suggestively until she felt herself grin. "You haven't changed at all."

"The old Jackson charm. Gets 'em every time." He leaned forward and shrugged off his bomber-style jacket. The brown leather had seen better days, but the faded patched garment suited the Chase she remembered.

She'd wondered how he'd dress, now that he'd made his own way in the world. For the past two days, she'd tried to prepare herself for pinstripe suits and wingtips. Instead, he looked like any steelworker, clad in blue jeans and a flannel shirt. Only this shirt had been washed so many times, the colors of blue and white blurred together in uneven lines. Her gaze drifted back to his, then skittered away when their eyes met.

"How about an omelet?" she asked.

"Sounds great. Got any coffee?"

"At midnight? How about cocoa?"

He grimaced, then stretched. With his long, lean body and powerful shoulders, he overpowered her small kitchen. From end to end, the room barely measured eight feet. The table, white tiles framed in pale oak, seated two, but even then knees bumped underneath.

Jenny pulled open the refrigerator door and removed three eggs and some raw vegetables. "Tell me about your dad. Did you talk to the doctor?"

"Yeah. Dr. Martin stopped by while I was there. She told me a little about his condition."

He hesitated and she looked up from her chopping. "What?"

"I don't know. I guess I'm frustrated that no one will give me a straight answer."

"Maybe there is no straight answer." She crossed the small room in three steps and rested her hand on his shoulder. "Your dad will be fine. He's a strong old bird. You'll see."

"I don't think so." He looked at the curtained window. "I think he's going to die."

"Chase."

"I'm okay," he said, still avoiding her gaze. "When I got the telegram, I started to prepare myself for the worst. I don't know if I'm angry at him for getting sick, or at myself for caring. I'd thought about coming back sooner, but I kept waiting for him to invite me." He gave a harsh laugh. She tightened her fingers. "You'd think I would have learned that lesson a long time ago. William Jackson never backs down."

"I wish . . ." Jenny blinked against the burning in her eyes.

"I know." He flashed her a grateful smile and her insides melted. This was the Chase she remembered. "How about my food, woman? A man could die of starvation in this place."

"Coming right up." She stuck two mugs with milk into the microwave, then went back to the vegetables. "Was Terry working the night shift tonight?"

"Yeah. Could have knocked me over with a feather. She's still as cute as ever. Said she'd married Tom."

"They have two boys and are very happy together." Jenny wasn't sure why she felt the urge to emphasize the couple's marital bliss, but continued to extol the virtues of their relationship until Chase's smile widened into a very male, very self-satisfied grin.

"You wouldn't still be jealous about me and Terry, would you?" he asked.

"I was never jealous." She pulled the mugs out of the microwave and stirred in the cocoa. Setting one cup in front of him, she frowned. "That you made a fool of yourself over her is really none of my concern."

The good humor fled as quickly as it had arrived. "I made a fool of myself over you. That didn't concern you, either."

Their eyes met. His anger didn't hide his hurt. She broke away first. "I'd better finish your meal or you won't get any sleep at all tonight. Was your dad awake when you were there?"

Chase hesitated as if he wasn't willing to accept the change in subject, then shook his head and cupped his hands around the mug. "They'd given him something to help him rest. I sat there watching him—for all the good that did. I expected him to be sick, but I didn't think he'd be old."

"It's been a long time," she said, breaking the eggs into a bowl, then beating them with a fork. "There's been a lot of changes."

"Did he . . ." She heard him shift in his seat, but didn't turn around. "I can't believe I have to ask you this, but did he get married or anything?"

Jenny couldn't imagine straight-laced William Jackson unbending enough to admit interest in a mere woman. "Not that I know of. He never dated anyone in town. He was gone on business from time to time, but I don't think he'd, ah, well, you know."

Chase exhaled, the sound seemed sad. "He wouldn't risk the emotion. To him, that was for the weak. After Mom died, he didn't have anyone. All he cared about was the mill."

"He cared about you."

"Yeah."

She risked a glance and saw him sprawled out on the chair. Long legs stretched under the table. The heels of his boots rested on the bottom rung of the chair opposite him. His fingers were laced behind his head.

After pouring the eggs into a pan, she dropped a slice of bread into the toaster and started to set the table. "He did care," she said, smoothing down a single place mat. "Every time you sent one of your letters, he'd read it over and over. I saw him sitting in his chair, staring at the pages. I could see that he loved you."

Brown eyes sought hers. She saw that he wanted to believe, but couldn't allow himself the luxury. "He never wrote back. Not once."

"I'm sorry." She added the chopped vegetables and turned over the omelet. "As soon as I found out why you left town, I went to him and told him the truth." The memory of the coldness in William Jackson's expression made her shiver. "He said it didn't matter, but I could see he missed you."

"Not writing seems to be a town failing."

"Yeah, I don't remember getting a letter from you," she said.

"Me? You're the one who—" Emotion flared. Then as quickly as it had appeared, it was gone, concealed behind a polite mask. "Sorry. Truce." He finished his cocoa and set the mug on the table. "So, what's been going on with your family? Your dad still raising hell with the union?"

"You bet. Although he's mellowed in the last few years. I think Anne's kids helped that process."

She slid the food on a plate and set it in front of him. Just as she reached to pick up his empty mug, he started to hand it to her. Her gaze fell upon his left wrist and the beaten-up old watch he wore. Deep inside, a knot tightened, then pressed against her heart. After all these years, he still had the watch.

She remembered that time like it was yesterday. Chase's birthday was in early November. She'd spent a whole summer vacation baby-sitting for the Van Ross kids, suffering their tantrums and wild stunts. Every hard-earned cent had been carefully saved. Then, in late October, her older sister, Anne, had driven her into the city and she'd bought that watch for Chase's birthday. Back then, seventy dollars had been all the money in the world.

When she'd given it to him, meticulously wrapped in floral paper with a store-bought bow, she'd been shaking so hard, she'd been afraid she'd throw up. He'd known, she remembered with a sad half smile. He'd seen that the gift was more than a watch, it was also her heart.

That had been the afternoon they'd admitted their love for each other. That had been the afternoon they'd begun planning their future together. The afternoon she'd realized there would never be another man for her. No matter what happened, or how much time they spent apart, she'd only ever love him.

"Jenny?"

"What? Oh." She stared at the mug she was holding, wondering if she had the courage to ask why he still wore the watch. She didn't allow herself to believe it had any sentimental value. "Let me fix you another cup."

"You feeling okay?"

"Yes. I was just, uh, thinking." Jenny pulled open a cupboard, grimacing when the handle came off in her hand. "This place needs an overhaul."

As he took a bite of toast, he looked around the tiny kitchen. "And about two thousand more square feet. It's like a dollhouse."

"Only to giants. It suits me perfectly."

He cut into the omelette. "You live here alone?"

"Yes. I rent it. The old lady who used to live here went to stay with her daughter. The family isn't sure whether to fix it up or sell it. In the meantime, the rent is cheap and I'm close to the mill and my family." She shrugged and stirred the cocoa. "When it rains, I have to put out about five buckets, the porch swing sticks and the railings are coming apart, but I still like it."

"Why?"

"It's mine. My first place and all that. Alec and I had talked about buying a house, but it didn't work out and I decided to stay here."

"Alec?" He said the name without any emotion at all.

Jenny took a breath and faced the table. "My ex-fiancé."

"What happened?" He calmly spread the jam on his second slice of toast; nothing in his face gave away what he was feeling, but she thought she heard a hint of relief in his voice. Hope fluttered in her chest. Foolish hope, she thought, squashing it with a large dose of reality. Chase was only in Harrisville because his father was in the hospital. If she'd meant anything to him over the years, he would have contacted her. He hadn't. End of story.

She watched as he finished off the omelette. It gave her time to figure out how to condense her relationship with Alec into one or two sentences.

"What usually happens. We grew apart, realized that we didn't love each other. Nothing spectacular."

"Did he live here with you?"

Her first instinct was to tell him the answer was none of his business. Her second was that the truth might serve as protection for her fragile heart. "Yes. For about two years."

"I see."

"What about you, Chase? Is there a Mrs. Jackson waiting back in Phoenix?"

He tossed his napkin on the table and glared at her. "No. You taught me all I needed to know about women. I don't trust 'em any farther than my bed."

So much for the truce. She didn't want to fight with him, she realized. She understood his need to lash out. Temptation stirred. It would be easy to tell the rest of the story, to defuse his temper with a few simple facts. But to what end? He was suffering so much already. In the past, he'd been her hero, she the innocent young princess waiting to be rescued. Now it was her turn to be strong. The truth would only hurt him. Between his father and the town, he'd had enough pain for one day.

She set the cup in front of him and lowered herself to the opposite chair. "What did you think of the mill?"

"I didn't go inside. Seems about the same."

"My dad says people are worried about their jobs. They're afraid the place is going to be shut down."

He frowned. "Why are you telling me this?"

"Because if anything happens, the mill will be yours."

"I don't want it." He pushed back the chair and rose to his feet. "Why the hell did I come back here?" He raked his hands through his dark hair and strode into the living room.

"Chase." She followed him.

"I can feel it, you know," he said, pacing her small living room. From end to end it was only four of his steps, then he had to turn and go the other way. "The walls, the town, everything is closing in on me. What do they all want?" He glanced at her, as if seeking an answer, then shook his head and kept on pacing. "I like my life in Phoenix. No mill, no iron ore. You can look out the kitchen windows and see across the desert. The air is clean."

"What do you do there?" She stood off to the side and watched him work out his frustrations.

"Construction. I have a couple of partners and we build offices, houses, just about anything new." He stopped in front of her and grabbed her arms. "I smell sawdust instead of iron. I spend a good part of my days outside on site. Nothing could make me go back into that mill again."

Jenny tried to ignore the panic welling within her. If William Jackson died, the mill would belong to Chase. A thousand people were employed by Jackson Steel, including her father, a sister, two brothers-in-law and herself.

Who would run it? Would he sell? Close it down? Either possibility was too awful to consider.

"What about you, Jenny?" he asked, his brown eyes blazing with confusion and anger. "Why are you still here? What happened to your dreams of getting away from this company town?"

"My family's here."

"So? They were here when we spent our nights planning our escape. What happened to you? Was it Alec?"

"No." She tried to twist away, but he held her firmly in his grasp. The past threatened to overwhelm her; she held on to the present. "I...I got lost for a while. Forgot about the dreams we had. By the time I remembered, it didn't seem to matter anymore."

He released her. His hands formed tight fists at his side. "Like me, you mean."

"Yes," she whispered, drowning in his intensity. This was the Chase she remembered. The man who radiated heat and passion hot enough to sear anything in his way. She'd always stood too close to the flame. Even now, it rippled across her skin, burning scars into her heart and soul.

How long had she waited for his return, praying night after night that he'd come back and make it all okay for her? How many years had she watched out the front window of her parent's house, waiting for the familiar rumble of his old Camaro? When had she at last realized that Chase Jackson never intended to come back for her? That he hadn't forgiven the lies she'd never spoken, had never even thought?

Dear God, she still wanted him. Every fiber of her being longed to be next to him, under him, joining in the one way youth and time had denied them. The need wasn't about sex, it was about healing—the completion of what should have been, if only fate had been more kind.

He reached up and touched her cheek, brushing away the tear she hadn't felt fall. "What happened to us, Jenny? Why did we have to become enemies?"

"I don't know. It's late. We both need to get some sleep."

He stiffened at her words. "I should leave."

"You don't have to." She held his palm tightly against her face, savoring the rough calluses against her smooth skin. He asked silent questions. "I have a spare room. You're welcome to use it. I know how you hate the big house."

His fingers tightened slightly, pulling her closer. His free hand cupped the back of her head. "You shouldn't trust me. I've turned into one hell of a bastard."

There wasn't a whole lot more damage he could do. The man had already broken her heart. "Maybe. But you can stay anyway."

She led him down the short hall. The spare room held a daybed and an old dresser. The white ruffled spread looked especially feminine as she watched Chase look around the small space.

"Thanks," he said. "I appreciate this. I really didn't want to go back to the house."

Jenny pulled linens and a blanket out of the hall closet, while Chase went to retrieve his luggage. Their good-night was brief and awkward, consisting of avoided glances and mumbled words.

Lying in her own bed, listening to the muffled noises of the shower, she wondered if she'd been mad to invite him to stay. If her father found out... Jenny chuckled, already hearing his lecture on morals and behaving like a lady.

Plumping up the pillow, she turned on her side. Part of her prayed that William Jackson would outlive them all. Most of her believed that was unlikely. That the old man had survived this long seemed a miracle. And when he was gone, Chase would leave, too.

It wasn't just about leaving, she thought, staring at the sliver of light shining under her door. Chase had always believed in looking out for himself. Time and both their fathers had only reinforced the lesson. Once, she'd believed that, too. But the last eleven years had taught her that family was everything. When she'd expected them to turn away from her shame, they'd stood by her, offering support and a place to live. She couldn't turn her back on what she owed them. Not for herself, not even for Chase.

Once she and Chase had been two halves of the same whole. Now they were just two people who'd once been in love.

Chase looked out the window and watched the sky lighten from black to gray to pale blue. From his place on the daybed, he could see a little of the roof and part of an old gnarled oak tree.

Sleep had been welcome, if unexpected, but he'd suddenly awakened a little after five a.m. and had been unable to relax since. His mind leaped from topic to topic, thinking about his father lying in the hospital, shying away from his responsibility to the mill, wondering how it was possible Jenny had become more beautiful and how he could still be attracted to the one woman he'd done his damnedest to hate.

He heard her alarm buzz, then the soft pad of her feet as she stumbled to the bathroom. She'd never been a morning person. He still recalled the time they'd gone camping together. He'd risen with the sun and caught fish for their breakfast. When he woke her up to proudly show her his catch, she'd screamed so loud, he'd dropped them in the fire and they'd ended up eating cold cereal, without milk.

Ah, Jenny, he thought. If only they could go back and make it all right between them. If he could take back leaving and she could take back being with—

He swore under his breath. After all this time, it still bugged him. Telling himself it shouldn't matter didn't seem to help. In Phoenix it had been easy to forget, but here, there were too many reminders. When would he learn to let go?

They were different people now; adults carrying scars too deep to ignore. Even so, she wasn't part of his agenda. He hadn't come back to stir up old flames—he was damn sure not going to get burned by this one.

Chase sat up, then swung his feet to the floor. The room was cold and he quickly reached for briefs and jeans. Last night he hadn't bothered to unpack more than what he'd need. A single shirt hung in the small closet. She stored her winter clothes in the cramped space. When he pulled open the door, the scent of cedar crept out to greet him. Underneath was the lingering fragrance of Jenny herself.

Chase caught his breath as the desire throbbed in his groin. He still wanted her. That hadn't changed. Whereas before, he'd longed for her with the undefined need of an untried boy, now he ached with the hard knowledge of a man. Their embrace last night had shown him that time had filled the lean lines of girlhood to the lush curves of a woman. She was still petite, with tiny bones that made him worry he could crush her without even trying, but the breasts pressing against his chest had been full and warm, straining with promise.

"No!" he growled, pulling out his shirt and tossing it on the bed. When his father was well—he didn't allow himself to consider the other possibility—he was heading back to Arizona. There was nothing for him in Harrisville.

He'd seen the look on her face when she'd gone on about the mill and the employees. Somehow she'd become a part of the town, even after swearing she'd never allow it to take away her dream. She'd been wrong. Whatever happened, Jenny's life revolved around Harrisville and her family.

The bathroom door opened and he heard her walk toward the kitchen. Chase gathered up his shaving kit and slipped into the steamy room.

An oversize T-shirt lay crumpled on the floor. A dab of makeup dotted the counter. The air was filled with the scent of soap and perfume and products he couldn't begin to identify.

It had been a long time since he'd shared close quarters with a woman and he found himself smiling as he spread shaving cream along his jaw.

When he'd finished washing up, Chase strapped on his watch and glanced at the dial. He still had plenty of time before Dr. Martin was due to start on her rounds. He pulled open the bathroom door and walked toward his bedroom.

As he crossed the threshold, a movement in the room caught his attention. Jenny turned swiftly, color flaming across her cheeks as her gaze fell to the floor.

"I was just bringing you coffee," she said, motioning to the mug perched on top of the dresser.

"Thanks." Chase tossed his shaving kit on the bed and crossed the hardwood floor.

She stood her ground, tilting her chin to look up at him as he approached. A soft cotton blouse covered but didn't conceal the fullness of her breasts thrusting forward in female invitation. Jeans, well-worn and faded, clung to her hips, then reached down to emphasize long, curvy legs. He could feel his dark emotions flowing away, diluted by clear, green eyes and a tentative but welcoming smile.

"Did you sleep well?" she asked, her voice lower and slightly husky.

"Yes. And you?"

"Fine." She licked her bottom lip. He followed the motion, then took that final step and rested his hands on her shoulders.

"Jenny," he whispered, needing to hear her name as much as needing to feel her in his arms.

Some small sensible portion of his brain called out a warning. Touching Jenny, kissing her, would only lead to trouble. He was here because of his father and nothing else. If he allowed himself to get lost in the past, he might never find his way back. He and Jenny had become too different to connect now. He knew he hadn't forgiven her. She belonged to the town and the mill; he'd never been welcome in either.

He acknowledged the reasonableness of the argument and started to move back. Then she placed her hand on his bare chest. Her palm burned him as she rubbed against the hair, as if seeking the warm skin below.

"Chase," she breathed, the single word sounding like a plea.

The hell with it, he thought and lowered his mouth to hers.

Chapter Four

She could have stepped away.

Jenny knew she'd remind herself of that fact over and over in the days that followed. Chase would never have held her against her will; he'd always been a gentleman. A single whisper of hesitation, a slight stiffening of her body would have been more than enough.

Instead, she moved closer and let her hands slide up his bare chest and shoulders until her fingers tangled in the thick, dark strands of his hair. In the split second before their lips joined, she murmured his name again.

He caught the sound, inhaled it, and the world became awash with sensation. Hard and soft, familiar and strange. Her eyes drifted shut as she felt his mouth mold itself to hers. Firm lips, confident and masculine but gentle enough to make her melt, moved back and forth, discovering anew what had once been known.

They pressed together from knee to shoulder, jean-clad legs brushing. She'd never thought the sound of denim on denim could be the least bit erotic, until now. How easy it would be to forget the present and return to that magic time long past. The years fell away—to when she was a teenager again and her whole world consisted of loving and being loved by Chase.

Powerful arms held her close; her breasts flattened against his chest. Her blouse and bra provided an unwelcome barrier to further intimacy. She parted her lips, eager to know more, straining to remember everything.

His tongue entered immediately, pushing past her teeth, searching the warm sweetness. Her body, never awake much before ten, rippled as if an electric current had been connected to each nerve ending. He tasted of toothpaste, the mint mingling with a half-remembered flavor. It was like trying to describe a childhood Christmas. There were no exact words for the memory, just feelings of the familiar, the comforting, the arousing. They dueled as they had a hundred, no a thousand times before, beginning a game of seek-and-destroy with the prize of passion going to both victor and vanquished.

The heat from his body inflamed her, while the strength of his arms offered a haven. His hands traced the length of her back, then slipped over her hips to cup her derriere and pull her firmly against him. Her fingers kneaded the strength of his shoulders, pressing smooth skin and hard muscle. No one had ever made her feel this way before; no one would again.

Past and present merged until the boy and the man were one and she knew she'd been a fool to believe she'd forgotten any of it. The truth brought pain. A lump formed in her throat and she stiffened slightly and swallowed. He released her instantly.

They stared at each other, their breathing rapid and shallow. Instead of giving off light, the fire in his eyes darkened the irises to smoldering black. But the shock was clearly visible. As was the desire.

"I thought it would be different," he said at last, turning away and walking to the window.

"Me, too."

"I won't apologize."

"Thank you." She glanced down and saw that her hands were clenched into tight fists. She relaxed each finger, then forced herself to smile, hoping that by ignoring the sudden awkwardness, she could make it go away. "I'm sure it's just left-over emotion. We never said goodbye to each other, all those years ago."

"Unfinished business?" he asked without turning around.

She stared at his bare back. Eleven years ago he'd been broad and strong, but she would have been able to feel the ribs through undeveloped muscle. Today the bones were hidden by sleek, defined flesh. Worn jeans hung low on his hips. The scent of him clung to her blouse. It would haunt her all day.

"Yeah. Unfinished business."

"Jenny, I—"

"Don't." She cut him off. "You said you wouldn't apologize. It just happened."

He kept his back to her and held the curtain slightly open. "I never forgave you."

"I know."

"I told myself it didn't matter."

"But it does."

"Yes. It does."

It shouldn't hurt, she told herself. She was doing this *for* him. With a single explanation, perhaps two or three choice phrases, she could tell him the truth. He wouldn't hate her anymore. But at what price? No. She'd made her decision eleven years ago. And then again yesterday. He didn't need to know what had really happened that summer. He had enough to worry about with his father.

"You're still angry," she said softly. "I understand."

"I'm not sure that I do. I've spent eleven years hating you and what you did. And here I am, in your house."

She wanted to go to him and offer comfort. But it wasn't hers to give. "Just accept it, Chase. Nothing is the way we thought it would be. In time—"

"In time, I'll be outta here." He let the curtain fall.

The lump in her throat returned. She coughed. "I've got to get to the mill. If you have a chance today, let me know how your father's doing."

"Sure. No problem."

She paused, hoping he'd turn around and look at her or say something, but he remained silent and still, his back to her, staring out at her backyard.

Her coat and purse sat by the door. Jenny grabbed her belongings and hurried toward her car. She wasn't late, but that didn't stop her from speeding down the street. She needed to put as much distance between herself and Chase as possible. They might have grown up in the last eleven years, they might have learned things and changed in more ways than she could tell, but his kiss had shown her that some things remained exactly the same.

"Do you have any *idea* of the rumors flying—"

Jenny held up her hand. Instantly the visitor stopped speaking, but continued to stand in the doorway of her office and tap her foot. Jenny hit several more keys on the computer keyboard to complete the report, then pressed the save function and swiveled to face her sister.

"Good morning, Anne," she said calmly. "What brings you to the mill today?"

"Oh, fine. Pretend like you don't know. The entire town is talking about you, Jennifer Davidson. I wouldn't have believed it if I hadn't seen it for myself."

Jenny glanced at her sister. Anne and Jenny were the most similar of the four sisters, in appearance, if not in temperament. But as the oldest, Anne was also the bossiest and most outspoken. Even a husband and three children under the age of six had done nothing to defuse her energy. Even now, with a baby propped on one hip, she fairly radiated indignation and a mother-bear-like willingness to do battle for her own.

"Well?" she said when Jenny didn't speak.

"You want some coffee?"

"I want some answers."

"Annie, I'm a big girl. I can do what I like." Jenny grinned. "And I have no clue what we're talking about."

Her sister sat in the chair opposite the desk and settled the baby on her knee. "Chase Jackson. He spent the night with you."

Jenny whistled. "News travels fast. What did you do? Send out a patrol to check on me in the middle of the night? I believe this is an example of Neighborhood Watch going amok."

"One of my neighbors has a little boy with an ear infection. She went to the all-night pharmacy to get a prescription filled and, on the way, happened to drive by your house. Her sister works in reception at the hospital. She'd seen Chase drive up in a Bronco. That same truck was still in your driveway not forty minutes ago."

"You drove by, too?"

"Of course. What are you thinking of? He's trouble. He's always been trouble, Jenny. Hasn't he done enough?"

Her family cared about her. That's what made it bearable. But sometimes . . . "Chase and I are friends. Despite everything that happened, we've always been friends."

Anne shifted the baby until she was lying on her back, then pulled a bottle from the diaper bag she'd slung over the arm of the chair. "Some friend. You haven't seen or heard from him in eleven years."

"I know that. But don't forget Dad beat him up and practically ran him out of town. You can't blame Chase for that."

"No, but I blame him for other things."

Jenny shook her head. "No. That was *not* his fault."

"Then whose was it?"

She stared at the sweet baby in her sister's arms. "The rapist's."

"Jen, I didn't mean—"

"I know." She tried to smile. "It's okay. Look, I appreciate your concern, but what I do with Chase is my business. For what it's worth, he needed a place to stay and I offered him the sparc room."

"A place to stay?" Anne snorted. "As if that mansion on the other side of town doesn't have enough empty rooms."

"I know it sounds funny, but it's true. He doesn't like the house."

Her sister began to feed the baby. "Are you still in love with him?"

"No." She answered without thinking. It was only after the word was out that she prayed it was true.

"Are you sure? There was always something between you."

"He was my first crush, my first boyfriend, my first kiss. And before that, we'd been friends, best friends, for years. Of course we had something. Something pretty wonderful. But we've both grown up and apart. Everything is different now."

She picked up a paper clip and willed herself not to blush. Not *everything* was different. The passion was exactly as she had remembered. Even an hour after the fact, she could still feel the strength of his body pressing against hers, taste him, hear the rapid pant of his breathing.

It was just hormones, she told herself firmly. Since she'd broken off her engagement with Alec, there hadn't been anyone in her life. Her reaction to Chase was perfectly understandable under the circumstances.

"I don't want you to get hurt," Anne said.

"I won't. It's only for a couple of weeks. When his father is better, it'll be like he was never here. I promise, I'll be fine."

Green eyes, so much like her own, studied her. "And if the old man doesn't get better?"

Jenny shrugged.

Anne brushed her daughter's cheek. "I may not remember that much about Chase Jackson, but I do know one thing. He hates this town and it hates him. He'll never stay here. Not even if his father dies and he inherits the mill."

"So?"

"So keep out of his way. You don't need more trouble in your life. None of us do."

The baby finished her bottle. Jenny held out her arms and took her niece. After positioning her over her shoulder, she patted the baby's back gently until a very unladylike burp filled the office. The infant, all warm and smelling of talc and formula, made her heart clench tightly.

She'd never had the chance to hold her own child. Had never seen the perfectly formed body. At the time, her family had been protecting her, but lately she'd wondered if she should have insisted. Maybe seeing the tiny coffin would have convinced her that her baby had really died. Maybe she wouldn't always be so aware of an empty spot deep inside, as though she'd lost a piece of herself.

"I've got to get going," Anne said, packing the empty bottle and pulling out an infant blanket. "Call me if you need anything—even just to talk."

"I will." Jenny kissed her niece on the cheek and whispered, "Goodbye, pumpkin."

Anne slung the diaper bag over her shoulder. "Oh, I almost forgot." She paused in the doorway. "Dad's here to see some guys in the mill. He's planning to come up and talk to you."

Her sister's tone warned her that the conversation wasn't going to be about her invitation to dinner the following Sunday. "Don't tell me—"

Anne shrugged. "He knows about Chase staying with you."

Jenny straightened in her chair. "I'm a grown woman. He doesn't scare me."

"Uh-huh. Just keep your butt covered, little sister. And if he starts to take off his belt, run like hell."

Jenny chuckled long after the footsteps had faded. Her father might yell a little, or a lot, but his bark was much worse than his bite.

She returned to the computer and printed out the monthly report. Income was down. It had been dropping steadily for several years. The reason wasn't difficult to figure out. Offshore steel production was cheaper and more efficient. Newer equipment, reduced wages, inexpensive land costs. Jackson Steel was surviving on investment interest and little else. What was going to happen if William Jackson died?

Not *if*, she thought. *When*. It was just a matter of time. If not this year, then next. Anne was right; Chase *did* hate the town. And with good reason. But if he turned his back on the company—

She walked to the window overlooking the mill. A thousand people were employed there. Friends, neighbors, family.

She'd been an employee almost ten years, but it seemed like only yesterday that she and Chase had walked along the river talking about the future. There had been so many plans. Dreams that had all started with their leaving Harrisville behind. Life had been simple; to find happiness they only needed to look to each other and the promise of tomorrow. Now she was all grown up. The dreams were a memory: the reality was she had an obligation to her family and the mill.

Jenny picked up the report and carried it to the controller's office. On her return trip, she stopped to chat with the secretaries in the large work area across the hall, then asked about the supply clerk's grandchildren. It was only when she glanced at her watch for the third time that she realized she was trying to stay out of her office longer than her father would be willing to wait for her.

Grinning wryly, she made her way back.

The large man filling the chair that Anne had recently vacated, sat stiffly, impatiently tapping his fingers. She slipped up behind him and wrapped her arms around his neck.

"I know you've come to yell at me, but I'm not going to listen, so save your breath."

Frank Davidson ducked to avoid her kiss on his cheek and untangled her hands. "Don't try to sweet-talk me, girly. The rumors are all over town this morning."

"So I've heard." She perched on the corner of her desk. "I'm all grown-up, Daddy. You can't tell me what to do."

He sighed. "Letting him spend the night? You should be ashamed."

"Be careful," she warned. "The last time you accused Chase you were very wrong."

Frank glanced away. "Maybe. About that. But he did other things that—"

"No. He didn't. You've always been quick to judge Chase, just because of his father, just as Mr. Jackson judged me by you."

"The boy's trouble. Barely back twenty-four hours and he's got the whole town talking."

"That's not his fault. I could have told him to go away."

"Why didn't you?"

A simple enough question. But she wasn't sure of her answer. Because of what they had once been, that she knew. Because deep in her heart, she felt responsible for his pain, even though she knew she wasn't. Because... "Because I've missed him," she said at last.

"He's used to getting what he wants. The boy was born with a silver spoon in his mouth. He hasn't changed."

"That's not true. He's very successful in Phoenix. He has his own construction company. You know he left here with nothing."

"Construction, eh? So the mighty Jackson boy has become a blue-collar worker like the rest of us." Her father rose to his feet. "Who would have thought?"

"Don't make trouble, Daddy," she said, going to him.

He gave her a brief hug. "Then keep him out of your house."

"No."

He tilted her chin up until their eyes met. "You've always been the most stubborn of my girls. I was too easy on you when you were growing up."

"Probably." She grinned.

"I'm going to pay my respects to the old man this afternoon. Has there been any news?"

"No. I called the hospital a little while ago. His condition is unchanged."

"If he dies, it's over. For all of us."

"You don't know that."

Frank touched her cheek. "You've always believed in that boy. I admire your loyalty. I wish you had the good sense to see the truth about Chase Jackson."

Chase pulled into the parking lot in front of the mill, then swore when he saw the crowd. A catering truck stood on one side, close to the office building. As he eased the Bronco to a halt, the people began to stare. When he stepped out onto the gravel lot, silence crashed over the group like a wave. Some people nudged one another. A few pointed. A couple hundred pairs of eyes bore into him as if they could drive him away simply by their combined force of will.

He'd almost forgotten what it meant to be the mill owner's son in a town that resented its main employer as much as it depended on him for survival. Many people believed they had been exploited by the mill, that their labor had provided the means to a luxurious life-style for the Jacksons. Two generations ago, that had been true. Government regulations and the union had made the employee-employer relationship more equitable, but old habits—and hatreds—died hard.

Chase's footsteps crunched loudly as he walked toward the truck. The line parted, allowing him to go immediately to the front. It wasn't, he knew, an act of politeness. They wanted him gone as fast as possible.

He paid for his lunch, then turned and moved toward the picnic benches set up under the tall oaks. A group of three women sat at the last table. Two of them stood up when he approached. The third remained seated, gesturing with her half-eaten apple for him to take the bench opposite.

"At last," Jenny said. "A friendly face." She smiled.

"My thoughts exactly." He could feel them staring into his back.

The conversation resumed around them. Murmurs and whispers, half-heard phrases. The hatred was all-encompassing, like a thick cloak that threatened to suffocate him.

"I'll bet your day's been better than mine," he said, then took a bite of his sandwich.

"Don't count on it."

He raised one eyebrow.

"My sister found out that you spent the night at my house. She's already been here to explain in detail the damage done to my reputation. My father also dropped by to discuss his feelings on the subject."

"What did you tell them?"

"To mind their own business."

Frustration grew inside of him. She looked exactly as he remembered from eleven years before. A little older, perhaps, more mature, but the essence of Jenny remained the same.

Dark blond hair fluttered around her shoulders. Despite the bright sunshine, the fall temperature was brisk. She wore a sweater. The burgundy wool hid her curves from view, but he could still feel the imprint of her breasts on his bare chest. The taste of her kiss lingered, as did the passion. He'd spent eleven years hating Jenny Davidson. Did, in fact, still hate her. And he'd gladly sell his soul to the devil for an hour with her in bed.

He swore again.

She finished her apple and licked the juice from her fingers. The sight of her pink tongue tasting her skin turned his sandwich into sawdust and his groin to fire.

"Don't blame them," she said.

"Who?" he managed after swallowing half his drink.

"My family. It's this town. Everybody knows everybody's business."

"I should never have stayed with you."

She shrugged.

"Why the hell didn't you send me packing?" he asked, his voice little more than a growl.

"Oh no you don't," she said, placing her forearms on the picnic table and leaning close to him. "Don't go blaming this on me. You're the one who showed up at midnight with nowhere to go. I did you a favor. You knew what could happen, what people would say. This is Harrisville, Chase."

"Why do you stay?"

She settled back in her seat. "Because I belong here." She opened a package of cookies and passed him three. "How's your father?"

"The same. I spoke to the doctor this morning. She says—" he rubbed his temple, but the ache didn't go away "—it's no good. Just a matter of time. There's been too much damage to the heart and he'd never survive surgery."

"She said he was going to die?"

He shook his head. "It's more what she *didn't* say. I understood the message."

"I'm sorry."

"Are you?" He glanced up and saw her face soften with compassion. "I'm not. The old man's a bastard. He never gave a damn about anything but the mill and getting his way."

"He loved you."

"Save the speeches for someone who cares." He bit into one of the cookies.

"I know you're upset, but—"

"Damn straight. Do you know I haven't even been back in this hole for twenty-four hours and all I can think of is leaving? How do you stand it, day after day?" He could feel his temper rising. With an effort, he tamped down the anger and rose to his feet. "I've got to get back to the hospital," he said. "I'll see you."

Jenny got up from her seat and stood next to him. "Not everything here is bad. There's a good side to a small town."

He glanced around at the lunch crowd, noticed how they were careful to avoid his eyes. "Having people know you, care about you? The camaraderie? Friends for a lifetime?"

A frown line marred her smooth forehead. "Yes. Exactly. How did you know?"

"I've seen it. All my life. But you're forgetting something. That's your view of Harrisville, not mine. I'm William Jackson's son and fitting in was never allowed."

He crumpled the wrappings from his sandwich and tossed them into the trash.

"Chase, don't go off like this."

She touched his arm. Her hand, so small and delicate, feminine despite the calluses and lack of nail polish, burned like a brand.

"It's always been like this," he said. "You never noticed before."

"It doesn't have to be. You could try to—"

He jerked his arm away. "I tried with you. I gave you everything I had and it wasn't enough. You were all I cared about in the world and you betrayed me. You lied. Even at the end, you didn't have the guts to tell me the truth—face-to-face."

She paled and took a step back. He could feel the workers listening. "It wasn't like that," she whispered. "I wanted to but there were things that had happened."

"I don't care. To hell with you," he said, then turned to the crowd. "To hell with all of you."

He stomped toward his truck, walking in a straight line, assuming the people would part to form a path. They did. No one would want to get too close to a Jackson.

He'd already started the engine when there was a tap on the window. He turned to tell Jenny to leave him alone, then scowled at the man standing beside the truck.

"Yeah?" he said after rolling down the glass.

"Hey, Chase. I just wanted to say hello."

"Mark?" He studied the tall blond man. "Mark Anders?"

The man smiled. "It's me. I wanted to tell you I'm sorry about your dad."

Chase brushed off the concern and offered his hand. "What are you doing here?" he asked. "Last I heard you were at Ohio State on a football scholarship. Rumor was you were going pro."

Mark glanced down at his leg. "Busted the knee my sophomore year. Patti turned up pregnant, so we got married. I never had the time to finish college. So here I am." He shrugged. "It's a living."

Chase turned to stare at the mill. Not in his mind, it wasn't. Working at Jackson Steel was a life sentence in hell. He shifted uncomfortably. "I guess."

"Heard you made it big."

"A couple of guys and I build houses and office buildings in Phoenix."

"I'm glad you got out."

Chase stared at his old friend. Back in high school they'd broken school sports records together. He'd thrown the football downfield and Mark had carried it across the goal line. They'd been unbeatable. He'd always assumed Mark had made it to the pros. Funny how nothing turned out like he'd thought.

He cleared his throat. "I got to get to the hospital, buddy."

"I hope your old man gets back on his feet soon."

"Me, too." He put the truck in gear.

"Maybe we can get together. Talk about old times."

He nodded at Mark. "Sure. I'll call you." Then he offered a wave and steered the car onto the main road.

The nurse tapped him on the shoulder. "There are a couple of other people here to see your father. Do you want me to tell them to come back later?"

Chase shook his head. The Cardiac Care staff preferred only one visitor at a time. "I need to stretch my legs. Are they waiting in the hall?"

"Yes."

He didn't know who was here, but he had a fair idea that he didn't want to talk to them.

"I'll tell 'em they can come in."

"Thanks. Why don't you get something to drink? It's almost four. You've been sitting with him for hours."

He looked at his father. The old man still lay silently, a ghost kept alive by tubes and machines. He'd hated him for years, despised the way William Jackson had let him walk out of his life, and yet this was his father, his own flesh and blood. God help him, he couldn't turn off all the feelings, no matter how hard he tried. Dr. Martin had urged patience and hope. Chase knew better. Time was running out. For all of them.

He walked through the double doors and saw Frank Davidson and his wife standing in the corridor. It had been eleven years since he'd last seen Davidson, eleven years since the union president had punched him in the face and accused him of knocking up his daughter. His hands closed into fists as he centered his weight over the balls of his feet. He wasn't a kid anymore. If Davidson tried something, he'd be ready.

The two men stared at each other, like lions warily circling before their fight for the pride. Mrs. Davidson, a slight, brown-haired woman with Jenny's eyes, took her husband's arm.

"I'll just be a minute, Frank. Then you can go in."

Her husband nodded.

She smiled at Chase. "It's good to see you. I'm sorry you had to come back to such sad news. We're all praying for your father's recovery." She sounded sincere.

"Thank you, ma'am. I'm sure he appreciates it."

As she walked past him, she paused, then raised herself on tiptoe and kissed his cheek. "Be strong," she whispered, then disappeared into the Cardiac Care unit.

Davidson continued to glare at him. Chase remembered Jenny's complaints that the entire town knew he'd spent the night at her house. Words of explanation formed on his tongue, but he refused to speak them. He didn't owe her old man anything.

The silence between them grew until it filled the hallway.

Finally, the older man shoved his hands into his pockets. "I won't apologize for hitting you that day."

He couldn't believe it. The urge to give back what he'd received was almost overwhelming. "You *can't* still think I got Jenny pregnant."

"No." Davidson scowled. "I know you didn't sleep with her. But she was out with you. You were so damn cocky all the time. The golden boy who could do no wrong. I expected more from you and I hold you responsible for what happened. You should have kept her safe."

"What are you talking about?"

"The night of the carnival. That last summer. When you got drunk and passed out."

"So?"

"Jenny got a ride home from a carny worker."

"She told me that. Things got out of hand—that's how she got pregnant. I had nothing to do with it."

Frank shook his head. "She's still protecting you, boy, and I'll be damned if I can see why. Things didn't *just* get out of hand. He *raped* her."

Chapter Five

*R*aped?

The word thundered through his brain, growing louder and louder until he could hear or see or feel nothing else.

No! Not Jenny. It couldn't be true. Not Jenny. There must be some kind of mistake. Her father could have misunderstood what she said or—

"No," he whispered. "No. She would have told me. I would have known."

The older man shook his head, his eyes dark and cold. "Nobody knew. She saw to that. But you could have stopped it in the first place. If for once in your useless life you'd thought of someone other than yourself."

Chase tried to draw in a breath. The band around his chest tightened until he thought his ribs would snap. Raped? It wasn't possible.

Without a word, he turned and started down the hall.

"That's right, boy," Davidson called after him. "Run away. And don't come back. My little girl doesn't need anyone like you."

The elevators were slow, as usual. Chase hit the down button again, then swore under his breath and headed for the stairs. He jogged across the parking lot to the Bronco, then slipped inside and started the engine. It was only after he turned onto the road that he realized he had nowhere to go.

There wasn't one person in a radius of a thousand miles that he could talk to. No home where he'd be welcome, no child that would smile at the mention of his name. He squeezed the steering wheel harder.

That wasn't completely true. There was one person who cared. Jenny. Even after all that had happened, she'd opened her door to him last night. She'd kissed him with all the passion he remembered. Had smiled when he'd walked up to her table at lunch. Dear God, what had he done?

The past appeared before him, flashing pictures of so many events that hadn't made sense. He remembered the night of the carnival, the way he'd gotten drunk and passed out. How the next morning, he'd been too hung-over to do more than lie in bed and groan. When he did get around to calling Jenny that evening, she'd claimed a summer cold and had stayed in her house for a week. At the time—he wrinkled his forehead, trying to remember—oh yes, he'd thought she was pissed about the brandy.

Raped. No wonder she'd avoided him. Everyone, really. That had been a summer of growing up for all of them, only Jenny hadn't deserved that kind of introduction to the real world. No wonder she'd resisted his suggestions that they make love.

He cringed as he recalled a Saturday spent by the river. It had been August. A hot, humid day when breathing had taken all the energy they'd had. They'd stretched out under the gnarled old oak tree. All those teenage hormones had been surging and he'd told her it was time. Even now he could see the fear that had darkened her eyes and paled her cheeks.

"I love you," she'd whispered. "But I can't make love to you."

Her pain, as real and tangible as the river itself, had frightened him. He'd kissed away the tears, as if by removing the symptom, he could erase the cause. Three weeks later everything had been over. In the space of an afternoon, he'd lost his home, his future and Jenny.

Eleven years, he thought, turning left at the signal. Eleven years he'd hated her for something that hadn't been her fault. The memory of the harsh words he'd spoken yesterday and that morning echoed loudly around him. He'd accused her of lying, had called her names. She'd never said a word—and one word of the truth would have vindicated her. Shame coiled in his belly and left a metallic taste on his tongue.

He'd sensed there was more to the story with the carny worker. Why hadn't he pushed her to tell him the truth? Why had he let his self-righteousness get in the way? Why in God's name had he let him spend the night? Why hadn't she shut him up with the truth?

Davidson was right. It *was* all his fault. He should have known, should have kept her safe. She'd needed him and he'd failed her. He should have been able to see what had happened. Rage joined the other emotions and he thought about how he would have killed the man who had hurt her. His right hand tightened on the gearshift, as if crushing the metal knob would punish the man who had violated her body and savagely stolen her innocence.

Chase pulled over and parked on the street. Taking slow, deep breaths, he tried to steady his breathing. Around him, people went about their business. A few stared at the truck; a couple recognized him. He saw the half frowns as they tried to place him, then their glares and hurried steps when they did. He'd come home a changed man, but he could feel those hard-won differences slipping away. It had begun the moment he'd seen the mill; it was completed when Davidson had told him the truth. He was now as he had been then—an angry, frustrated man who would never fit in. Jenny had been the only friend he'd had in Harrisville and he'd let her down.

He gazed across the street. A new mall took up two city blocks. On the opposite side of the road sat the old stores. A butcher shop, the dry cleaners. Modern glass and brick blended with small-town architecture. Those were the changes he'd expected. He hadn't allowed himself to picture Jenny still around and he'd never dreamed it would matter. It had. And now—

Why? Why hadn't she told him? He would have listened. Pain joined the rage and frustration until he thought he'd explode.

He closed his eyes and remembered the last time he'd seen her. It had been less than three hours before. If he recalled correctly, his parting shot had been to tell her to go to hell. He winced. Did the right words exist for an apology? Would she understand?

For a moment he thought he'd lost everything, but then he remembered the way she'd looked in her tiny kitchen the night before. He'd baited her with his anger. She'd shuttered her expression, hidden her feelings, but even then he'd known she'd never throw him out.

Chase propped one booted foot on the opposite seat and leaned his head against the window. There was only one solution. He'd make things up to her, fix what had been broken. Despite what had happened at the end of that summer, she'd been his best friend for more years than he could remember. He owed her nothing less than making it right.

With that decided, he started the truck and pulled out into traffic. Her house was only a few blocks away. He glanced at his watch. She'd be home within the hour. He'd tell her that he knew, explain how sorry he was, that he hadn't meant the things he'd said. Her secret had trapped her here in Harrisville. There was no reason for her to stay if she didn't want to. He could help her leave, give her money or something. The plan was vague, but that didn't matter. Between now and the time he left for Phoenix, he'd take care of Jenny's future. Then the debt would be paid.

He pulled into the driveway. The small red house looked worse for wear in the afternoon light. Cracked paint peeled off from the front corners and the porch steps sagged. There were a couple of plastic chairs in front of the living-room windows. He locked his vehicle and climbed up to sit and wait.

A few minutes later, a blue sedan stopped in front of the house. He rose to his feet. But the large car didn't look familiar. And the woman stepping out, while Jenny's height and coloring, wore her hair long, in a braid.

Her face had the same heart shape as Jenny's, but the angles were slightly off, as though a sculptor had designed one from the memory of the other. A similar likeness, but not exact. In the world's eyes, Anne would probably be considered the beauty of the two, but to him there had only ever been Jenny.

Anne marched up the front path. "I might have known I'd find you here," she said as soon as she was within earshot. "If you think you're going to weasel your way back into my sister's life, you can just forget it. She doesn't need you. Go away, Chase. Go back to your fancy home on the rich side of town. We don't want you here."

"You haven't changed at all Anne. Still protecting your own," he said.

"Someone has to." Her chest rose and fell with each agitated breath. "How dare you sit on Jenny's porch advertising your presence."

"I needed to talk and—"

"Oh sure. Talk. As if that's what people are going to think you're doing. Don't you care about her reputation? This is still Harrisville. It might be the nineties in the rest of the world, but we have small-town values here. Haven't you done enough?"

Chase walked to the end of the porch. Anne stood on the first step. He was taller by several inches to begin with, but now he towered over her. Rage returned. And frustration. He knew it showed on his face. He waited, but she didn't back down.

"I don't scare so easily," she said softly. "I love my sister."

"Once I loved her, too."

"A lot of good that did her."

The shot hit home. Chase turned away and walked over to the railing. "I have a couple of things to say to Jenny. When I'm done, I'll leave her in peace. As soon as things are taken care of with my father, I'm out of this town. You'll never see me again. Satisfied?"

"No."

He glanced at her over his shoulder.

She shrugged. "You could have waited on the back porch."

"My truck would still be parked in the driveway. Is it that terrible that the neighbors see me here? Jenny and I used to be friends."

"Some friend you turned out to be."

He knew she was trying to get a rise out of him. What she couldn't know was that nothing she could say was worse than what he'd already told himself. He was all the things Anne thought of him and more. His anger faded as quickly as it had flared.

"You're right," he said, holding her gaze. "I am responsible for what happened. I can't change the past, but I can try to make up for—"

"Make it up?" She climbed up until she stood next to him. "Are you crazy? This isn't some broken doll you can fix with a little glue. We are talking about a person. What happened to Jenny—" She paused. "Wait a minute. How do you know? She didn't tell you, did she?"

"No. Your father had that pleasure."

"Oh."

"It's not important how I found out," he said. "What matters is that I know now. I understand I can't completely erase what happened, but there are things I can do to make it easier. I owe her that."

"Then leave her alone."

"No."

Anne shook her head. "You don't get it, do you? We don't need you. Jenny doesn't need you. We look out for our own here."

"And I've never been one of your own."

She shrugged as if to say why dispute the obvious.

"It always comes back to that damn mill."

"Us against them," she agreed. "It'll never change."

It would when his father died, he thought grimly. But this wasn't the time to go into that. "You're right, Anne. Nothing ever changes in Harrisville."

"Except Jenny," she said softly.

He shifted until he was sitting on the porch railing. "I know that."

"No. You don't. You plan to fix her." Green eyes met and held his own. "But she's all grown-up. The past is behind her. What will you do if she doesn't want or need fixing?"

A beep from a car horn interrupted them. Chase turned and saw Jenny pulling into the driveway, next to his truck. She opened the door and climbed out. A combination of shame and anger and pleasure and guilt flooded his body. The urge to run battled with the need to ask for her forgiveness. If Anne hadn't been standing beside him, he would have raced off the porch and pulled Jenny next to him just to reassure himself that she was okay. But he couldn't. After all, the neighbors might be watching.

"Anne," Jenny said as she walked up onto the porch. "What brings you here?"

Her sister offered a half smile. "Just stopped by to welcome Chase home. We've been catching up on old times, haven't we?"

She dared him to speak the truth. He would. But not like this. "Yeah. A welcoming committee of one."

Jenny glanced from one to the other. The skeptical look on her face told him she knew they were lying. He waited, but she didn't push for the truth.

"How's your father?" she asked.

"A little better. They took him off the breathing equipment, but he still hasn't regained consciousness. Dr. Martin says maybe tomorrow. I hope so. I'd like to talk to him for a few minutes, at least."

She moved closer and reached out to touch him. Then she dropped her arm to her side. He winced at the insecurity in her eyes. Damn. It was his fault. He remembered how he'd blown up at her at lunch. The way he'd told her to go to hell. Even now, he could see the hurt on her face as he'd turned and stormed away.

The light cotton of her blouse had been muted by the ash and grit that belched from the mill. The gold in her hair had been erased by the soot. A smudge stained one cheek. God, she was beautiful, he thought. How could he not have seen it yesterday? Had he been so blinded by rage, so caught up in avoiding the past that he'd ignored the pleasure of watching her live and breathe?

"Jenny, I—"

"I'd better be going," Anne said, interrupting. "Goodbye, Chase. A pleasure and all that. Do remember what I told you."

"No problem. I'll send you a postcard from Phoenix."

"I'll look forward to it." She kissed her sister on the cheek. "Talk to you soon."

"Do I want to ask what that was all about?" Jenny asked as Anne drove away.

"Not really."

"She didn't bother you, did she? Say things that—"

"Let it go." He took her arm and steered her toward the door. "Maybe we could continue this conversation inside."

"What conversation? Why?" She pulled her arm free. "What's gotten into you?"

He glanced over his shoulder at the neat rows of houses across the street. "I have a lot to answer for."

She smiled and reached for her key. "If you mean about last night, forget it. So little happens around here that people are dying for something to gossip about. You and

I both know you spent the night in the spare room. And even if you hadn't, it's really none of their business."

She pushed the door open and motioned for him to precede her. He walked into the small living room and turned to face her.

"I don't mean about last night," he said, stuffing his hands into his pockets. "I mean about before. That summer. I spoke to your father at the hospital. I know—" he glanced at the ground, then lifted his head and stared straight at her "—I know about the rape."

Jenny felt the blood drain away and wondered if she looked as shaken as she felt. No! He couldn't know! Fiery shame filled her, sweeping across her body like wildfire. Her hands clutched the keys so tightly, she could feel the cold metal digging into her skin.

This was the moment she'd dreaded for the last eleven years. Seeing the pain and disgust in Chase's eyes, hearing the pity in his voice. Why now? she wondered. Just when she'd managed to pull her life together, it all began to unravel again.

"He had no right to tell you," she said at last, staring at the third button on Chase's shirt.

"He had every right. You're his daughter. He was trying to protect you."

"I don't need his protection." She drew in a deep breath and forced herself to raise her eyes to meet his. "Or yours. So if that's what this is about, you can just forget it."

His face was as expressionless as it had been yesterday. She didn't know what he was thinking, but it was just a matter of time until he blamed her, or got angry. She'd been the only one in the support group without a husband or boyfriend, but she remembered the other women talking about the men's reactions. Some had turned into a one-man vigilante force, swearing to hunt down the rapist and punish him. Others had withdrawn slowly, day by day, until the relationship was little more than a fragile shell, shattered at the first sign of discord. Alec had been different. She'd told him about the rape, but it had occurred so long before they had met that he had no personal feelings save concern for her. There hadn't been any macho posturing, little desire for revenge, no sense of violation. He had healed her with his easy smile and gentle touch.

Regret joined the apprehension. Regret that she hadn't been able to forget her past enough to enjoy the present and the potential future. Alec had seen that there was more holding her back than the rape. He'd known that she'd never recovered from loving and losing Chase. He hadn't known the other man's name, but had felt his presence in their lives. In the end, he'd asked her to choose. She couldn't, in good conscience, deceive Alec any longer. She'd let him go.

"I don't want to hurt you," Chase said, taking a step closer.

She stiffened. "Then forget everything you heard today. It doesn't matter anymore."

"How can you say that? I've treated you so badly since I've been back. Why didn't you tell me? Why did you let me walk away all those years ago? How could you let me think you'd betrayed me? How could you let me think you didn't care?"

It was beginning, she thought. "I did care, but at the time I didn't know what..." She sighed. "Do we have to talk about this? I'm fine now."

"Are you?" He took another step, stopping only inches from her. Then he cupped her chin in his hand and forced her to continue to hold his gaze. "I don't believe that."

Alec hadn't believed it, either. Oh, he'd known she'd recovered from the trauma, but he'd suspected there was another secret. Not as dark or as scary, but more powerful. The secret of loving and waiting for Chase.

"Why didn't you tell me?"

His pain was her undoing. If he'd been angry or ashamed of her, she would have been able to tell him it was none of his business and send him on his way. His fingers felt warm against her skin. Calluses, earned through physical labor and time, rubbed against her cheek. His mouth, firm but tender, pulled into a straight line. Only that morning she'd tasted his desire, had feasted on passion long-denied. Now deep lines bracketed the straight lips. A frown drew dark eyebrows together. Stubble shadowed the hollows of his cheeks and outlined the strength of his jaw. This face, familiar and strange, all man, but retaining echoes of the boy, weakened her resolve.

"I would have slain dragons for you," he whispered. "Conquered the world." He swallowed. "Sold my soul. You never gave me the chance."

She closed her eyes. A single tear escaped and rolled down her cheek. He brushed the moisture with his thumb. The gesture, one he'd performed so many times before, made her smile.

"I wasn't looking to be rescued," she said. "I needed—"

"What?"

"A magical way to turn back time so it never happened in the first place. No one could do that. Not even you."

He swore violently under his breath. She flinched. He dropped his hand and swore again. "It's my fault. If I hadn't gotten drunk, I would have been able to drive you home. Then it would never have happened."

"That's not what I meant."

He turned away and leaned against the doorframe, facing the tiny hallway. "It's the truth."

"No." She touched his arm; he shook her off. "Listen to me." She moved to face him. "It *just happened*. It's nobody's fault. There's no blame here. Not for you or me. I asked you to get the alcohol. You didn't want to. You could have easily said no, but I knew you'd do anything for me."

He looked haunted. She knew how that felt.

"There's nothing you could have done," she said.

"I could have done something. Beat him up. Made him marry you. Something to make it right."

She shook her head. "Do you think I'd want to marry the man who raped me?"

"No, of course not."

"My father sent the police after him, but he'd left the carnival. We talked about hiring a private detective." She rubbed the side of her head as if she could force the memories back into the dark corners of her mind. "I just wanted to put it behind me."

"I would have found him." Chase's hands clenched into fists.

"This is exactly why I didn't tell you. I knew you'd get crazy and want to punish the guy."

"Is that wrong? Should I be happy about what happened?"

"No."

He frowned. "I don't understand any of this."

"Come here."

She tugged on his arm. He resisted at first, then allowed her to lead him to the small sofa under the living-room window. The sun had begun its nightly descent. After seating Chase, she reached over and turned on the lamp in the corner, then went into the kitchen. She returned carrying two long-neck beer bottles and handed him one.

She sat on the floor, with her back to the couch, then took a long drink. She hadn't told the story in years. Time was supposed to be the great healer, but she could already feel her stomach tightening up in knots. Clearing her mind, she forced her emotions to the back of her consciousness. It had been over a long time ago. It couldn't hurt anymore.

Chase's long legs stretched out beside her. She studied his worn leather cowboy boots, the much-washed denim covering his calves.

"It happened so fast," she said at last. "One minute we were talking and the next—" She took another swallow. "I fought. As much as I could. He was bigger and for several minutes I didn't realize he meant to go all the way."

Beside her Chase stiffened. She didn't dare turn and look at him. The fear of his disgust and pity was too great.

"When it was over and he drove me home, I couldn't even get out of the car. He told me to go, but I just laid there. Stunned, bleeding, crying." She stared at the carpet, noting it, like many other things in the house, needed replacing. "Finally, I crawled out and went into the house."

"Jenny—"

She shook her head to silence him. "The worst part was I blamed myself. I felt responsible, as if I'd done something wrong. Getting in his car was stupid. I see that now, but no one deserves to suffer that badly for a mistake. This was Harrisville, for God's sake. Things like that don't happen here."

She paused, unable to go on. A few deep breaths and she got control again. Chase touched her head. Long fingers toyed with the strands of hair, pressed reassuringly against her neck. She leaned back, savoring the warm contact, then continued with her story.

"I was afraid to tell anyone. I thought I'd get in trouble. That my family would be ashamed of me and know that I'd done something so awful."

"It wasn't your fault," he said.

"I know that now. But it's taken me a lot of time to figure that out."

"I would have listened."

"Would you? Really? Think about it, Chase. We were kids. You would have wanted to run off half-cocked and kill the guy. Admit it, that's what you're feeling."

"You're right," he said softly, continuing to stroke her hair.

"And I was too afraid of losing you. I thought I'd get over it in a few days. I'd been raped, but I hadn't made love, so I knew you'd still be my first time."

The tears burned hot, but she blinked them away.

"Why didn't you tell me yesterday?" he asked. "Why did you let me go on the way I did?"

"I made the decision to keep silent when it happened. There's been so much going on. It's been eleven years. I wasn't sure the past would still matter to you. I knew you were upset about your dad and everything, it just seemed easier to keep quiet."

"Easier for me, you mean."

"Yes."

"Jenny, I—" he cleared his throat "—I understand why you didn't tell me, then or now, but I wish you had." He sighed.

"I know. When I found out I was pregnant, I had to tell my parents. It took me a long time to work up the courage to tell them about the rape. By then it was too late—you were gone."

His fingers stilled. "I would have come back if I'd known."

She bowed her head. "I would have told you if I could have found you. It's silly, but that still hurts."

"Yeah."

The room was silent. Jenny traced circular patterns on the carpet with the beer bottle. In the hallway, an old clock chimed the hour.

"Did you get help?" he asked.

"About a year later, I started seeing a counselor. She got me involved with a group. It took some time, but I've healed."

"I should have been here with you. I would have stood by you no matter what."

"You can't know that."

He set his beer on the floor and leaned forward, lacing his fingers together. "I can and I do. Dammit, Jenny, you meant the world to me. I would never have turned my back on you."

"We were so young. We had all these plans. That night changed everything. I'm glad you got away. You were supposed to." She half turned and looked up at him. "Getting out of Harrisville was what you always wanted."

He stared down at her. His tan couldn't hide the ashen tint underneath. "It was supposed to be *our* goal. I thought we wanted to get away together."

"It was a beautiful dream, Chase, but it would never have worked."

"Why?"

"We were children, with the hopes and plans children make." She glanced at her clothes. "Look at me. I'm blue-collar, through and through. And you—"

"I'm a construction worker."

"No. You're the steel mill owner's son. It was fun to be Cinderella. You made high school magical. The son of the richest man in town falling for the union president's daughter. It plays great in literature or on TV, but not in real life. I grew up."

"You sold out." His dark eyes glittered in the lamplight. "You had the chance, but you didn't take it. You could have left, but you were afraid."

"In the beginning I stayed because I had nowhere else to go. But in the end, I stayed because I wanted to."

"And now?"

"I belong here."

He shook his head. "Not me. I've never belonged. And as soon as I can, I'm leaving again."

It was right for him to get out, she acknowledged. Chase had made his dream come true. He'd earned his reward. But why did it have to hurt so much? She'd barely survived losing him eleven years ago. Then she'd been a teenager, full of hope for the future. It had never occurred to her she wouldn't forget him.

But Alec had showed her the truth. She might not still love Chase, but she'd never love anyone else. Her life was in Harrisville; as for Chase, he was counting the hours until his escape.

It was already too late, she thought. It was like trying to stop a speeding train. Heartbreak was rushing to mow her down and she could only stand helplessly and wait for it to happen.

Chapter Six

The phone rang, the shrill sound cutting through the silence of the night. Jenny scrambled to her feet and walked across the room. She picked up the receiver.

"Hello?"

She listened for several seconds, then covered the mouthpiece. "It's Terry, from the hospital. She says that your father seems to be regaining consciousness."

Chase rose. "Tell her I'll be right there."

Jenny concluded the conversation and hung up. "He's pretty out of it and not making much sense, but you might be able to talk to him."

He started toward the door, then paused. "I feel like we haven't finished all we had to say."

"I know, but you need to be at the hospital right now."

"I'll call you later."

"No. Don't call."

He looked surprised. "Why? Don't you want to—"

"Just come back when you're done."

"Here? It might be late."

He was offering her an out. The problem was she didn't want one. "The guest room and I will be waiting."

"I don't want to make trouble." She could read the indecision in his eyes.

"You mean the neighbors might talk?"

He nodded.

"Let them." She smiled. "I'm a big girl, Chase. I can take care of myself. I answered all your questions about the past. The least you can do is be honest with me. Or don't you want to stay here?"

His half smile, so full of pain and need, made her long to go to him. But this wasn't the time.

"I'll be back before midnight," he promised. "If it's going to be any later, I'll call." He opened the front door, then turned back to her. "Thanks."

"My pleasure." She walked to the open door. Placing a hand on his arm, she rose on her toes and kissed his cheek. He was warm and alive. The stubble tickled her lips; his scent made her long for his embrace.

A declaration, not of love but of need and compassion, hovered on her lips. She swallowed it knowing he would misunderstand her purpose. He needed time to absorb all that had happened. So did she. When he returned, they'd pick up where they'd left off.

Chase walked down the path toward his Bronco. The temperature had dropped with the falling sun. He shrugged into his worn leather jacket, then slid onto the seat and started the engine. Disconnected thoughts whirled through his head. Kaleidoscope pictures blending and blurring, overlapping until he couldn't separate what he remembered from what Jenny had told him.

Over the sound of the engine and the soft country song from the radio, he heard her cries of distress, the ripping of her dress, the panic of her "No!" He could taste her tears, smell her fear, feel her blood. Dark and ugly, the urge to kill a man—*the* man—burned hot and low in his belly.

And he did nothing. She was right; he would have sought revenge. Exacted a price for the crime. Standing by her would have been easy, staying beside her on her terms, impossible. Even now he reacted from instinct.

The hospital loomed up ahead. For the third time that day, he made his way through the halls. This time, he didn't bother buzzing before he entered the Cardiac Care unit. Terry, looked up at his approach.

"I'm glad you could make it," she said, coming forward and smiling. "He's not all here, but he is talking. The medication to help his rest will start to work in about fifteen or twenty minutes, then he'll sleep through the night. If all goes well, he should be awake in the morning." She studied him. "You look awful."

"Is that your professional opinion?"

"You bet. Have you eaten today?"

"Lunch."

"It's already seven-thirty. Your blood sugar is hanging down around your knees. Don't you know how important it is to eat well-balanced meals, properly spaced?"

Chase reached out and tapped her nose. "You must be a great mom."

"Sweet talk will get you absolutely nothing. So save it for the day staff."

She led the way into the small room. Leaning over his father, she took his pulse and spoke softly. "Mr. Jackson, your son is here. Can you hear me?"

"Denise?" the old man on the bed murmured. "I can't see you. Where are you?"

"Right here," Terry said, smoothing back his thin white hair. She looked back at Chase. "Denise was your mother's name, wasn't it?"

He nodded.

"He's been talking to her for about half an hour. Maybe if he hears your voice..." She shrugged. "Buzz me if you need anything or if he gets agitated." She glanced at the clock. "He's going to be asleep in a few minutes. Don't worry if he doesn't make sense. The drugs help him rest and heal, but they also make it hard for him to concentrate."

She straightened and stepped back to allow Chase to sit in the chair beside the bed. After patting him on the shoulder, she left.

"Hey, Dad. It's me. Chase."

The old man moved his head back and forth. His eyes were closed. "Is that you, son?"

"I'm here." He leaned forward and took his father's hand. Once again the clammy skin reminded him of a fish. Long, sticklike fingers curled around his.

"You've got to try harder," the weak voice demanded. "You're a Jackson. That means something in this town. Can't let those mill boys show you up."

"Dad," he interrupted. "That was a long time ago. Everything is—"

"Listen to me, boy. I said listen." The voice grew in volume. His father's eyes opened and he glared right at Chase. "You always were a trial to me."

"That's all in the past, Dad. It's been eleven years. Maybe we should—"

"No!" His father cut him off. "Denise, the boy needs to make his way. We can't send him to a private school.

He's going to be in charge of those other children. He needs to learn early about authority and making people listen. I don't care if they like him. Respect is more important.''

The argument was familiar, Chase realized. It was one he'd heard over and over, right up to the day his mother was killed in a car accident.

"What's he going to turn into, without me pushing him? The boy has no ambition. Never did. It's a failing from your side of the family."

"Dad," he said, leaning closer. "It's okay. I did make it. All on my own." He wanted to withdraw his hand and any comfort it might offer, but he held on.

"Denise! Denise!" His father raised up slightly, then fell back on the pillows. "I can't see you anymore." His eyes closed. "Come back. I need you. What am I supposed to do with the boy? I can't—"

His father drew in a deep breath and the hand holding Chase's relaxed.

"Dad?" he said. "Can you hear me?"

There was no answer. Only the sound of William Jackson's shallow breath and the quiet beeping of the heart monitor.

Chase sat there for another hour, willing his father to wake up and speak to him. It did no good. His side and back tightened from leaning forward at an awkward angle, but he didn't release the old man's hand. Tomorrow, he thought. Tomorrow his father would be more lucid and they could talk. Maybe mend a few fences.

For eleven years, he'd waited to be called home. Gradually anger had replaced hope, then resignation had set in. When he'd received the telegram, he'd felt nothing. Or so he'd thought. But now, in the hospital room, the regret surprised him. He'd never meant to care that his father was dying, but he did. He didn't love the old man; certainly he didn't want to be anything like him. Yet the thought of the world without his father was more than he could imagine.

Nothing was how he had thought it would be. Nothing was easy. Seeing Jenny again—he sighed—that hurt, too. He almost wished he hadn't pressed her to tell him the truth. It had been better when he could hide behind his hatred.

The feeling started slowly. A slight tremor in his legs, a tightening in his gut. It grew until the message pounded in his head.

Run.

Chase released his father's hand and shifted on the chair. The command flashed again. If he started driving tonight, he'd be in Phoenix by Monday. Sooner, if he drove straight through. His bag was on the back seat; he wouldn't have to tell anyone. They'd figure it out when he didn't show up again. The town and the mill had gotten along fine without him for eleven years. Someone else could handle his father's estate, when the old man died. Someone else could endure the glares and not-so-subtle comments whispered behind his back. Someone else—

Jenny. She appeared before him as real and vivid as his father's vision of his mother. He couldn't leave her. Not yet. He had to make things right. He owed her for what had happened; he had to fix what had been broken. He couldn't run. Even if it seemed the easiest plan.

At nine-thirty he rose from his father's side and moved out of the small room. Terry sat behind the nurses' station. When he approached, she looked up and smiled.

"How was he?" she asked.

"Like you said, pretty out of it. I thought he recognized me, but—" He slipped into his jacket. "He was talking about some stuff from when I was a kid. I doubt he knew I was here."

"Don't get discouraged," she said, coming out from behind her desk and standing next to him. "These things take time."

"Sure." It was the one commodity that he didn't have an abundance of. "I'm going to head home. I'll see you later."

"Okay. I don't work for a couple of nights, but I'll be in touch."

Chase walked toward the door, then turned back. "How long does he have?"

Terry stared, startled. "The doctor can tell you better—"

"Don't give me that crap," he said softly. "I want..." He took a deep breath. "I need to hear the truth. Everybody's so careful about what they *do* say. I have to listen for what they *don't* put into words. Please."

"There's always a chance. We can't know for sure." She pushed up her glasses, then folded her arms over her chest. "A few days, maybe a week. He's off the ventilator, but he's not getting stronger. I'm sorry, Chase."

"Hey, it's not worse than I suspected." He patted her shoulder. "I appreciate the honesty. Tell Tom he's a lucky guy."

"He knows already. I remind him every day."

He waved goodbye and left.

What must it be like, he wondered as he took the stairs two at a time, to live a normal life? Go to work every day, come home to a wife and kids, mow the lawn Saturday mornings, take out the trash on Tuesdays. He and Jenny had planned on escaping Harrisville. They'd talked about what the future would be like, but except for the leaving, their ideas had been broad strokes of an ideal life. They were going to work their ways through college. Find an apartment together. Get married and pursue their careers. See the world, then have children. He frowned, trying to remember exactly. Oh yes. One of each. Two years apart.

Only none of it had happened. She'd been raped and he'd been forced out of town.

At her house, he walked across the porch and tapped on the door. There was no answer. He tried the knob and found it unlocked.

"Jenny?" he called as he walked inside and toward the living room.

She lay curled up on the sofa. Her head rested on a throw pillow, one arm tucked under her ear, the other clutched the collar of her robe. The navy terry cloth covered her from neck to ankle, but the front opening gapped enough to give him a glimpse of long, slender legs up to midthigh and the hem of her T-shirt. She'd showered and her hair glowed golden in the lamplight.

"Aw, Jenny," he murmured as he moved closer. "You didn't have to wait up."

He crouched beside her, gently brushing the hair from her face. She stirred slightly, moving her head toward the warmth of his hand.

"Hi, honey," she whispered, not bothering to open her eyes. "I tried to stay awake, but I couldn't. Everything go okay?"

He froze in the act of touching her. She was still asleep. And dreaming of another man. She thought he was Alec.

It was as if a giant fist clutched his midsection and squeezed. Air rushed from his lungs and his stomach jerked violently.

"You must be hungry," she said, rubbing her cheek against the back of his hand. "I left you a plate in the fridge, Chase. All you have to do is heat it in the microwave. Or I could do it.''

He inhaled and relaxed. She knew it was him. The panic receded slowly. Damn it, why would it have mattered one way or the other? he asked himself. He wanted to make up for the past, not relive it.

''No. I think you need to be in bed, young lady.''

She opened one eye. Without makeup, the flush of sleep lingering on her skin, she looked about fourteen. All sweet and innocent.

''You sound like my dad.'' She rolled on her back and stretched. The action parted the robe the rest of the way and he saw the curves of her body outlined by the thin material of her T-shirt.

Heat flooded him, washing his soul with desire, drowning his body with need. If she had been any other woman of his acquaintance, he would have gathered her close and shown her how much he wanted her. Instead, he rose to his feet and stepped back.

She sat up and smoothed down her hair. ''I look a mess, huh?''

''No.''

The sound, more a low growl than a word, caused her to glance up at him. She blinked several times, as if trying to bring him into focus. He saw the exact moment she connected the controlled stance and tight fists with what he was thinking.

''Chase?''

''Go to bed.''

''But you—''

''It's just a reaction, Jenny. It doesn't *mean* anything.''

She looked away, but not quickly enough to hide the flash of pain.

He swore and dropped onto the couch next to her. "Don't be upset. I'm confused. There's too much happening too fast. You, my father, the town. It's all I can do to keep from running. Nothing is what it's supposed to be. Dammit, you shouldn't even be living here anymore."

She nodded in agreement, but the hurt in her eyes didn't fade. He started to reach for her, then paused. Was it okay? Would he scare her with a friendly hug? Did she think of the rape when a man touched her?

Questions tumbled over each other and he didn't have any answers. In the end, he folded his arms over his chest and rested his head against the sofa back.

Jenny fought the urge to whack him over the head with the table lamp. Maybe then she could knock some sense into him. "I'm not a porcelain doll," she said, picking at the sleeve of her robe.

"I know."

"Then?"

"Then, what?"

"Why did you start to hug me and stop?" She glanced at him out of the corner of her eye. He was staring across the room.

"I don't want to scare you. I have certain, uh, feelings that are inappropriate for the circumstances."

"You mean sex?"

He winced. "Not exactly."

"What exactly?"

"It's hard to explain."

She bit down on her lower lip to keep from smiling. "Because I'm a woman?"

"Maybe." He frowned in concentration.

"Oh, Chase. Sell it somewhere else. Of course it's sex."

He turned to look at her. She saw his outrage.

"Don't go all manly on me," she said, shifting closer and tugging his arm until she forced it around her shoulders. "Eleven years ago we wanted each other more than anything in the world. Those feelings are still here. For both of us. They're mixed up with guilt and affection and memories and nothing makes sense. You don't know if you should or I can. You're leaving town as soon as possible. I'm committed to staying. It's more than geography, it's a symptom of everything that's wrong between us."

"And?"

"And we keep on going. Muddling through as best we can. Trying to be friends. I've missed you so much."

"I've missed you, too." He pulled her closer, settling her head on his shoulder. "When I left here, I thought I'd die. I was so hurt and angry."

"I know." It was painful to hear the truth, but she'd learned the hard lesson that hidden feelings only got more painful and festered into ugly wounds.

"Now I don't know what to think," he said. "I hate what happened to you. I want to make it better."

"You can't."

"I have to."

He sounded determined. She shifted until she was kneeling beside him. Cupping his face, she stared into his brown eyes. "Accept the past. Make peace with it. I have. There's nothing to fix, nothing to atone for."

"You're wrong," he said. "I have to—"

She silenced him with a kiss. Words of duty and promise would only bring regret later.

Her mouth molded against his, absorbing the strength, the taste. His stubble rasped along her palms as she slid her hands back to touch his hair. His tongue pushed forward to meet hers. She allowed them a moment to caress, then she pulled back and trailed kisses along his jaw.

He tasted salty. The bitter flavor of his after-shave made her wrinkle her nose and chuckle. Large masculine hands tugged at her sleeves, forcing her arms down and the robe to pool at her hips. The thin shirt provided no protection against roving fingers. He spanned her waist, then moved up her ribs. Tiny ripples of sensation preceded his touch. But the movements were tentative, planned. She nipped at his neck, drawing a moan.

He slid toward the center of the sofa, then shifted her until she straddled him. Her bare thighs cupped him, lace panties and straining denim the only barriers to their joining.

His hands returned to her body, moving slowly toward her breasts. She drew in her breath in anticipation.

But he didn't move farther. His arousal pressed hard against her, but he was still. She sensed the war raging within him. The knowledge of her past lay between them like an unbridgeable wall. She opened her eyes.

Indecision tightened the lines of his face. Apprehension straightened his mouth and drew his brows together. His chest rose and fell with heavy passion, but his eyes questioned their actions. Instinctively, she arched forward slightly, as if to force the contact. Her breasts, swollen and heavy with desire, pressed against his shirt. His hands moved up a fraction, his thumbs barely touching the inside curves.

"This is as far as we've ever gone," he said.

"Second base." She forced herself to smile. The timing couldn't be worse. "Although there was that one night—" She paused, not wanting to bring up the time he'd slipped his hand inside her panties and stroked until she felt ready to explode. With the perspective of an adult, she knew that she'd asked him to stop just short of completion. As a teenager, she'd been worried about dying from pleasure. "At least this time we didn't steam the windows."

He didn't return her smile. "I want you. As much as I ever did."

"I know."

"There's so much happening so fast. When this is over—"

"You'll be gone," she reminded him.

"I wish it could be different."

"Me, too."

She tried to look away, but couldn't. Deliberately, she moved his hands up until they cupped the weight of her breasts. Long fingers kneaded. Ribbons of pleasure tightened through her body. Then he flicked his thumbs over her tight nipples. Her muscles clenched, forcing her thighs against him. They both swallowed.

"It's late," he said, dropping his arms to his sides. "You'd better turn in."

She slipped off the couch and gathered her robe around her. The needing ache inside would keep her awake most of the night. He knew that as well as she did. But making love would only complicate everything. He needed time to come to grips with his new knowledge. She was already having trouble thinking of Chase leaving. At least now she could only imagine what it would be like to make love with him. If she had the actual memories to call upon, his absence would be unbearable.

The argument sounded hollow, but it was the best she could do at the moment.

It was barely dawn when Chase picked up his boots and crept down the hall. He paused outside Jenny's door and listened for any sound.

Last night he'd heard her restlessly tossing and turning in bed. Long after midnight, they'd both lain awake, staring at the ceiling. Even when the physical evidence of his passion had faded, the wanting inside had stirred him. The little sleep he'd managed had been filled with violent or sexual dreams.

Cautiously he opened her door and peeked inside. She slept on her stomach. The blankets covered her completely, only her face and tousled hair showed.

"I promise I'll make it up to you," he whispered fervently. "No matter what it takes, I'll fix it. I swear."

Leaning on the wall by the front door, he pulled on his boots, then let himself out and started toward his truck.

After stopping at a fast-food joint for coffee and breakfast, he drove to the mill. The first shift came on about an hour and a half before the office staff started. He parked the Bronco in an out-of-the-way corner of the lot and counted the number of cars pulling in.

Since he'd refused to ask Jenny to show him the books, he didn't have any idea about the financial state of the business. The brief glimpse he'd had of the mill yesterday showed him that the equipment hadn't been improved in years. With today's economy, an American steel mill would require the best machinery and management to survive. Offshore companies had the advantage of reduced overhead. He'd bet his contractor's license that Jackson Steel hadn't shown a profit in a decade.

He watched the parade of cars quickly file into the parking lot. And he counted. By the time the whistle blew signaling the beginning of the first shift, he had his answer. Production was down. There was about half the workers that there had been eleven years ago.

He sipped his coffee. His father was going to die and there wasn't a thing he could do to stop it. And when the old man was gone, Jackson Steel would pass down the family tree. To the oldest son. The *only* son.

"I don't want it," he said, speaking aloud.

He stared out the window and frowned. In the half hour he'd been sitting there, a fine coating of ash had covered his windshield. He looked around. Most of the cars had rust spots on the paint, a legacy from the mill.

A man walked toward him. Chase recognized Frank Davidson and grimaced. Hell of a way to start the morning.

"You here to count your chickens?" Davidson asked when Chase got out of the truck. The older man carried a cup of coffee. He paused and took a sip.

"I came by to see how the mill's making out."

"Times are hard. People worry about being laid off. They have families to support." Jenny took after her mother in looks. There was little of her softness in the older man's craggy face.

"This company is a dinosaur. It should have been extinct a long time ago."

"There's still a way to turn a profit at steel. With the right man in charge."

Chase leaned against the hood and folded his arms over his chest. "Don't look at me. I'm just some rich kid. Never amounted to much."

"That used to be true. The way my daughter tells it, times have changed and you've gone and made something of yourself. I might have been a little too quick to judge you yesterday. 'Course that don't excuse you spending the night at her house. Again." Davidson finished the coffee and tossed the paper cup into a nearby trash can.

In spite of himself, Chase grinned. "Is there anything you don't know?"

"Yeah. I don't know what's going to happen to my people when your father dies. Your great-grandfather started this company. My grandfather worked for him. That used to mean something. Now it's all changed." Davidson shoved his hands into his pockets. "William Jackson has turned his back on his people. He won't listen to reason. I don't mean to speak ill of the dead, but—"

"He's not gone yet. Let's put off the funeral arrangements until the body's cold."

Davidson had the grace to look ashamed. "Sorry. You're right. But we're going to have to talk about the future of Jackson Steel soon enough."

Chase opened his door. "It has no future. There's nothing to say."

"The problem's not going away. Decisions have to be made."

"Forget it. I'm not going to run the mill."

"There are a thousand people still employed here. You going to forget about them, too?"

Despite the crisp morning air, Chase could feel the walls closing in again. "I've got to get to the hospital," he said. "The doctor is expecting my father to be fully conscious today and we have a lot of things to say to each other."

"I bet you do." Davidson leaned closer and stared. Chase wondered if he'd nicked himself shaving. "I broke your nose, didn't I?" the older man asked.

He rubbed the bump marring his profile. "If Jenny had been my daughter, I would have done the same."

Davidson raised an eyebrow. "We couldn't possibly agree on something, could we?"

"I always cared about Jenny. You're right. I *am* responsible for what happened to her that summer. It's not something I'll live with easily. But I want you to know I intend to make it up to her any way that I can."

"It seems a little late for that, but I'll leave the two of you to decide. Just know that if you hurt her this time, I'll do more than break your nose." He offered his hand.

Chase stared at him a moment, then clasped it in his own and shook.

When the men stepped apart, Davidson turned and looked at the mill. "Lot of things are going to be different real soon. You might think you won't be a part of it, but responsibility has a way of changing a man."

"Not me."

"Keep saying that, son, and you might make it true."

Chapter Seven

Chase glanced at his watch, then buzzed the speaker at the Cardiac Care unit. When the nurse came on the line, he announced himself. She told him to come in.

He pushed the door open slowly. The shift changed at 7:00 a.m., so Terry had already left. A different nurse greeted him. Youngish, close to thirty, she had a slight protruding belly under her smock.

"When's the baby due?" he asked as she greeted him.

"Another four months. Feels like an eternity." The nurse smiled. "Your father is awake and feeling pretty good. We've given him breakfast, although we don't expect him to eat that much. You can talk to him. Just don't get him too tired, and don't let him move around. We don't want his heart rate any faster than it has to be."

"Fine."

Chase squared his shoulders and walked toward his father's room. Tension stiffened his spine. He was a Jackson; he wouldn't show fear. Ironic that the training he'd despised would serve him so well when he faced his father.

The door to the room stood ajar. He knocked once and stepped inside.

William Jackson sat upright, his back supported by the hospital bed. A tray sat on the table pulled over his lap. Someone, probably the pleasant nurse, had shaved him and dressed him in a clean gown.

"Hello, Father," Chase said. "I'm glad you're feeling better."

"Well, well." The old man set down his spoon. Gray eyes, exactly as cold and judgmental as he remembered, met and held his own. "So you finally came back. I always knew that you would." He motioned to the chair. "Tail between your legs. Couldn't cut it, could you?"

Chase frowned, not understanding what his father was going on about. Had the medication affected his—

He tightened his jaw. William Jackson wasn't crazy because of the medication, he was gloating. Apparently he didn't know Jenny had sent a telegram recalling his only son. The old man thought he was returning in defeat.

Chase sat in the same chair he'd been using since his first visit to the hospital. "You're looking well, Father. You gave everyone quite a scare."

Jackson brushed off the implied concern. "They haven't seen the last of me yet, even though the vultures are probably circling overhead. So. How much do you need? A million?"

"Dollars?"

His father nodded. "I might have spent my life in steel, but I understand about construction. Lose a couple of backers and the whole project falls apart. Times have been tough. I'll loan you the money, with interest. Of course the best thing would be for you to come back and work in the mill. It's not too late.''

''Wait a minute.'' Chase leaned forward and linked his hands together. ''First, I am not going to work in the mill. Second, I don't need your money. My company is doing fine. We had to turn down a hotel expansion last month because we're too busy.''

''There's no need to exaggerate your position in—''

''I'm not exaggerating,'' Chase said loudly as he came to his feet. ''Why do you assume I've failed?''

''Because I know you don't have what it takes to make it, boy. You've always—''

''Stop.'' Chase walked to the end of the bed and braced his hands on the metal footboard. ''It's been eleven years and you don't know a damn thing about me.''

The older man pushed away the tray. ''I know you're my son.''

''Some father you turned out to be. You let an eighteen-year-old kid run off on his own. You never tried to find me, or write me. What the hell were you thinking of? If I made it—and I did—it's no thanks to you.''

William Jackson pursed his lips. ''You needed to learn about your responsibilities. We didn't know that Davidson girl was going to lose her brat. If you hadn't run away—''

''I didn't get Jenny pregnant. I tried to tell you that, but you wouldn't listen. You're still not listening.'' Frustration added an edge to his voice.

''I'll admit I was hard on you, but it was for your own good.''

Chase turned away and ran his hand through his hair. Hard? He thought back on the beatings, the cold words, the obvious disappointment in his father's voice every time they spoke. "Hard doesn't quite describe it," he said softly.

"You're a grown man now, Chase. What do you want from me?"

The question, spoken in that impatient why-are-you-bothering-me voice he'd always hated as a child, brought him up short.

He folded his arms over his chest. "Guess what, Dad? I don't want a damn thing."

The room was silent. He forced himself to look back at his father. The man had aged suddenly. His hands shook as he lifted his juice glass. Something hot and gritty burned at the back of Chase's eyes, and he stared at the floor. He didn't want to see the old man like this. It was better when they yelled at each other.

"They sent you a telegram, didn't they?" William asked.

"Yes."

"So you're here out of obligation."

There was no good answer to that question. "It's been a long time, Dad. Let's just let it go. You need to think about getting better."

"I've left you the mill."

"I don't want it." He spoke without thinking.

"You are my son and you *will* be responsible. I don't give a damn about your petty little construction business."

Chase looked longingly at the door. "I employee forty guys."

"*We* employee a thousand."

"I'm not coming back."

"You don't have a choice."

He spun to face him. "The hell I don't. You can't make me do anything anymore." Anger boiled inside. Clenching his jaw, he forced himself to relax. "I didn't come here to fight with you. I was concerned, so I flew home."

"You must stay. The mill is your heritage."

"It's a death sentence."

"Not to the people employed there."

"Don't give me that crap. When have you ever cared about the people of this town? One of the last things you told me before I left was that it didn't matter that I'd gotten some girl pregnant, only that she was the union president's daughter. It's always been about what you want and no one else. Don't pull this noble act now. Not on me. It won't work."

His father leaned back against the pillows. "You've gotten good at speeches. Maybe you should go into politics. The doctor says that I'll be in the hospital for at least two more weeks. That will give you enough time to return to Arizona and pack up your house. When you get back—"

"Have you listened to one word I've said?"

William offered a half smile. "I heard, but it's not important. The mill—"

"Is just a factory. Dad, I'm your son. Don't you care about what I want?"

The elder Jackson raised his head slightly. "No. I don't. The mill must continue. You will inherit everything eventually. You must learn how to run it. I tried to explain this eleven years ago, but you were too caught up in feeling sorry for yourself. I won't live forever."

He continued to speak, but Chase didn't hear anything. He felt battered, as if he'd had a run-in with a two-ton flatbed. They'd been talking at cross-purposes and he'd finally figured out what was going wrong. He'd come home looking for a change in his father, some sign that the years apart had mellowed him. He'd hoped to find parental approval, a happily-ever-after ending to a tragic relationship. It had been a nice dream. But meaningless. The old man hadn't changed at all. He had his priorities. Years ago, they'd never included a small boy. Now they couldn't include a grown man.

"...just in time delivery systems," William continued. "You can research that when you get back."

"Dad, I—"

"Hi. Am I interrupting?"

Chase turned at the question and heaved a sigh of relief when he saw Jenny standing in the doorway. "No. Come in."

"Mr. Jackson." Jenny set a large flower display on a table in the corner. "I called to make sure you were allowed plants. I'd wanted to bring them sooner, but with the oxygen and all—" She shrugged, then smiled. "You look great. How do you feel?"

"Just fine. And who is balancing the books if you're wasting your time here?"

His father wasn't making a joke, Chase knew, but Jenny brushed his comments aside and moved closer to the bed. "I came to work early today just so I could stop by and see you. Everything is going well at the mill. I don't want you to worry about anything but getting better."

As they talked, Chase studied her. Carefully applied makeup hid most of the dark circles. A green sweater, the exact shade of her eyes, hugged her curves, reminding him of what he'd come so close to possessing the previous night. The wanting had never left him and even seeing her was enough to fan it into fire.

Oh, Jenny, he thought. What kind of a mess are we in now? He'd always known her father's dedication to the mill workers. Somehow his fight had been passed down to his daughter. Jenny was tied to this town with the unbreakable tentacles of obligation. He didn't understand the whys of what had happened in the years that he'd been gone, but the result was plain to see.

And somehow, amidst his father's illness and the problems of the mill, he had to find a way to make up for the past. If only he could convince her to leave, he could—

His gaze slipped past Jenny toward the heart monitor. The wavy line that represented his father's heartbeat seemed to be moving faster. In the outer room, a machine beeped softly, then hummed as it spit out paper.

He glanced at his father. The old man's coloring was good, but his breathing had grown more shallow.

"Jenny, I think we'd better let—"

"All right, Mr. Jackson." The pregnant nurse entered the room. "You've had about all the excitement you need for one day." She looked at Chase. "His heartbeat is elevated. I'm going to give him some medication to bring it down and something to help him relax. There's nothing to worry about, just too much activity on the first day awake." She gave William the pills and a cup of water. "No more visitors for you today, Mr. Jackson."

"I have to see my employees."

"Tomorrow," she said firmly. "You need to rest. All this moving and talking isn't good for your heart."

Chase watched his father swallow the medication. He wanted to say something meaningful, find the words that would bring them closer together.

He took his father's hand. "Get better, Dad. And then we'll talk."

The old man shook his head. "They won't get rid of me this easily. Think about what I said, boy. You need to recognize your mistakes. Time's a' wasting. We've got a mill to run. Thanks for the flowers, Jenny. Now get back to work so I don't have to dock your pay."

The nurse ushered them out of the room.

"Is he going to be okay?" Chase asked.

"You'll have to ask the doctor," she said. "The rapid heartbeat isn't that unusual. Right now he needs rest. Call me in a few hours and I'll give you an update, but don't plan on stopping by until tomorrow morning."

He smiled his thanks, then turned to Jenny. "Why did you come by?"

"To see if the two of you had come to blows yet."

He grimaced. "He sure hasn't softened any."

"He loves you, Chase."

"You said that before. It's obvious he doesn't care about anyone. Why do you defend him?"

"I keep thinking about my own family, how they stood by me. I can't help looking for the same with him." She linked her arm through his. "He has trouble admitting his feelings. It seems to be a Jackson failing."

Her perfume enveloped him, the sophisticated scent making him think of tangled sheets and whispered passion. "I'm sorry about last night." He pushed open the double doors leading to the main corridor.

"I understand. It's been a tough couple of days."

"Have dinner with me."

She stopped outside the Cardiac Care unit and stood in front of him. "I have a better idea. There's a carnival at the high school tonight. It's the yearly fund-raiser."

"Carnival?" He frowned. "But that's what—"

"It's okay. This is the little one the high school puts on every year. I'll admit, the first time I went, it was a little spooky, but now I look forward to going. It'll be fun. What do you say?"

Refusing her became a pipe dream the minute she placed her hands on his arms and smiled up at him. Despite all that had happened to her, she looked as trusting as a child.

A strand of blond hair fell into her eyes. He brushed it back, lingering as he touched the softness of her face, felt the warmth of her skin.

"Yes," he said. "What time should I pick you up?"

"Six. I gotta run back to the mill." Raising herself onto her toes, she kissed him on the mouth, then grinned and ran down the hall.

Chase stood staring after her. It didn't matter that they had no future together. He'd traveled eleven years and several thousand miles only to find out he'd never gotten over Jenny Davidson.

Jenny glanced in the mirror for the hundredth time. She'd already changed twice. The cream-colored sweater she'd chosen dipped low enough to make her blush, but she was on a mission. She had to convince Chase to let go of the past and make the most of the time they had together. One way or the other, he was leaving and when he did, he'd never come back. She'd accepted that. This visit was a gift and she intended to make use of it. When he was gone, she'd pick up the pieces of her life and move forward, but for now, all that mattered was Chase.

She heard footsteps on the porch, then a knock. Her heart bounced against her ribs and her palms grew moist. Geez, it was like being a teenager again.

She pulled open the door. "I'm ready if you—" She swallowed. Hard. "Oh, my."

He was still dressed in jeans, but the old, worn denim had been replaced by a newer pair. The deep blue fabric clung to slim hips and powerful thighs, and continued down the long length of his legs to shiny black leather boots. A cotton shirt, white, with the sleeves rolled up to the elbows, emphasized his chest's breadth and strength. Hair, still damp from the shower, had been brushed away from his face. He'd shaved and it was all she could do not to touch the smooth line of his jaw.

The heels of her cream-colored cowboy boots gave her a couple of inches of height, but she still had to look up to meet his eyes. Fire flickered in the brown depths. Fire and appreciation.

"You look great," she said, stuffing her keys and a few dollars into her pants pocket.

He stood there, staring at her. "You, too."

Butterflies soft-shoed their way across her stomach. "I'm, ah, ready. If you are."

"Sure."

He stepped back and allowed her to precede him. After pulling the door shut and making sure it was locked, he placed a hand on the small of her back and guided her down the path.

The sun had already set. The Bronco sat under a streetlight, the freshly washed paint gleamed.

"What ever happened to that Camaro?" she asked as she settled onto the seat.

"I got rid of it about five years ago." He closed the car door and walked around to the driver's side and slid inside. "I miss it, though."

"Me, too." He glanced at her and she shrugged. "I spent a lot of hours in that car with you. Even today, if I see some teenage boy driving one, it makes me remember." She smiled. "You always had the coolest car, Chase. That hasn't changed."

He started the engine and winked. "And you're still the prettiest girl in town."

"You haven't seen my nieces."

He chuckled and she felt the butterflies begin to fade. It was going to be all right, she thought. If they could just keep remembering the good times.

As they turned the corner, a glint from his wrist caught her eye. The watch. Again the question formed itself. This time, she took the chance.

"You still wear that old watch."

He glanced down for a second as if in surprise. "It keeps great time. I wear it at the construction site. All that dust and grit doesn't hurt it at all. I was working when I got the telegram."

"Oh." Not exactly the answer she was looking for. She chided herself for being disappointed. It was foolish of her to hope Chase had kept the gift she'd bought him for purely sentimental reasons.

The high school playing field was brightly lit. Tinny music from the rides competed with screams from the riders. Barkers called out to invite revelers to play their games, while children shrieked as they darted between people in a complicated game of tag. The odors of oil and gasoline from the rides mingled with the smells of popcorn and barbecue beef.

Jenny smiled as Chase helped her down from the seat. His hand felt warm and strong as it held hers. Their fingers linked together. His thumb brushed against the back of her hand; the familiar sensation threatened to drag her back to another time. Undiluted joy, as liquid as the tears that burned unshed, filled her body, bringing with it hope and promise. The second part of their story would end as unhappily as the first, but she had today and as many tomorrows as were allowed.

"Cotton candy," she said, when she'd cleared her throat.

He groaned. "Already? You always were a bottomless pit at the carnival. Cotton candy it is." He steered them toward the food stands. "Then what? A hot dog?"

"Uh-huh. And a frozen banana and licorice and ice cream and popcorn."

He rubbed his stomach. "How do you keep from getting sick?"

"I live a pure life."

"Yeah. Pure junk food."

Their feet crunched on the peanut shells littering the ground. The crowd jostled around them. She saw the glances sent their way, heard the whispered comments. A couple of people said "Hello." Chase answered casually, but she could feel his tension. It had always been like this, she remembered. The disapproving stares from those who refused to understand or tolerate.

A tall man with a beard brushed hard against her, causing her to stumble slightly. Chase stopped and turned toward the intruder.

"Let it go," she said, refusing to drop his hand. "It's not worth it."

"He could have hurt you."

"But he didn't. Don't start anything."

He looked down at her. All the happiness had faded leaving behind that haunted look she'd always tried to forget. Tremors of rage rippled through him. "I'm not afraid of them. And I don't care about that damn mill. Why can't they understand that?" His fingers tightened around hers.

"They're the ones who are afraid," she said. "They worry about the future, about what will happen when—I mean—if your father dies."

"I should never have come back."

"Chase!" She tugged her hand free. "Stop squeezing. I'm not as tough as I used to be."

"Sorry."

He rubbed her bruised fingers, then kissed each soft pad. The erotic touch sent shivers down to her toes.

"Better?" he asked.

She felt like the wicked witch in *The Wizard of Oz,* and fought the urge to scream that she was melting. "No. I need sugar to start the healing."

"When we were in high school you told me my kisses could fix anything." He took her hand again, careful to hold it lightly.

"I lied."

He gave her a mock glare. "You have not grown up into an especially kind young woman."

"Who says I grew up at all? Last one to the cotton candy stand has to buy."

"What? Why you—"

Jenny darted away, following her nose and the crowd. One quick glance told her Chase was gaining. She saw her father, offered a quick wave, then ducked behind a man walking on stilts. She heard her mother call out Chase's name and giggled. She'd won! His good manners would never let him ignore the woman's greeting.

The stand appeared up ahead. She slowed and walked toward the red-and-gold kiosk designed to look like a miniature train car. She was almost to the counter when powerful arms swept her off her feet and deposited her on the other side of a three-foot-high fence protecting a patch of grass beside a tree. Then a tall figure in jeans and white shirt sauntered to the stand and ordered a single cotton candy, pink, "And the lady will be paying."

"You cheated," she said as she climbed over the railing.

"Me? You started it. I only sank to the level of my competition. Thanks." He took the confection from the vendor and reached into his pocket.

"No, I'll get it," she said, sliding a dollar onto the counter. "A deal's a deal."

They strolled off together. Jenny pulled off wads of the fluffy candy and licked it from her fingers. She offered some to Chase.

"No thanks," he said. "But you've got some stuck on your face, right here." He leaned over and kissed the corner of her mouth.

The caress, sizzling despite its brevity, made her smile. "Is it all gone?"

He studied her thoughtfully. "No, I see another bit on the other side." He kissed her again, this time fully on the lips.

She leaned into the embrace, letting his body support her. The crowd surged around them until a familiar voice said, "Excuse me, you two. I see that some things haven't changed at all."

Jenny turned and saw Terry standing behind them. Tom, her husband, had one boy on his shoulders, the other by the hand.

"Fancy seeing you guys here," Jenny said, hoping she wasn't blushing as much as she thought.

"What a surprise." Terry grinned, then glanced at Chase. "How's your father doing?"

"Better. He was awake this morning. His heartbeat got going a little too fast, but they gave him some medication to slow it down and it seems to be working. I called about five-thirty and the nurse said he was resting comfortably."

"Good." She picked up her youngest son and held him in her arms. "We have an appointment with the carousel horses. Have fun. We'll see you later."

"Bye."

Jenny dropped the cotton candy wrapper in the trash and wiped her fingers on a napkin. "Now what?"

"Can you go fifteen minutes without food?"

"Maybe. But not more than twenty."

"Great. I need to work off a little frustration. How about if we try some of the games?" He looped his arm over her shoulder.

"Is this some kind of manly thing, shooting the woolly mammoth and all that?"

"Sort of. I like the idea of throwing something hard."

"I'd hoped we'd have fun. Maybe I was wrong to suggest coming here." She looked up at him. "We can leave if you want."

He glanced around at the crowd. Several people nodded in his direction, but most were careful to avoid his eyes. "No. They can't make me run."

She stopped and rested her hands on his chest. "It's my fault. I should have realized you'd be uncomfortable."

"Hey, no big deal. I want to win you some big, ugly stuffed animal. Something to—" He paused, then shrugged and urged her to keep walking.

Remember him by, she finished silently. Didn't he know it was already too late to try to forget?

Chase found several games he liked. After tumbling weighted milk bottles, he shot moving tin bears, then used a squirt gun to blow up and pop a balloon. The only game he didn't win was the ring toss. Three stuffed animals and a goldfish later, she cried "Uncle."

"No more," Jenny said firmly, juggling the giant panda in her arms. "We can't carry them and my house is too small. Besides, what am I going to do with a goldfish?" She jiggled the plastic bag she held.

"You always said you wanted a pet."

"I was thinking of something warm and fuzzy."

He leaned over and rubbed his face against hers. Despite his recent shave, stubble scraped her skin.

"I said fuzzy, not scratchy."

"I'd be a great house pet."

She tried not to smile. "Too much responsibility. Now a cat you can leave alone all day."

"Cats are a little standoffish for me. A dog is always happy to see you."

She glanced up at him. He had a yellow giraffe under one arm and a huge lime green cow under the other. Her heart filled with hope and regret. There was a time when she would have known him as well as herself—better, even. That time was long past. She realized she didn't know anything about him or his life in Phoenix. "Do you have a dog?"

"No. The company has one." He chuckled at her frown of confusion. "We found a mutt on a construction site. He was skinny and dirty. The guys started feeding him, so he kept hanging around. When the job was done, we drew straws to see who would take him home." Chase shrugged. "First time in my life I wanted the short straw. Anyway, John, one of my partners, got it. He and his wife have a couple of kids, so the dog was in heaven. John still brings him to work a couple times a week."

They stopped by the hamburger stand. After settling their prizes on a table, they stood in line for food.

"You could have gotten a dog of your own," she said.

"I still might. But a pet—it's more for families."

A lock of dark hair fell across his forehead. Jenny leaned forward and brushed it out of the way. He offered her a half smile, full of promise and pain, desire and defeat.

"You mentioned you aren't married now," she said. "Were you ever?"

He stared over her head toward a time she couldn't see, and shook his head. "Came close once. I met this associate producer working on a movie they shot in the area. But Jolie wasn't interested in settling down and I didn't fit in with her world. Last I heard, she'd married some guy and is living the good life in L.A."

She understood his fury at her mention of Alec a few days ago. She wanted to find this Jolie woman and beat her within an inch of her life. "Do you miss her?" she asked.

"Sometimes. But it's for the best."

"So she's not the one who got away?"

His expression changed from pensive to watchful. "Don't play games, Jenny. Not now. I can't be a cold bastard much longer. You know you're the one who got away."

The man in front of them picked up his food and they moved to the counter. Chase ordered, then handed her a hot dog and a soda. They walked back to the table.

"I didn't mean—"

He cut her off with a glance. "I know. It's okay. I never let myself think about how things could have been because I always thought you'd betrayed me. Knowing what really happened changes the past as well as the present. I never forgot any of it."

The urge to tell him how she felt swelled up inside. She wanted to erase his concerns with confessions of affection and promises of tomorrows. But before she could speak, an employee from the mill approached them.

"Hey, Chase."

"Mark. How's it going, buddy?" The two men shook hands.

Jenny greeted Mark's wife, then spoke to their daughter. Conversation flowed, as a few more people stopped to chat. Her hot dog grew cold, but she kept talking as best she could. Part of her attention focused on Chase. He seemed to be handling the crowd well. He thanked people for their inquiries about his father. His replies to questions about the mill were vague, and no one pressed for more. She suspected that they, like herself, were too afraid of the answers to want to hear the truth.

"Where'd they come from?" he asked, when the last family had drifted away, leaving them to eat in peace.

"Despite your opinion to the contrary, not everyone hates you."

"And I should be grateful?" He took a bite of his hot dog.

"Word is getting out that you made something of yourself in Phoenix. Everyone knows you left with nothing. They respect what you've done with your life."

He grunted.

"Even my father was impressed, although he'd rather be tortured than admit it."

Chase swallowed some soda. "Your old man's not so bad."

She raised one eyebrow.

"We spoke this morning," he explained. "I understand his concerns about you. He's a little myopic about the mill, but..." He shrugged as if to say everyone has their failing.

"Do you think—"

"Aunt Jenny, Aunt Jenny, look what I got!" A five-year-old whirlwind flew into her arms. "It's a magic wand. See?" She held out the treasure. "It has fairy dust and if I wish real hard, I can make dreams come true."

Jenny kissed her niece on the forehead, but her gaze was drawn to Chase. If only it were that easy, she thought. There were a couple of dreams she'd like to use that magic wand on.

"It's lovely, honey." She pulled the girl up on her lap. "Where's your mom?"

"Back there." The little girl waved behind them, then eyed Chase distrustfully. "Who are you?"

"Tammy, this is my friend Chase. And this is Tammy, Anne's oldest."

"Pleased to meet you," he said, formally offering his hand across the table.

The girl giggled and shook it. Then she frowned and glanced up at Jenny. "He's not the one who's going to take you away, is he?"

"What?"

"Mommy says that there's a man here. That he's going to take you away and shut down the mill. She says that she'd like to take the silver spoon from his mouth and stick it up—"

Jenny covered Tammy's mouth. "I don't think you were supposed to hear that, little one. So why don't you try to forget what Mommy said, okay?"

Tammy nodded. "But you won't leave, will you, Aunt Jenny?"

"I'm not going anywhere." She didn't dare glance up at Chase.

"Are all those stuffed animals yours?" Tammy pointed at the pile.

"Uh-huh. Chase won them for me."

"That's a lot. I have stuffed animals."

Chase picked up the small plastic bag and grinned. "Do you have a fish?"

Tammy's eyes got round. She wiggled on Jenny's lap and reached for the container. "A real fish? You mean it's alive?"

The goldfish spun suddenly, as if it had heard the questions.

The little girl squealed excitedly. "It's beautiful. Look at the pretty colors."

"It's yours," Chase said. "If you don't mind, Jenny."

"I don't," she said. "But Anne might."

"Tell her she can stick it—" he met Jenny's gaze "—in an aquarium."

Jenny shook her head. "I'll never understand why the two of you don't get along."

"Maybe because we want the same thing, but don't trust each other's motives," Anne said, coming up behind them. She had a baby on one hip. "There you are, Tammy. Your father is standing in line at the bumper cars. If you want to ride with him, you'd better hurry."

"Okay." Her daughter slid to the ground, the plastic bag held carefully in her small hands. "Thanks for the fish. Bye." She headed toward the rides.

"Wait," Anne called. "I'm coming too." She turned back. "Did she say 'fish'?"

He grinned. "It's from me, Anne. I'll send a bowl and food tomorrow."

"Damn you, Chase. A goldfish! What am I supposed to do—" She shook her head in disgust and disappeared after her daughter.

"You shouldn't have," Jenny said, gathering up her trash.

"But you're glad I did."

She paused for a second, then grinned. "Yeah. Come on, I want to ride the carousel horses."

They ended up going on every ride. When she tried to beg off the Upside-Down Death Spiral, he threatened to win her another goldfish. It was after midnight when they pulled into her driveway. Her stomach was full, her senses had been scattered by the rides, she'd spent time with her family, and a man she'd loved since she was sixteen stood at her side. Life didn't get much better than that.

"How about a nightcap?" she asked, holding the panda in one arm and digging her keys out of her jeans pocket. When the door opened, she stepped inside and waited for him to follow.

He set the giraffe and the cow on the floor. "I'm not staying tonight, Jen."

"Why?"

"Because I want you."

"But, Chase, I want—"

"No." He touched his index finger to her lips. "Please don't say it. It's not right. None of it. I can't give you what you need. Hell, what you deserve. There are too many reasons, people really, in the way. I want things to be better, not worse, and making love isn't the answer."

"I wasn't aware anyone had asked a question," she said softly, surprised at the quiet strength filling her. She wanted him, but she didn't *need* him. She'd come a long way in eleven years. Maybe she'd finally grown up. "You're afraid."

"I'll admit to that. But I'm not a fool. See you in the morning."

She felt calm and detached. Was it real, or would the delayed heartache kick in later? "It's Saturday. I won't be at the mill."

"I know. I meant here. I thought I'd work on the roof. You said it was leaking."

"You don't owe me anything."

"I want to do this. I owe you for your hospitality. I'm a contractor in my other life, I think I can handle a leaky roof."

In the porch light, she could see his expression. He believed what he was saying, that fixing the leaks was a simple thank-you. But was it? she wondered. Or did the house represent something else—was it his symbolic way of trying to fix the past, to fix her?

She rubbed her temple. Too much philosophy at midnight, she thought.

"Thanks," she said, at last. "I get tired of putting out buckets. But only on the condition that you let me pay for supplies."

"Deal." He stepped back. "Good night."

Chase was hard at work by nine-thirty the following morning. He propped up a ladder he'd found in the gardener's shed at the big house and brought along, then strapped on the tool belt he'd bought at the local hardware store.

"Is that you already?" Jenny asked as she walked onto the porch carrying a cup of coffee. She wore her robe, but bare feet peaked out below. She'd painted her toes a bright red.

"We can't all be lazy," he said. "I've already got the supplies to fix the roof, been to the hospital and had breakfast. Oh, I also dropped off the bowl and fish food for Anne."

"I'll bet she was thrilled."

"I didn't stop to ask," he admitted. "Just left 'em on the porch and ran."

"Coward." She sipped her coffee. "Even that's too ambitious for me. Do you want some?" She waved at her cup.

"No thanks."

"How's your dad?"

"He was asleep when I stopped by. I'll go back this afternoon." He put a foot on the ladder and checked to make sure it was secure. "Go on about your business. Pretend that I'm not even here."

"Fine." She yawned. "I'll just read the paper and think lazy thoughts."

He smiled as she stumbled back into the house. God, she was beautiful in the morning. The tousled hair and sleepy eyes made him think of a night making love. Need tightened his groin. He pushed the desire away and climbed.

Once on the roof, he located the loose shingles and made a note of how many needed replacing. Turning Jenny down last night had been a hard decision, but he knew it had also been the right one. Neither of them needed the complication of a relationship. Besides, he wanted to fix things, not make them worse. He couldn't offer her security or promises; hell, he didn't even know how long he was staying in town. If his father's condition continued to improve, he could be out of here in about a week.

Terry's comments about the old man not getting stronger drifted through his mind, but he ignored them. William Jackson *had* to get better. Chase refused to be responsible for that mill and the town. Pulling a handful of nails out of his pocket, he straightened a loose shingle.

He worked through the morning. It was almost noon when Jenny appeared at the base of the ladder.

"Chase?"

"Yeah?"

"The hospital called."

He leaned over the edge and stared down at her. All the color had faded from her face. Her eyes were wide and worried.

"What did they say?"

"It's your father. He's taken a turn for the worse. You'd better get over there right away."

Chapter Eight

Jenny stared up at the big house. Despite the heat of Indian summer and the bright blue sky overhead, she felt a chill clear through to her bones. She folded her arms over her chest and shivered. She hadn't been warm in days, not since Chase had called to tell her the news. She remembered the stunned quality of his voice as he'd spoken of the arrangements. When he'd asked her to come to the house and wait for the caterers, she'd agreed. It was the least she could do. She didn't mind missing the funeral. Last night, she'd gone to the mortuary and said her goodbyes to William Jackson.

She glanced around and frowned. The perfectly manicured lawns and trimmed roses should have made the house a showplace. Instead, the yard looked temporary and artificial, as if waiting to be photographed for some trendy magazine. And after the shoot, everything would be taken away and only a naked building would be left.

She forced herself to climb the stairs leading to the double-wide front door. Chase had left the key to the Jackson mansion in her mailbox. She frowned as she realized she hadn't seen him in four days. Not since Saturday morning when the hospital had called. He'd barely made it in time. His father had died a half hour after he'd arrived.

The house made her uneasy. She'd never been inside it before. When they'd been in elementary school, she'd often wondered why Chase didn't invite her home—he was at her house almost every day. Weekends had been a problem; her father didn't like him around. They'd often gone down by the river to play and talk. Whenever she'd teased him about not wanting to share his toys, he'd shrugged and said the big house didn't like kids.

Jenny turned the key, then pushed open the door and stepped into the black-and-white tiled foyer. A huge chandelier hung from the two-story ceiling. To her right was the living room. She walked across the floor, her black pumps clicking loudly in the silence. Now, looking around at the elegant furniture and dark paintings, she understood Chase's need to escape. Even the atmosphere was stiff and unfriendly. He'd called the house a mausoleum. He'd been right.

When she stepped onto the thick Oriental carpet, the hush swallowed her up. Sofas and tables sat in groups to better allow conversation. The back wall of the living room consisted of a series of panels. Someone had slid them aside so that the area opened up into what used to be the ballroom.

The showplace had been built by Chase's great-grandfather almost a hundred years ago. At one time, parties and dances had been the norm. There hadn't been a large gathering since before Chase's mother had died almost twenty years earlier. Gilt-edged love seats hugged the walls of the ballroom, while tiny tables and straight-backed chairs had been scattered around the center. Several long tables, covered with white cloths, stretched across the left side of the room. She was expecting at least a couple hundred people to stop by after the funeral. The old house would handle that number easily. She glanced at her watch; the caterer was due any minute.

Jenny returned to the foyer and went in search of the kitchen. She passed through a library, a darkly paneled formal dining room and finally found the cheerful yellow kitchen. An eight-burner stove and extra-wide refrigerator dominated one side of the room. Two metal coffeemakers stood on the counters, ready to be started. Serving dishes in crystal and silver filled the counters, but the worktable in the middle of the floor had been left vacant.

In the front yard, a truck pulled up. She hurried to greet the workers. They carried in platters of food and boxes of liquor. Within minutes, a bar was being set up in a corner of the ballroom. Salads, cold meats, breads and hot dishes were all laid out. Someone found the sound system and classical music filled the house. She hovered in the background, answering the few questions they had and generally trying to stay out of the way.

Jenny checked the time again and saw that she'd have another half hour or so until the mourners returned from the graveside. The bustling activity was giving her a headache. She grabbed her purse and climbed the steep staircase to the second floor.

Three doors down, she reminded herself. Chase had told her the location of his room a hundred times. Three doors down, on the left. It would be the only place in the house that would make her feel safe. The elder Jackson had died; the mill belonged to his son. Nothing would ever be the same again. For a few minutes, she needed to hold on to the past, remember what was, cry for what could have been, and then she'd have to let go and face the future.

The door stood open. The duffle bag at the foot of the bed was the only sign that Chase had slept in this room. Otherwise it looked like a museum. High school sports trophies lined most of one wall. A baseball glove sat on the desk, a football nestled next to it.

She searched for something meaningful, something to connect to, but there were only impersonal things. The room didn't welcome her or insist she leave. No trace of the boy remained, and the man—he had never been hers. Even the memories had been dusted away.

She turned to go. A picture on the nightstand caught her eye. She stepped closer. The photograph, taken her junior year, was a duplicate of the one on her parent's mantel. Only this frame was bent, the glass broken, the picture cut. She traced a bit of glass stuck in the corner. Had he destroyed it in a rage when he'd found out she was pregnant? Or was the damage new?

She replaced the photo, then hurried down the stairs. There was no comfort to be found in this house. No place for her. Funny, all these years she'd known he was the mill owner's son, but they had just been words, not really meaning anything. Today, seeing where he grew up, touching his belongings, remembering the payroll of the mill, she saw for the first time that they came from different worlds. Even through leaving, he had highlighted their differences. He'd gone on to make something of himself in construction. He owned the company, employed other men. She was the daughter of a blue-collar family. A bookkeeper. She'd never gone to college, had only left Harrisville on vacation twice.

The servers had finished setting up. She knew Chase had paid for the caterer out of his own pocket. Glancing around at the selection and quantity, she calculated the cost. It was more than she made in three months. She'd been fooling herself to think they might have a chance at happiness while he was in town. He was Chase Jackson, mill owner, successful businessman. Rich. She was just the girl he'd left behind.

Storing her purse in the coat closet, she returned to the kitchen and made sure the coffee had been started. After chatting with the woman in charge of the food, she returned to the foyer and waited. The mourners would be arriving any moment. She was ready; her pride would see to that.

Her father drove up first. He parked by the wide, green lawn, and took the stairs slowly.

"How are you doing, Daddy?" she asked, coming forward to hug him. He looked old and tired. Deep lines fanned out from his eyes. The dark suit, the best one he owned, hung loosely around his shoulders and back. "You've lost more weight. Do you feel all right?"

"What is it about funerals?" he asked, smiling gently and kissing her cheek. "I'm healthy as a horse. It's the mill that's got me up nights. What do you know of young Jackson's plans?"

"Nothing. I haven't seen him in four days. We've spoken by phone, but only briefly."

"I need to know what's going to happen. Everyone fears losing it all. If the mill shuts down, the town goes with it."

"I know, but I don't think Chase would do that."

He patted her shoulder. "You've always thought the world of that boy. I hope he's worthy of it—especially now."

"He is. I know Chase. He's confused, but he'll do the right thing. You'll see."

"A lot of families are praying you're right, little one."

Three more cars pulled up with a black limousine following. "He's here," she said. "Go on into the living room. I'll send the others in. I want to talk to him for a moment."

Chase didn't wait for the chauffeur to open the door. He stepped out as soon as the vehicle pulled to a halt. Family, or the lack of it, had never bothered him before. But standing alone beside the grave had shown him that dying alone and unloved was the worst thing that could happen to a man. He regretted asking Jenny to help out at the house. As the minister had talked about William Jackson's service to the community and the cycle of ashes to ashes, Chase had missed her presence. Despite her slight body and sweet nature, she was a rock of strength. He could have used a rock to ward off the waves of animosity crashing against him.

"Chase?"

She stood on the top step of the house. The black dress, relieved only by a white collar and cuffs, drained the color from her face. She'd worried away any lipstick.

He took the steps two at a time and held open his arms. She flung herself against him.

"I'm so sorry," she whispered. "I wanted to be there for you."

He wrapped his arms around her. "I know. Thank you."

"I've been worried about you. Are you eating, sleeping? Do you need anything?"

"Jenny." He studied her face, noting the changes time had wrought, the similarities. "I can't believe he's gone."

"But you said you knew he was dying."

He sighed. A few guests passed by them. They offered sympathetic smiles, but didn't intrude.

"I thought I was prepared. At the end—" He took her arm and led her around to the side of the house. A stone bench stood in the middle of a garden. A few last hardy roses clung to the bushes, but most of the shrubs were already bare. "When I got to the hospital, it was too late. He was unconscious. We never spoke."

He sat down and pulled Jenny onto his lap. Burying his head against her chest, he allowed the heat of her body to warm the coldness in his soul. His jaw pressed against the soft curve of her breast.

"He loved you," she whispered, stroking his hair and face.

"You keep telling me that."

"It's true. He just didn't know how to show you."

"He wanted a replica of himself. I was only a disappointment."

"Then it's his loss."

He tightened his grip, trying to bring her closer, inside him to where the pain had left a gaping hole. "I need you. I've always needed you."

"I'm not going anywhere."

He wanted to make love to her. Here, on the lawn, with the sun caressing and healing their bodies. Only by being with her could he forget what awaited him. While his father had lived, there had been a reprieve from the duties. Now, he had no escape.

"Jenny?"

He didn't know if she understood the question, but her soft kiss on his forehead was all the encouragement he needed.

His hand slid up her leg, moving under her dress toward her thigh. Instead of seamless panty hose, he felt the lace edge of her stocking, then bare skin and the elastic of a garter belt strap.

He swallowed. "This is new."

"I wasn't trying to be sexy," she said. "They were the only black hose in the house."

"I'm not complaining." His fingers traced the lace, then dipped down to brush her panties. His other hand cupped the back of her head and urged her mouth to meet his.

"Chase," she whispered. "You're expecting a couple hundred people and they're already starting to arrive." She shuddered as he breathed against her nipples. "This isn't—"

"The time. Yeah."

He helped her stand up, then followed her around the front. "I don't suppose you could make them all go away?"

"No."

He took her hand. "Then do me a favor. Don't leave my side."

Her green eyes met his. He saw the concern and the affection. "I promise."

"I don't deserve you."

"My dad would agree with you."

For the first time in four days, he smiled. "Let's go get 'em."

She was as good as her word. For the next few hours, over two hundred people crowded into the house. Whenever a waiter approached, Jenny spoke in hushed tones about the food and drinks, but she never went into the kitchen, or left him alone with the mourners.

"So sorry about your father," a matronly woman said. "He was a good man."

Chase repeated words of agreement and thanks. When the woman moved away, he turned to Jenny. "Who is the man they're all talking about, because it sure isn't my father. Most of the people here hated him. Why are they acting like his death means anything?''

"They didn't hate him, exactly."

"What would you call it?"

"They resented his power and control over their lives. The peasants have always lived in fear of the lord of the manor."

He glanced around the room. A crowd milled by the buffet tables. The clink of glasses and silverware threatened to drown out conversation. "They seem happy enough to eat and drink in his house. I'm surrounded by vultures."

She cupped his hand in both of hers. "Not everyone is a hypocrite, Chase. I liked your father. I could never understand why he treated you so badly. I believe that he cared a lot more than he let on."

"He treated you like a slave. Jenny, he threatened to dock your pay for visiting him in the hospital."

"He was afraid of feelings. If I'd told him I cared about him, he wouldn't have known how to handle it. I think he kept everyone at a distance, because the thought of affection terrified him."

"Your imagination is working overtime. He kept everyone away because he was a cold bastard who never cared about anything but the mill."

She leaned close and placed her hand on his chest. "I don't want to fight with you."

"Sorry." He closed his eyes. "How much longer are they going to stay?"

"Not much longer. Here comes someone you like."

He glanced up and saw Terry and her husband approaching.

"I'm so sorry, Chase," she said.

"Thanks." He bent over and hugged her. "I'd forgotten how tiny you are. A midget."

She swatted him. "Almost five feet is *not* a midget."

He pushed up her glasses and turned to Tom. "Thanks for coming." The two men shook hands.

"If there's anything we can do," Tom said. "Just holler."

"I appreciate that."

"We're leaving. The sitter has a test she needs to study for." Terry glanced at Jenny. "Do you want me to come back later and help you clean up?"

"The caterers are taking care of that when everyone's gone. But thanks for offering."

"No problem. Keep in touch." Terry offered Chase a smile and she and Tom left.

"See," Jenny said when they were alone again. "Not everyone hates you."

"I know, it's just—"

"Chase. I'm sorry about your dad."

He turned and saw Mark approaching. "Thanks, Mark. It was good of you to stop by."

His former teammate shifted uncomfortably. His black suit, old and ill-fitting, hung awkwardly. "I guess you've got a lot to think about now, huh? What with the mill and all."

Why the hell couldn't they all forget about the damn mill for ten minutes? He started to tell his friend exactly what he could do with that particular mill, when he felt Jenny's warning squeeze on his hand.

"I do," he said, trying not to let his irritation show.

"Have you, ah, decided what—"

"No!" He took a breath and lowered his voice. "I haven't. Look, this has all been pretty sudden and I don't want to be hasty. But don't worry. You're young and healthy.''

Mark's hopeful expression changed to defeat. "Meaning I could get another job?"

Chase nodded.

Mark looked around, as if searching for someone. "The mill's all I know. And Patti's pregnant again. We've got a house here, a kid in school. Sorry." He laughed insincerely. "You must be getting tired of hearing sob stories. I gotta run. See you later."

He stepped back and disappeared into the crowd.

Chase felt the knot in his stomach double in size. "What do they want from me?"

"Answers," Frank Davidson said, walking up and handing him a plate. "You eat yet, son?"

"No." Chase stared at the food. "I can't."

"Won't help anybody by getting sick. And you and I need to have a talk."

Chase stared around the room. Didn't anyone else feel the walls closing in? He had to get out of here. "Not now," he said, thrusting the plate back at the older man. "Not today."

"When?"

"Soon."

"Don't wait too long. You've got a thousand people on the line here. They all want to know what you're going to do."

"You think I don't know that?" He saw another man start to approach him. He couldn't connect the face with a name, but knew he'd seen him at the mill. "I've got to get out of here, walk around and clear my head." He touched Jenny's cheek. "Can you handle things?"

"Of course. I'll wait till you get back."

"Thanks." He turned to Davidson. "I know my responsibilities to the mill and the union. I'll make some decisions and get in touch with you by the beginning of the week."

Jenny watched him thread his way through the crowd. A couple of people tried to stop him to talk. He shook his head and kept going.

"That boy's a powder keg," her father said.

"Can you blame him? It's been a rough week."

"Is that all the time it's been? Almost feels like he never left town at all." Frank motioned to the food he was holding. "You'd better eat something, too. You're looking peaked."

She rolled her eyes, but took a bite out of a roll.

"Has he talked to you about his plans?"

"No, Daddy."

"If he does—"

She dropped the roll back on the plate. "I won't spy for you."

"I'm not asking you to spy. Just to keep me informed. I'm worried about my people."

"And you think I'm not? You, me, Anne's husband, all our friends work at that mill. I know how important this is. But don't ask me to make a choice."

"A choice?" Frank steered her into a quiet corner. "Have you forgotten how your family stood beside you when you needed us? When you came out of the hospital—"

"I know," she whispered, remembering the size of her debt. "But I won't sneak around like a double agent."

"Have you thought about what would happen if Jackson Steel shuts down?"

She'd be free to leave.

Jenny's mouth dropped open. She pulled it shut and drew in a deep breath. Where had that thought come from? She didn't want to leave. Her whole life was here. Friends, family.

What about the dreams? a small voice asked.

"I know the consequences if the mill closes," she said at last. "I don't want that to happen any more than you do. I owe you and the family and I'll do whatever I can. But I won't deceive Chase. Not again."

Her father put a finger under her chin and forced her to look at him. The familiar craggy face with the love shining from his eyes made her heart ache.

"That man is going to leave you, one way or the other. Even if he stays he'll never be yours. I've told you time and again, our kind don't mix. You've seen the house for yourself. Could you live here?"

"No."

"And if he leaves, could you go with him?"

The answer was harder to say, but still the same. "No."

"You don't fit in with him, Jenny. I don't want to see you hurt."

"Oh, Daddy, it's been too late for that for years."

"Then I'll be here, whatever happens."

"Thank you."

"Eat this." He handed her the food. "I'm going to go find your mother and take her home."

She watched him move through the crowd, speaking with one employee, then another. By the constant shaking of his head, she knew they were asking if there was news about the mill and he was telling them no.

It should have been so cut-and-dried, she thought. Her duty and loyalty lay with her family. Perhaps it was the threat of change brought about by William Jackson's death, but something was calling to her. Those forgotten dreams still spoke from a place deep inside. Chase had made it. Could she? Was it wrong to want to try?

"Excuse me, Ms. Davidson. Do you want us to start cleaning up?"

Jenny followed the server toward the kitchen and wondered when Chase would find his way home.

The last guest left an hour and a half later. The caterer's truck pulled out on their heels. Jenny stood in the center of the living room, trying to imagine what the house must have been like in the old days, back when the rooms had been filled with laughter and love.

If only Chase's mother hadn't died. He'd been so young to lose her, not quite twelve. She'd wanted to go to that funeral, too, to stand beside her best friend. Her father had told her she wasn't old enough, that she didn't belong. That afternoon, she'd sat by the river waiting for Chase to show up. In his suit and tie, he'd been a stranger, until the tears and pain in his voice had shown her that he was still her friend.

All those years ago, she'd hugged him tight, promising with a child's wisdom that it would get easier, that she'd always be there for him. They'd sworn to be best friends forever, had sealed the pact with pricked fingers and the mingling of blood. That night, and every one after for the rest of the summer, he'd snuck out and joined her in the tree house in her backyard. They'd slept side by side in their sleeping bags, and when the bad dreams had come, she'd offered hugs and the comfort of her favorite stuffed bear. If her mother had guessed why Jenny had spent so much time in the tree house, she'd never let on. Her father, like old man Jackson, couldn't have known the reason; each would have put a stop to the nightly visitations at once.

The living room seemed cold and empty. Even with the panels back in place and the ballroom hidden from view, she could feel the vastness of the house echoing around her. Her gaze fell upon the marble fireplace and the stack of logs sitting neatly beside the screen. She wanted to start a fire and warm herself, but this wasn't her home.

Instead, she returned to the kitchen and poured herself a cup of coffee. Then she walked back to the foyer, sat down on the second step from the bottom and waited for Chase.

He returned twenty minutes later.

"I was afraid you'd have left," he said, pulling the front door closed behind him.

"I wanted to make sure you were okay." She scooted over and made room for him on the stair.

"It helps that everyone is gone. Did the caterer clean up?" he asked as he sat next to her.

"Yes. They did a great job. How are you doing?"

He ran his hand through his dark hair, then shrugged out of his black suit jacket and loosened his tie. "I walked down to the river. When I was little, my mother used to take me there. We'd watch the boats go by, throw bread to the birds. She'd tell me what it was like a hundred years ago, when there were only farmers in the valley."

Jenny offered him her cup of coffee. He shook his head.

"I remember how she'd hold me close," he continued. "Even when I got older. When my dad was around, she'd treat me like a man, never offer a hug or anything, but when he was gone, she would tuck me in. She used to tell me she loved me and that she'd always be there."

"I was just thinking about her, too," she said. "I guess the funeral reminded us both."

"Yeah." He tugged on the end of his tie and pulled it free, then draped it over the bannister. "When she died, I couldn't imagine life without her. If you hadn't been my friend, I wouldn't have made it. But with my father, it was so different. He was always a cold bastard. I hated him for what he made me do. I hated him for never caring about me."

"He—"

"Loved me. You keep saying that, but I don't believe it."

Jenny leaned her head on his shoulder and sighed. She wished she could take away his pain, even for a few hours.

"I told myself he was going to die," he said, taking her hand in his. "I thought I believed it. But that day...I guess I wasn't as prepared as I thought. And now I don't know what to think. There's this knot inside." He made a fist and hit his chest. "Here. It hurts like hell. I've spent eleven years wanting to punish him for what he did. How can I care that he's gone?"

"Oh, Chase." She turned toward him and pulled him close. "He's your father. You can't help but love him."

"That's not possible." His voice muffled against her shoulder.

"I won't tell anyone," she whispered. "I promise. But you need to admit you cared. That's the beginning of the healing."

He stiffened and she was afraid he'd pull away. She tightened her hold on him, murmuring soft words of comfort. The sound of his breathing, the scent and warmth of his body, filled her senses.

"I did," he said at last. "God help me, I loved that old man. And I had no earthly reason to."

"You don't need a reason. He was family."

"That's something you'd know better than me."

They sat in silence for several minutes. Jenny kept her eyes tightly closed, allowing Chase the privacy to mourn.

Finally he straightened, but kept his arm around her shoulders.

"I need to ask another favor," he said.

"Sure."

"I'll have to go through the house and separate what I want to keep." He laughed harshly. "Offhand I can't think of anything, but there are some boxes stored on the third floor. I remember a few things that belonged to my mother. I was wondering if you could help me?"

"When?"

"Tomorrow?"

"It's Friday. I have to work. I could come by later or—"

A slow grin spread across his face, crinkling the corners of his eyes and making her heart pound faster.

"What are you smiling at? Some of us do have to work for a living."

"I know. But I believe I recently inherited the position of your boss, so if it's okay with me for you to take off Friday, there shouldn't be a problem."

"Oh." How could she have forgotten that he owned the mill? "I never thought of it in those terms, but I guess you're right. What time do you want me here?"

"Whenever you get up. Say ten?"

"I usually start work at eight-thirty."

"Consider it a bonus."

"Thanks." She stood up and pulled on his hand. "Come on."

"Where are we going?"

"Home."

He squeezed her fingers briefly, then released them. "I'm going to stay here tonight."

"Why?"

"It's easier for you. Your dad and Anne have reminded me that you have a reputation to preserve."

"It's my reputation and I don't care what people think." She studied his face, but the mask was slipping into place. She couldn't read past the handsome lines and familiar features. "You'll be alone. You said you'd given the housekeeper the rest of the week off."

"I don't mind." He glanced around. "The old man is gone and the ghosts with him. This is where I belong."

Jenny stepped down to the floor of the foyer. Isn't that what she'd already figured out? This house, less than two miles from her own, was light-years away in style and substance. Their only bond was the memories they shared. Even those had begun to fade.

But all the rationalization in the world didn't stop the disappointment and hurt. Foolishly, she'd hoped he'd come home with her and they could finish the passionate dance they'd begun twice before. Today, of all days, making love would be healing. And they both had plenty of open wounds.

"Then I'll be going," she said, walking toward the living room.

After collecting her purse, she moved toward the front of the house. Chase held the door open.

"What are you going to do about dinner?" she asked, hating herself for the show of weakness, despising the hope that he'd invite her to come back.

"Probably just order in a pizza. Or eat the leftovers. I'll be going through papers tonight," he said. "Bonds, investments, that kind of thing. My father's broker sent over a copy of his portfolio."

In the afternoon light, his dress shirt gleamed like fine linen. The expensive watch on his wrist was not the one she'd bought him so long ago. Her father was right; she didn't fit in Chase's world. She never had. Funny how the truth hadn't changed, just her perception of it.

Ask me to stay, she pleaded silently.

He offered a smile. "Thanks for your help." The dismissal was obvious.

"I'll see you tomorrow," she said, then walked quickly out the door and down the steps. When she reached her car, she turned back. The huge, three-story house loomed over her like a dark, forbidding dragon. She thought of how only a few days before, he'd offered to slay her dragons.

For eleven years she'd mourned the loss of the only man she'd ever loved. Now she knew that loss was as empty and hollow as the promises they had shared. She could not have lost what she could not have had. She'd loved a dream, a fantasy, memories left over from childhood. The reality was as cold and unwelcoming as the Jackson family home.

She would be here at ten tomorrow morning, as he had asked. She would do whatever she could to speed him on his way. The mending of her broken heart would wait until he had made his choices and moved on. One last gesture of concern, one last act of kindness. Not because she loved him, but because they had always been more than friends.

Chapter Nine

Chase looked out the front window for the third time in as many minutes. It was only nine-thirty. Jenny wouldn't arrive for another half hour, but he couldn't stop looking for her.

He'd sent her away the previous night with claims of paperwork to get through. The stacks of papers still waited on his father's desk, as untouched as they'd been yesterday. He'd spent a couple of minutes on the phone with his partner in Phoenix, making sure the business was surviving without him, but other than that had wasted the night thinking.

In truth, he'd been afraid to leave with her. The feelings he'd experienced had terrified him; they still did. He'd needed her so much in the past and, except for that last September day, she'd always been there. But his father's death had shifted everything. A line had been drawn and he stood on one side, alone.

Jenny had become a part of everything he hated about the town. He couldn't fault her decision; they had each made a choice. What he wanted to know was why she'd sold out.

The sound of a car door cut through his musings. He glanced up and saw her walking up the steps.

"You're early," he said, opening the door and grinning.

She didn't return the smile. Half circles under her eyes marred the creamy paleness of her complexion.

"What's wrong?" he asked.

"I couldn't sleep."

"Me, either," he admitted. "I should have taken you up on your invitation."

She wore jeans and a sweatshirt. The faded logo for an ivy league school matched the green of her eyes. Her hair, layered and feathered around her face, glowed in the morning light. She hadn't sprayed on her usual perfume, but he caught the scent of her body. Fragrant soap combined with her heat to produce something heady.

But there was nothing soft or willing about the way she stood in front of him. Her feet braced against the floor, legs stiff, her hands tightened into fists.

He reached out to touch her. She stepped away.

"Last night I wasn't offering you the spare bed, I was inviting you into mine."

Involuntarily, his head jerked as if he'd been slapped. "I didn't know."

"You didn't listen. You couldn't get me out of here fast enough."

"You're angry."

"No. I'm hurt. Yesterday, I saw you clearly for the first time."

He didn't like the sound of that, or her. "What do you mean?"

She folded her arms over her chest and stared out the front window. "Even when I knew it wouldn't have worked out, when I told myself the union president's daughter and the son of the mill owner couldn't have made a go of it, I believed it was all about circumstances. That we were star-crossed lovers. A modern-day Romeo and Juliet. I saw yesterday that it's more than where we grew up and what our fathers did for a living. It's us." She looked at him, the pain visible in the trembling of her mouth. "You and I are not what *I* thought we were. You can tell me what time to show up for work and where to be. You control the destiny of my family. You're not the boy I fell in love with—you are William Jackson's son."

"No!" he roared, backing away from her. "I'm not. I won't be."

"It's too late, Chase. You never had a choice."

"You can't make me do this. No one can." The rage grew, ugly and out of control. "Dammit, no!"

He walked out of the foyer and down the hall, moving faster until he was running. But somewhere he took a wrong turn. There was no exit from this part of the house. The tall double-doors at the end of the corridor led into his father's study. Chase burst through, then glanced around. Bookcases stretched to the ceiling. Leather-bound volumes, dusted, but never read, stared back.

In front of him stood the old wooden fireplace, and above it, a mirror. Reflected in the glass was the portrait of his father, painted many years ago. The older Jackson, barely forty in the picture, sat at his desk in this very room. No wife, no son, no family pet. He'd been painted as he'd lived and died. Alone.

Chase looked at his own reflection, then up at the picture. The mouth, the eyes, the jawline, they were all the same. Fate or time or God had played a cruel trick, he thought. But the last word would be his.

He heard a soft step, then saw Jenny also reflected in the mirror. Regret and compassion mingled on her face, and the hurt he had so callously caused. And through it all, his father's portrait stared down.

"Go to hell," he shouted, then picked up the bronze Remington statue on the coffee table and flung it at the mirror.

The glass shattered with a loud crack. Shards fell. The bronze hit the marble floor, cracking the tiles and breaking off the horse's tail. A cold sweat broke out on Chase's back.

"Do you feel better?" she asked.

He took a deep breath. "Yeah, I do."

He felt her small hands on his arms, urging him from the room. "I guess this isn't the best time to ask you for a raise," she said.

He risked a glance. She was smiling.

"What's wrong with you?" he asked.

"What do you mean?"

"I just destroyed an antique mirror and a priceless piece of art. You should be pissed or screaming for help. Not laughing."

"I hardly think a sculpture of some nameless cowboy smoking and sitting on a horse is priceless."

"What do you know about Western art?"

"Nothing," she said cheerfully.

The delayed reaction set in. A tremor rippled though his body. He stiffened his muscles. "Why aren't you frightened of me? I've never lost control like that before."

"I know you wouldn't hurt me. And I provoked you."

He stopped walking and turned to face her. "You did it on purpose?"

"I was telling you the truth. I wanted to make you think about everything that's been going on."

"That's all I have *been* doing."

"No. You've been running. And you still are. But you're going to have to stop pretty soon. You can't hide from the mill forever."

"I know. But one more day won't hurt." He glanced over his shoulder at the library door. "Guess we won't start in there. That is if you're still going to help me go through the house."

Her smile faded. "You remember how in eleventh grade I had all that trouble with quadratic equations?"

"Yeah."

"And I told you that if I got a *B* in the class, I'd owe you forever?"

He grinned. "Now that you mention it—"

"After we're done with the house, we're even."

Their first stop was the kitchen. While he filled a thermos with coffee, Jenny grabbed a couple of apples and a bag of cookies. He wanted to make a joke about it being like it used to be when they got ready for a study session, but he knew the humor would fall flat. It wasn't the same. They weren't in high school. They'd both changed. Funny how, in the space of a few days, his whole world had spun out of control. The house, the mill, the town, even Jenny, stood poised, waiting for his decisions. He was a Jackson, after all, born and bred to lead the masses to victory.

Right. The only thing he wanted to lead was a parade out of town. The urge to run and never look back swept over him. He pulled a couple of mugs out of the cupboard and followed Jenny across the foyer and up the stairs. He was getting used to fighting his natural inclinations. In all the years he'd been gone, he prided himself on his control and good sense. Now he knew it wasn't anything that mature, he thought with a frown. He'd never been tested like this before. In Phoenix there had been no expectations, no past, no responsibility save what he had chosen to take on. Here—

"You're looking pensive," she said, pausing on the second-floor landing.

"Just thinking."

"A dangerous occupation for a jock."

"It's been a lot of years since I've been classified as a jock."

"Good. Then I'll race you to the third floor. Loser makes lunch."

She ran up the first few stairs.

"You're cheating again," he said, following right behind.

"And you're losing again."

"Watch me, woman. I might not be able to throw a football a hundred yards, but I can still—" He drew in a deep breath and passed her on the turn. Taking the last ten stairs two at a time, he jogged onto the third floor and smiled victoriously. "Beat you."

"I let you win," she wheezed, stopping short of the landing and sitting on the top step.

"Liar."

She nodded. "I need coffee. It might be ten by the clock, but according to my body, it's the middle of the night."

He settled next to her and poured them each a cup from the thermos. After screwing the top back on, he leaned the container against the wall and stared out the window.

Big, square panes of glass illuminated the top of the house. Behind him was the long corridor with guest rooms.

At the end of the hall, where the building branched into wings, began the old servants' quarters. It was in there that the boxes had been stored. The musty odor of abandoned house clung to the walls and freshly vacuumed carpet. No cleaning product could erase the scent of disuse.

From this elevation, the sky soared on forever. Treetops, some leaves still green, others gold and red in the autumn morning, reached high toward the light. Past the grove lay the river, and to the east, the town. He was king of all he surveyed. And he'd give it away to the first person who asked. If he could.

Jenny stirred next to him. Except for a light gloss on her lips, she didn't seem to be wearing much makeup. A pale hint of color stained her cheeks. The profile, strong, yet feminine, made his heart pound with both desire and regret. He was supposed to be fixing things for her, atoning for the past. Instead, he only seemed to be making things worse.

"Is it too late to apologize?" he asked.

"For?"

"Everything."

She glanced at him. "That's quite an apology. Maybe you could be a little more specific."

"I guess this is where I tell you I've never stopped wanting you, and you tell me that it's too late."

Green eyes flickered over his face, as if picking out the features one by one. Her gaze seemed to linger on his mouth. "I wish I was strong enough to say that."

"But?"

"We both know I'm not. For the next couple of hours, I'll continue to hold on to how angry I've been. Yesterday I left here hurt, and staring at the ceiling for most of the night has a way of fanning my temper. I'm sorry, too."

"You're cute when you're angry."

She rolled her eyes. "The line is 'you're beautiful when you're angry,' not cute."

"You *are* beautiful."

She moistened her lips. "Chase?"

They had a ton of work to do, he reminded himself. They should get started. Instead, he tucked a strand of hair behind her ear.

"I've always believed that about you," he said. "Even when I hated you, I never stopped wanting—wondering." He thought about the years apart, what he had accused her of. "Tell me how it could have been."

She turned to look out the window. "Tell me about the watch. It's the one I gave you. I noticed you're wearing it again."

"My watch?" He stared at the timepiece strapped to his wrist.

"Why do you wear it?"

"You asked me before."

"I know."

He'd told her it was old and convenient to wear at the construction site. He'd lied.

She'd given him the watch on his birthday. A cold November afternoon they'd stolen between football and cheerleading practice and study time. A laughing conversation when she'd told him he was getting old and he'd realized there was something different about Jenny these days. She'd grown up. Not just the body that was beginning to drive him wild, but her mind, where she kept track of their plans and reminded him of what their future together could be.

The slim, elegant box had been store-wrapped, an unheard of luxury for a blue-collar town. Her hands had trembled. Even the tiny card, edged with gold, told him this was no ordinary gift. She'd signed her name, but above that, the phrase: With love.

He'd looked at her then, a question forming that he didn't dare ask. What if he was wrong? What if she'd meant the kind of friendship-love they'd shared for years. What if he'd been the only one to sense the difference when they touched?

So he'd gathered his courage, his voice cracking for the first time in three years as he spoke the single word.

"Love?"

She'd blushed and glanced down at her tightly clasped hands. The tiniest of nods had given him hope.

"Do you love me, Jenny?"

She swallowed, then had nodded again.

He hadn't cried since the summer his mother had died, but that day in his car, as they sat by the river, he'd felt the burning behind his eyes and the lump in his throat.

"I love you, too."

They'd come together in a glory of words and promises, kisses and laughter. Only after he'd brushed away her tears and heard the magical words again, had he thought to open the package. He recognized the brand, knew what the gift had cost. For him, not even two weeks' allowance, for her, a summer of hard work.

"I'll treasure it always," he'd said, holding her close. "And you. I'll love you forever."

Chase rubbed the metal band. Scratches marred the finish; he'd had to replace three links after a construction accident. There weren't any more secrets between them. They'd lost as much as they could.

"When I left town that day eleven years ago, I drove until sunup, then stopped at a motel to rest. All I could hear was you telling me you wanted to see other people, then your father saying you were pregnant." He wasn't looking at her, but he could feel her stiffen. "Eventually, I gave up trying to sleep, got dressed and walked to my car. As I opened the door, I saw a trash can on the side of the road. Your words got louder. I remember wondering how they could drown out the sound of a big rig thundering by on the highway. Before I knew what I was doing, I'd slipped off the watch and thrown it across the parking lot. Actually, it fell about two feet short of the trash can. Kind of like that time I joggled the winning pass to Mark at the playoffs."

"We went all the way the next year," she said. "State champions."

"I know. But dammit, I still remember that missed throw." He shrugged. "Anyway, I got about a mile down the highway when I stopped and came back. The watch was lying there, in the dirt. Still ticking. I couldn't leave it behind. I've worn it ever since."

She smiled shyly. "Thank you for telling me that."

He wanted to tell her something more, something that would make up for the past, but words eluded him. There was only now. He grinned broadly to break the mood. "No big deal. Hey!" He poked her in the ribs. "We've got work to do. Break's over."

He led the way toward the servants' quarters.

"Most of what's in the boxes is old junk. There's some first edition books I'd like to keep," he said, pulling open the last door in the east wing. "When my father remodeled the library, he wanted only leather-bound books, and sent anything old into storage."

She set her cup, the apples and cookies on the floor and joined him in the room. Stacks of boxes lined the walls. An uncovered window allowed in light.

"There's no furniture," she said.

"A couple of the rooms still have beds and dressers, although there's no electricity in most of these bedrooms."

"You're kidding?"

"Nope. Great-Grandfather didn't want the expense of wiring back here. He always said that servants didn't need to do anything in their rooms but sleep. There are a dozen or so oil lamps somewhere up here."

"That's positively feudal."

He ran his finger over the top of a stack, then brushed the dust on the tip of her nose. "That's us Jacksons. Generations of trodding on the little people."

But she didn't smile at his attempted humor. Instead, she looked back down the long corridor.

"Looking for an escape?" he asked quietly.

"No. Wondering what the square footage is in this place."

He shook his head. "You don't want to know."

The boxes were labeled. Chase left most of them in place. The few he opened contained knickknacks and samplers.

"What are you looking for?"

"My mother stitched a few things when she was growing up. I'd like those."

"What will you do with the rest of it?" She lifted a large needlepoint and stared down at the picture of a very ugly dog. "This is scary. A pet like that would give kids nightmares."

He leaned over her shoulder. "That's no pet. That's Great-Grandfather Jackson."

"Right. I take it this goes in the discard pile?"

"Sure thing. I'm having an antique dealer come through on Monday. He's going to give me a price on everything."

"You're selling the furniture?" Her head was buried inside a deep box, but he was sure he'd heard something in her tone.

"I can't keep it, Jenny. Even without the ghosts, this isn't my idea of a home."

"Makes sense," she said brightly, sitting up and smiling. "And you won't be here much longer anyway."

"I don't belong here."

She glanced around the crowded room. "What will you do with the house?"

"Who knows. There aren't many takers for turn-of-the-century mansions in steel-mill towns."

"If you gave me that raise I mentioned earlier—"

Despite the friendly teasing, she was hiding something. But what? He wasn't sure he'd like the answer if he asked; better not to know. They worked for another half hour, speaking only of trivial things. How Tammy loved her goldfish, how he'd better stay clear of Anne. She brought him up-to-date on a few friends from high school. She'd been on the reunion committee last year.

"Why did you stay in Harrisville?" he asked. "When I first came back you said you'd stayed because you had to. Why didn't you get out?"

"Is this the day for confessions?"

He pulled down another box and opened it. "I guess it is. I showed you mine."

"I don't think—" She pushed her box away and nodded. "Okay. You're right. I told you I lost the baby."

"Uh-huh."

"But it was really late in the pregnancy." She sat crosslegged on the floor. Sunlight shone through the window, surrounding her in a golden glow. "They had to induce labor. I lost a lot of blood, got an infection and didn't take it easy long enough. I ended up back in the hospital. It took me almost a year to recover.''

Her description told him the basic facts, but he knew her well enough to read between the lines. She'd almost lost her life. He'd been clear across the country hating her and she could have died. Cold fear sliced through him as he realized no one would have been able to find him to tell him she was gone.

"You were going into your senior year when I left. Did you graduate?''

"No.''

She picked up another sampler and showed it to him. He motioned to the discard pile.

"I lost the baby right after Christmas and didn't get back to school.''

A bitter taste coated his tongue. "And never got to college?''

"I didn't have the right. The insurance covered some of the medical expenses, but not enough. By the time I was back on my feet, my parents had gone through all their savings. Mary and Randi were entering high school, but I'd used up their college fund.''

"They wouldn't have blamed you.''

"They didn't. But I felt responsible.'' She opened the box he'd pulled down, and reached inside. The top frame contained a linen sampler with the alphabet and a proverb from the Bible. "Is this what you're looking for?''

"You found it. I remember this used to hang in her reading room.'' He took the needlework and placed it in the hall. "I don't think there's anything else in here. Let's try next door.''

He helped her to her feet and brushed the dust from her nose. "So to pay back the money, you took a job in the mill.''

It wasn't a question. Her expression closed slightly, as if to ward off any judgment.

"You've always been a stubborn one," he said, tracing her mouth with his index finger. "Beautiful when you're angry and stubborn as a mule. Hell of a combination."

"So you lucked out not having to marry me."

There was a sharp pain in the vicinity of his chest. "I wouldn't say that." He let go of her and opened the door to the next room. "I'm surprised my father hired you."

"I got my general education diploma and applied for office work. I'd been at Jackson Steel almost a year before he noticed." She grinned. "You should have seen the look on his face. I thought he'd have a stroke and die right there in the accounting department." She instantly sobered. "Sorry. That was in poor taste."

"Go on."

"He didn't say a word, and when I got promoted to head bookkeeper and started going to those meetings he always held, it was like I was just another employee."

He lowered a box to the floor. Jenny knelt down and pulled back the flaps. "What on earth?" She pulled out several toy soldiers and a handful of blocks. "Toys. I think they're antiques."

"They might be my grandfather's." He crouched beside her and took one of the soldiers. The hand-painted wooden figure was scarred and battle-weary, but the miniature sword at his side gleamed with flecks of gold paint. "This is great. I'm keeping these."

"For your kids?" she teased.

"You bet."

Their eyes met and the room became charged. Not with sensual energy, but with memories.

"I'm sorry about the baby," he said. "That you lost it."

"Funny how you assume I would have wanted that child. Most people told me I should have been grateful he was gone."

"A boy?"

She nodded.

Chase pressed the toy soldier back in her palm and closed her fingers around the small figure. "You would have loved him however he'd come to be born."

She bowed her head and let her hair fall forward, creating a shield between them. He kept his hand around hers. A single tear fell from her cheek onto his thumb.

"Why didn't you come to me when you got better?" he asked quietly. "I think I secretly waited for you to come and explain, to tell me that it had all been a giant mistake."

"Did you? I wanted to believe you'd forgiven me, but—" She half swallowed a sob. "I never heard from you. All those years. Six months after I got promoted, your father called me into his office. He—"

"Hush." With his free hand, he stroked her hair. "It's okay."

She sniffed. "He handed me an envelope with your return address. Never said a word, just passed it across the desk, then told me to get back to work."

"He always was a warm and friendly guy."

"Sometimes." At his *hmmph* of disagreement, she glanced up. Her eyes glistened with tears. "He didn't have to let me know."

"You never wrote."

She smiled. The corner of her mouth quivered slightly and a tear slid down her cheek, but she held the smile firmly in place. "Three years had gone by. I knew that if you'd wanted to get in touch with me, you would have. I was obligated to my family. Randi only finished college eighteen months ago. Even if you'd wanted me to join you, I couldn't have said yes. It was too late for us."

He released her and moved to the window. These rooms weren't cleaned, and dust caked the panes of glass. "You're wrong," he said, staring out at the landscaped garden below.

"Why didn't *you* get in touch with *me?*" she asked.

"Pride."

"No. You never forgave me for what you saw as my betrayal."

"I didn't know about the rape."

"Would it have mattered?"

"Of course." He turned to face her. "How can you ask that? I loved you."

Do you still?

She didn't voice the question, but somehow the words echoed in the room all the same. *Did* he love her?

Chase studied the slight figure standing with the toy soldier clutched in her hand. She was his past, the only decent memory in a past full of bad ones.

"You forgot the dreams," he said. "Why didn't you leave when Randi graduated and you were free to go?"

"I owe my family for what they did for me. It's not a debt I can pay with money. I still remember what you and I had planned, but now it seems so selfish and unimportant."

She'd sold out to Harrisville and the mill. He owed her, as she had owed her family. He still planned to fix Jenny, although what exactly was wrong seemed hard to define. He was responsible for the tragedy that had destroyed her life. When the debt was paid, he'd move on. They didn't belong together anymore.

The work continued in silence. A stack of children's books joined the growing pile in the hall. The rest of the things were left for the antique dealer to look over.

Chase glanced at the labels on the final stack of boxes. One more contained toys. "I'll keep this one," he said, moving it out of the room. "The rest of the stuff is just old clothes. Does anyone buy those?"

"Antique clothing?" she asked, stepping closer to the boxes. "Sure." She moved around him to study a trunk in the corner, then frowned. "Who was Elizabeth Jackson?"

"My great-grandmother. Why?"

"This trunk has her name on it. Anything from the nineteenth century would be valuable to collectors or a museum."

"Old clothes?"

"Absolutely. Can I open this trunk?"

"Be my guest."

Jenny tried the latch. It caught for a second, then lifted. She pulled up the top of the leather trunk. The smell of cedar drifted out.

Blue tissue covered the clothing inside. Moving it aside, she sighed. "Oh, look."

Beads and lace covered the bodice of the dress and the high neck. The thick, once-white silk had darkened to a rich ivory color. A wide ribbon wrapped around the waist. Gently holding the shoulder seams, she lifted up the gown.

Yards and yards of fabric formed a long, full skirt. A tulle overskirt, delicate and hemmed with lace, fell to the floor. The sleeves had been stitched with fine thread in the pattern of lilies of the valley.

"It's a wedding gown," she said, holding the garment in front of her. "It must be over a hundred years old. Look at the stitching and the lace. Everything is made by hand. It's stunning.''

Chase bent down and looked into the trunk. ''There are a couple more boxes.'' He opened them. ''Some weird shoes and a hat.''

She leaned down and took the hat. The silk and lace matched the gown. Swirled roses on the crown matched those on the back. Reverently, she placed the hat on her head. ''How do I look?''

Chase studied her. A frown drew his dark brows together and she wondered if she looked silly. Just as she was about to pull off the hat, he grinned. ''Incredible. I think there's a mirror in the room across the hall. See for yourself.''

She picked up the dress, holding it carefully over her arms, then made her way to the larger servant's room. An old-fashioned free-standing mirror reflected the meager contents of the room. She stepped in front of the bed and let the hem of the dress fall to the ground. The light from the window caught the shine of the beads; the aged lace and silk glowed like candlelight.

''Wow,'' she breathed. ''Imagine dressing like this every day. I've never seen anything so beautiful.''

He moved behind her. Their image, hers full-length, his shoulders and head, reminded her of the scene in the library. But this time there wasn't any anger in Chase's eyes, only admiration and a little confusion left over from the emotion of their recent conversation.

The ''if onlys'' crashed upon her with all the subtlety of a bar of steel. Without even closing her eyes, she could see him in a morning coat, the deep gray wool a perfect foil for his good looks. The room faded into another time and place. She saw a white tent set on a green lawn, crowds of celebrating people, a minister asking "Do you take this woman?"

She blinked and the tent became four dusty walls; the lawn, wooden flooring; the crowds, a few pieces of furniture. And the man—he remained, but as distant and unobtainable as the fantasy itself.

"You look like a princess," Chase said, leaning forward and straightening the hat. As he adjusted it, he snagged a length of tulle. "What's this?"

"The veil."

She pulled it down over her face. The woven net fabric softened her features, erased the signs of tears.

"What do you think?" she asked.

He placed his hands on her shoulders. In the aged mirror, their eyes met. Fire flickered in his, the brown depths darkening. Would he tell her that he too had imagined a happy ending?

"I'd like you to keep the dress."

Doing her best to hide her disappointment, she spun to face him. "I couldn't. Chase, this is an heirloom. You should save it for your daughter." Another thought occurred to her and she had to swallow the lump in her throat before she could say, "Or your wife."

He touched the sleeve, fingering the fine stitching on the cuff. "No. It seems to belong to you. Please, take it." He dropped the sleeve. "Unless you already have a wedding gown."

She pulled off the hat and set it on the bed. "Why would I?"

"You were engaged to Alec."

"It never got that far." She looked back in the mirror. It wasn't right for her to accept the gown. The last thing she needed was another reminder of Chase Jackson. But the gown was too beautiful to refuse. "If you're sure?"

"I am."

"Thanks, Chase."

She leaned forward to kiss his cheek, but he'd already turned away and moved into the hall.

"I'll check what's left to go through," he called.

"Okay."

She stared at her reflection. All their talk had left her feeling melancholy, she thought as she swirled the skirt and watched the beading catch the light. Lost children and forgotten dreams.

She picked up the hat and carried it and the gown back into the storage room. After placing them in the trunk, she shut the lid. Had Elizabeth Jackson had dreams? Had they come true for her? Jenny sat back on her heels, remembering what she and Chase had planned. It had been so long ago; she couldn't recall the particulars. Fragments of vague hopes drifted through her mind. Did it matter? She'd made her life here. She belonged.

"I've looked at the other room," Chase said, standing in the hall. "There's not as much as I thought. I appreciate your help, but I can handle the rest."

"Are you sure?"

He nodded. "Take the day off."

"I've got work at the office."

"Whatever." He took a step away, then paused. "I'll be at the mill on Monday to go through the books. Could you have everything ready?"

"Of course." She rose to her feet and rubbed her arms. The air had grown cold. "Does that mean you've made a decision about the mill?"

"No." His clipped answer didn't invite comment.

"Then I'll be leaving."

He walked back into the room and hoisted the trunk to one shoulder. "Don't forget the dress."

"Thanks." She moved to follow him and kicked something with her foot. It was the toy soldier he'd pressed into her hand. She bent over and picked it up. Surely he wouldn't miss one. Squeezing it, she went down the stairs.

Chase placed the trunk in the front seat of her car. "I'll be by either this weekend or Monday to finish working on your roof."

"You don't have to do that."

"I want to."

She stared at him for several seconds, but the mask was firmly in place. Without a word, she got into her car and drove away.

He'd shut her out again. Too much emotion, too many shattered dreams. He wasn't running yet, but it was just a matter of time. He was bent on fixing her. It was obligation, she told herself. And another way of avoiding the mill. Could she allow herself to hope that Chase would find his way out of the past? Or would he be lost there forever, never able to forget what had been a lousy twist of fate?

Chapter Ten

"Morning, Mr. Jackson."

Chase froze in the act of opening the door of the office building.

"Morning," he answered as the mill worker stepped past him.

Mr. Jackson? What the hell had he meant by that? Mr. Jackson was his father. He was just—

Chase sighed heavily. Along with the mill and the rest of the headaches, he'd also inherited the title. He climbed the stairs to the second story, then stared down the hall.

"Good morning, Mr. Jackson," said a young clerk as she hurried past him.

"Morning," he mumbled in return.

"Good morning, sir." A secretary smiled as she passed.

He half waved a greeting. It was worse than he'd feared. If they couldn't scare him off with sob stories, they'd kill him with courtesy.

When he reached Jenny's office, he paused and leaned against the wall. What was he going to say to her? After the way he'd hustled her out of the house on Friday, he wasn't sure they were still speaking. He hadn't meant to be rude, but seeing her modeling that wedding gown had made him feel as if he'd gone ten rounds with the heavyweight champ. And lost.

There had been something so old-fashioned and innocent about the way the dress had made her look. And sexy as hell. Those buttons running down the back must have driven men wild. The thought of undoing each one, imagining the secret pleasures concealed beneath—he'd seen more than he could stand.

For the past two days he'd struggled to find a solution to the Jenny Davidson problem. In between, he'd wrestled with paperwork. His father had left a sizable portfolio, but he would have given it away without another thought if that would have made everything all right with Jenny.

Yet another secretary walked past, greeting him. He forced himself to smile as he made his way into Jenny's office.

"Hello, and don't call me Mr. Jackson," he said, collapsing in the chair across from her desk.

"I won't, but can you explain the request?"

He motioned to the hallway. "Them. They're calling me by his name. Gives me the willies."

"Get used to it. You're the big boss these days."

As she smiled, he searched for a trace of anger or hurt. She seemed normal enough.

"I meant to get by your house this weekend," he said, resting his ankle on his opposite knee. "But I never got past the paperwork."

"I've already told you to leave my roof alone. It's not your problem."

"I *want* to fix it. Humor me."

"You're the boss."

"Don't *you* start."

She leaned back in her chair. "No humoring and no calling you 'Mr. Jackson.' I don't remember you being this bossy when we were growing up."

"Back then I was only heir apparent."

"And now you're the king."

He rested his elbow on the arm of the chair and dropped his head into his hand. "Want to play Mrs. Simpson to my Edward VIII?"

"You can't abdicate your responsibility."

Maybe not, but he could do the next best thing. "You win. All right, Ms. Davidson. I'm ready to see the books now."

She led him toward his father's office. Although Jenny walked right into the room, Chase hesitated. He hadn't been inside the old man's domain in over eleven years. It didn't matter that his father was dead and buried, his presence dominated the building as it always had.

Chase cautiously crossed the threshold, suspecting that, at any moment, he might plunge back in time. But there was no bright light, no sizzling flash, no vision of the elder Jackson seated behind the wide oak desk. The leather chair, ordered especially for the owner's tall frame, faced the window and the mill. The seat remained empty. As it always would. Chase had no plans to take his father's place.

A conference table sat on one side of the huge room. Jenny straightened several files. "I got out everything I could think of. Income statements, balance sheets and statements of cash flows, through last month. The auditor's report is from the beginning of the year." She tucked her hands into the front pockets of her jeans. "There are a couple of outstanding loans, and I have the current balances on those. Then here—" she pointed to a thick sheath of papers. "—is the investment information. The income is quite substantial. Can you think of anything else you'll need?"

"Coffee?"

"Sure. Do you want to talk to anyone else?"

"No." He stared at the tableful of reports and groaned. "I'll yell if I have a question."

"Fine." She turned to leave. "Oh, I did think of something." She walked out of the room and returned shortly with a cup of coffee and a thin folder.

"What's this?"

She handed it to him without meeting his eyes. "A list of employees. Just their names."

He tossed the folder on the table. "It won't work."

"What?"

He wasn't fooled by her innocent tone. "Trying to make me feel guilty. It won't work," he repeated.

"It has to. You're our only hope."

He cupped her chin and forced her to look at him. "As you just pointed out, it's *my* responsibility and I can do any damn thing I want."

"We're depending on you. *I'm* depending on you."

"I've got you covered, kid. Don't worry."

"I can't help it. There are a thousand people employed here. My family, my friends. The whole town depends on Jackson Steel."

He dropped his hand and turned away. "The town and I have never been close. Why should I care about it now?"

She didn't answer. There was silence, then the sound of the door closing quietly behind her.

* * *

Three hours later, he stormed into her office and tossed a report on her desk.

"Is this correct?" he asked.

She glanced at the income statement. "Yes."

"No. That's not possible. You can't have a business lose money for ten years and still keep going."

"It's true."

Chase started to sit down in the extra chair, then bounced back to his feet and paced to the window. "It's insane. If the company didn't have a huge investment portfolio, Jackson Steel would have gone bankrupt a decade ago."

"I know."

"You know!" he shouted. "You know! What the hell has been going on around here? Perhaps everyone is unclear on the concept. Businesses are supposed to make money. Not a lot, but enough to pay the goddamn bills." He reached across her desk and grabbed the report. "These losses run into the millions."

"If you would sit down and listen—"

"To what?" He tossed the papers in the air and let them fall. "Fairy tales about how the American steel industry can turn it around? Guess what? It can, but not here. Look at that place." He motioned to the mill. "I haven't been inside, but I'll bet my life the equipment is old. It would have to be refurbished from the ground up. Even then, there's no guarantee that the union won't strike for more benefits or salary, then there goes your profit margin. What was my father thinking of?"

"You're upset."

He leaned his head back and laughed. "A prize for the pretty lady in the red blouse. Damn right, I'm upset. I'd thought I could at least try to sell this white elephant, but who's going to want it? The only good news is that the company isn't in debt.''

She rose and walked toward him. ''The employees—''

''Are sucking this place dry. Thanks to your father.''

She planted her hands on her hips. ''Leave my father out of this.''

''Fine, let's talk about you.'' He leaned forward until their noses were inches apart. ''You knew about this. All along you've been keeping your little secret. What were you hoping for? That I'd agree to run this sinkhole? That I'd leave you in charge and let the company continue losing money until there was nothing left?''

''I thought you'd at least try.''

''Give me one reason why I should?''

''It's your birthright. Your father left you this company because he wanted you to make it work. He could have closed it years ago.''

''Why didn't he?''

''I'm not sure.'' She shrugged. ''Family duty?''

Duty. He swore. The four-letter word dropped into the silence of the room like a ton of raw steel.

''I don't want it and I don't need it,'' he said.

''You don't have a choice.''

He pointed at her. ''Watch me.''

There was a knock at her open door. ''Jenny, I brought—'' A young woman paused and stared at them. ''I can come back,'' she said, her gaze going from Chase to Jenny.

''Good idea,'' he said.

''No wait, Connie. I'll take the papers.'' Jenny looked back at him. ''Don't be a jerk,'' she whispered heatedly.

''Me?'' He shook his head in disgust.

Jenny spoke to the other woman, took the papers she offered, then shut the door behind her. ''Connie was delivering the monthly newsletter from the printer. I wanted to see how it came out."

"You interrupted our discussion for a newsletter?"

"Not *a* newsletter. *My* newsletter."

"Wait a minute. You write it?"

She set the sheet on her desk, then perched on the corner. "Edit it mostly. The employees provide the articles. I take care of design and the layout, then get it ready for the printer."

His anger dwindled in the face of confusion. He held out his hand. She gave him a copy, then folded her arms over her chest.

"Don't get all defensive," he said. "I'm not going to jump down your throat."

"Once a day is your limit?"

"I'm ignoring you." He scanned the sheet. The newsletter, eight pages in all, was professionally put together. Clear photos and eye-catching headlines dominated the first page. He flipped through the rest. "This is better than the brochure my bank puts out."

"Don't patronize me."

"I'm serious. Can I keep this?"

She raised one shoulder. "I don't see why you'd want to, but sure."

He frowned. "You have a real talent for this. Why are you spending your days balancing books?"

"You really like it?"

"I said so." He collapsed into the chair in front of her desk.

She sat up straighter. "I've been looking at the catalog for the local junior college. They have a certificate in graphic design, working with different computer programs." Her arms moved as she spoke, illustrating the conversation with graceful movements. "I was thinking of taking a few classes in the evenings and—'' The animation faded from her eyes. "You think it's silly."

"Of course not. I think it's terrific. And again, I ask why are you here at the mill?"

"I have a responsibility."

"To your family." He rubbed his temples. "I've heard it a thousand times before. You're Joan of Arc, and I'm a selfish bastard. Spare me the lecture." He rose to his feet and glanced at the papers littering the floor. "Sorry about the mess."

"Don't worry about it." She slipped to her feet. "Now what?"

"Now I collect the financial statements and take them home. Tomorrow morning, after I've made my decision, I'll go have a talk with your father."

Jenny touched his arm. "Go easy on him, Chase. The mill is his whole world."

"Go easy on *him!* Your concern seems a little misplaced. He's the one who beat me up and ran me out of town on a rail."

"That was a long time ago."

The anger, defused by his glimpse of her talent, flared back to life. "Not long enough. I'm reminded every time I look in the mirror."

"He was protecting his daughter."

Chase grabbed the doorknob. "He threatened to kill me. I was eighteen and I believed him."

Behind him, she drew in a loud breath of air. "I didn't know."

"Well, now you do."

If Monday had been bad, Tuesday showed every sign of being a disaster. Chase slipped on his sunglasses, but the glare still pierced his eyes like shards of glass. The lack of sleep would have been enough to make him edgy, but combined with the hangover, he looked and felt like road-kill.

"Hell," he muttered, as he started the Bronco, then shifted it into gear. He'd spent the previous afternoon going over the financial statements, and most of the night thinking about Jenny. By dawn, both problems had been solved, but the solutions would please no one.

Across town, he turned into a parking lot and stopped next to a wooden, two-story building. He'd never been here before, but then the mill owner's son hadn't had a reason to visit union headquarters. He collected the folder he'd brought, wished he'd taken four aspirin instead of two and stepped out of the truck.

The receptionist recognized him immediately. Without saying a word to him, she picked up the phone and spoke softly into the receiver.

"Mr. Davidson will be right down," she said, motioning to a worn vinyl sofa against the far wall.

"Thanks," Chase mumbled and tried to smile.

No go. It hurt too much. Somebody had fired up a jackhammer in his brain. His eyes felt ready to explode and the painkiller was eating a hole through his gut. No more Jim Beam for dinner.

He studied the inexpensive prints on the wall and wondered who'd chosen the Impressionists. Somehow he'd thought they'd hang that painting of the dogs playing poker. Ah, that was the mill owner in him, he realized, assuming union men would have bad taste.

Then he laughed—hard and loud, despite the hangover. He was a contractor; *he* belonged to a union. Frank Davidson would lose it right in his chair if Chase whipped out his local card. It showed dues paid up to the end of the year.

"Mr. Jackson."

Chase winced at the loud voice. "Mr. Davidson," he said, turning to meet the older man. "But call me Chase. I'm having a little trouble adjusting to this Mr. Jackson thing."

"My office is down here." Davidson led the way.

Chase pulled off his sunglasses and squinted in the fluorescent light. The jackhammer dropped into low gear. The long hall was filled with activity. Everyone stopped to watch him go by. They didn't say anything, they just stared. He thought about slipping the glasses back on, but didn't. He wouldn't give them the satisfaction of knowing he noticed.

"Have a seat."

Chase looked at the hard chair beside the modest desk. Frank Davidson didn't believe in letting people get too comfortable. Probably made for short meetings.

"I'll stand. Why don't you take a look at this."

The older man took the folder and flipped through it. "More management lies?"

"I don't know what my father told you or how you handled things before and I don't give a damn. Your daughter printed these out for me yesterday. If you want to confirm the numbers, call her and ask."

Frank frowned at him. "Why are you willing to tell me the truth?"

"Read it and find out."

Chase prowled the medium-size room. The walls, bare except for a bookcase, could use a coat of paint. The concrete floor was clean but cracked in places. There wasn't a window. This was the office of the union president? Where were the original Oriental rugs and the fancy leather sofa? The conference table that sat twenty? He shook his head as he realized he was describing his father's office.

Davidson scanned the papers quickly, turning the sheets over one by one. Chase studied him. There was more gray at his temples, although he looked fit enough. He had a temper—the one Jenny had inherited—and a deep devotion to his workers.

He finished reading and looked up. Under his tan, his skin had paled to an unhealthy gray. "I didn't know."

"Now you do."

"I can't believe this. There have been losses the last few years, the shifts have gotten smaller, but Jackson never said a word."

"He wouldn't. My father admit that the mill was less than perfect, that *he* might have made a mistake? He'd rather die than admit—" Chase sank into the chair. "I'm shutting it down."

Davidson stiffened and leaned forward on the desk. "No! You can't. There are a thousand people employed there. This town depends on Jackson Steel. It's the primary source of income for the community. Shut down the mill and the town dies."

"It should have died a long time ago."

"My God, what about the employees? You're going to put everyone out of work. The union contract—"

"Has clear procedures to be followed. I'm not going to cheat you or the workers, Davidson. I'll be more than fair. As of today, I'm delivering notice. The mill closes."

Davidson shook his head. "Don't talk to me about cheating. I won't deny your legal right, but how can you do this? There are ways—an infusion of capital, new equipment. We could work something out, concessions—"

"Would be too little, too late."

Chase thought about the projections he'd done on his father's computer. The options he didn't have. He wasn't interested in sticking around to try to bail out a drowning company. "Closing is the only solution."

Davidson glared at him. "Explain how putting everyone out of a job is a solution."

"The investment portfolio will allow everyone to stay on severance pay for over a year. The union and unemployment benefits will supplement the rest. No one is going to starve, and you damn well know it." Chase squinted against the light, hoping to reduce the throbbing in his head. "After selling the inventory and machinery and paying outstanding bills, there will be money for job training. I'm counting on you to coordinate that. When everyone is settled, the investments can be sold and the money distributed to the employees. They'll get usable job skills and cash in their pockets. It's a fair plan."

Davidson shook his head. "You can't fix this with money. People have homes and families. They'll have to move. Even if you pay to relocate them, you've destroyed their way of life."

"Everybody needs to move on sometime."

"That's what this is all about, isn't it? You don't want the responsibility. Dammit, boy, this is one time you've got to stand up and accept what's happening."

Chase straightened in his chair. "I have accepted it. What the hell do you all want from me? I'm doing every damn thing I can to make sure my employees—don't look so surprised, I know they're mine—have a chance at a decent life."

"They have a decent life here. Harrisville is their home. They don't want to change that."

"This place will suck them dry and spit out the remains. Trust me, I'm the expert on small towns."

Davidson rose and came around the desk. He bent over and braced his hands on the arms of Chase's chair. "And what about my daughter? Does she get tossed aside like the rest of us?''

"I'm taking her with me.''

The older man swore. "She know?''

For the first time since the beginning of the interview, Chase was on shaky ground. "I haven't told her, if that's what you mean, but she needs to get out of here. She has talent and potential and she deserves more than what the mill has to offer.''

"And you're going to see that she gets it?''

"You bet I am.''

Davidson straightened and arched one eyebrow. "You spent your whole life turning away from your father. When you were a little tyke and he used to bring you to the mill, I could see it in your eyes. You wanted something he couldn't give you. I felt sorry for that little boy. That's why I never forbade Jenny to see you. By the time I realized you were going to break her heart, it was too late to change things. I understand you, Chase Jackson, more than you think. I thought you'd turned into a man I could respect, if not like. I was mistaken. You turned into your father.''

"You're wrong.''

"Am I?'' He folded his arms over his chest. "I'll fight you on this, with every breath I have. Now get the hell out of here.''

Chase rose slowly, then walked to the door. When he reached the hall, the older man spoke.

"When are you going to tell Jenny about your plans?''

"Tonight.''

"She won't take kindly to your shutting down the mill.''

"It's for the best. She'll understand.''

"Maybe I was wrong about you. Maybe you aren't just like your old man. William Jackson might have been a sonofabitch, but he was never a fool.''

* * *

Jenny pressed hard on the accelerator. Her tires squealed as she rounded the corner. Of all the stupid, insensitive, thoughtless, selfish things she'd ever heard in her life!

She'd kill him. And she didn't care if she went to jail.

The Bronco sat in her driveway. She pulled her car behind it, slamming on the brakes so that her bumper stopped inches from his.

"Chase Jackson!" she yelled as she slammed the door shut. "Where the hell are you?"

"Jenny?"

She looked up and saw him staring down at her from the roof.

"What are you doing up there?" she asked.

"Fixing shingles."

In the warmth of the afternoon, he'd taken off his shirt. Bare, broad shoulders, tanned from the desert summer, blocked the sun. His sunglasses hid his expression, but the straight line of his mouth told her he knew.

"Damn you," she said.

"I can explain."

"That's an explanation I'd love to hear. Lucky for you my daddy never taught me to use a gun."

He made his way down the ladder, then followed her onto the porch. "I never thought of you as the violent type."

He pulled off his work gloves, then pushed the glasses up until they rested on the top of his head. Sweat beaded on his face and torso. A single drop slipped down his throat and chest, only to get lost in the light matting of dark hair.

Jenny planted her hands on her hips, pleased to note that her sensual awareness did nothing to defuse her temper.

"You are the lowest form of life, Chase. There are several words I could use to describe you, but that would cause me to sink to your level. You are a selfish bastard. Of all the—"

He held up one hand. "What happened to not sinking to my level?"

"Don't joke with me."

"With that temper? I wouldn't dare."

He took her arm. She jerked away from him, then walked over to the swing in the corner. After plopping down in the exact center, she glared, as if daring him to try to find room. He took one look at her face, then settled on the porch railing.

"You spoke to your father," he said.

"It was a very enlightening conversation. I won't even talk about the mill. What you're doing with that is too despicable for words." She covered her face with her hands and took a deep breath. A band twisted around her chest, the tightness more from fear than exertion. When her heartbeat slowed some, she looked up at him. "So you're planning on taking me away from all this? When were you going to tell me? Have you picked the date yet? Should I start packing? Or is my life here so unimportant that I should drop what I'm doing and just walk away with you, leaving everything behind but the clothes on my back?"

"I didn't mean it like that."

"Oh?"

"I wanted—" He turned and stared out toward the street. "I owe you. I wanted to do something, but couldn't figure out what until I saw the newsletter. I want to send you to college. Pay for it. You deserve a fresh start. It's the least I can do."

Was he crazy? "Send me to college? Support me? What am I, your pet project for the month?"

He faced her. She saw the confusion in his eyes. "No. It's not like that."

"Then tell me what it's like. Would I live with you? Am I your mistress? Your daughter? Some street kid you're taking in to show how magnanimous you are? What the hell have you been thinking?"

"Why are you making this so hard?" he asked, coming to his feet and glaring. "I want to help."

"Why?"

"I want to make up for what happened."

She rose also and stepped toward him. "This is all about the rape, isn't it?"

"I want to make it like it never happened."

"Oh, God." She inhaled slowly and walked to the stairs. Standing on the top one, she collected her thoughts. "I am not a leaky roof," she said softly. "Or a broken porch, or a shattered lamp. You can't 'fix' me, Chase. It's not your job and I don't need your help."

"I want—"

"Listen to yourself." She whirled back toward him. "*I want. I want.* That's all you've been saying in this whole conversation. Here's a news flash. It's not about you. It's never been about you. Ever since you drove back into town flashing your expensive rental car and your self-made success, you've been wallowing in your own feelings."

Stepping closer, she pointed her index finger at her chest. "I'm the one who was attacked. I'm the one who got pregnant and lost the baby and had my dreams sucked away by circumstances. I'm not saying you didn't get some bad breaks. My father had no right to accuse you, and your father could have handled the whole thing a little more graciously, but that's all over. Let it go."

He folded his arms over his chest. The mask had returned, slipping down to hide his feelings. "I'm not living in the past, Jenny. I don't need the lecture."

"The hell you don't. You found out about the rape less than two weeks ago. To you, it's fresh and tragic and you're reacting. I understand that. Believe me, I appreciate the white-knight routine. I think it's swell that you care."

She moved closer and touched his upper arms. The thick muscles tightened, but he didn't step away. "You want to find the guy and beat him up," she said. "But that only makes you feel better. It doesn't help me at all."

"But I want—"

He stopped speaking. The mask slipped a little, and she glimpsed hurt and confusion.

"It's been over a long time," she said. "I've dealt with it. I can't ever forget, not because that night haunts me but because of all the tragedy it caused. I lost my future, I lost a baby. And most of all, I lost you."

He looked away. She touched his chin and urged him to meet her gaze. The deep brown of his eyes dulled with her confession.

"Don't fix me," she said. "That's not what I want. It's not what I need."

"I don't know what to say," he admitted, then shrugged. "That's a new one."

Tears burned and she blinked. A single tear rolled down her cheek. He brushed it away with his thumb. Holding his wide palm against her face, she pressed a kiss to the callused skin.

"You should have been my first time," she whispered, trying to smile. Another tear fell. "And I should have been yours. We should have learned about love and passion together—fumbling and giggling on that bed of yours in that big old house. We should have spent afternoons tangled in the sheets, listening for the sound of your father coming home. I always thought—'' her voice cracked "—it would be you.''

"Jenny.'' He pulled her close.

He cradled her head against his chest, while strong arms held her tight. She choked back a sob, not sure if the salt on her lips came from his body or hers.

"You had a choice,'' she said, tightly closing her eyes. "And you chose to leave.''

"I thought you'd betrayed me. I left here thinking you'd betrayed me.''

"But you made a decision. My future—our future—was stolen from me in the front seat of a car. I never had a choice. And now you waltz back in here and want to fix me.'' She pushed away and stared up at him. "Everything can't be made right. The bottom line is when things got tough, you ran away. And you're still running.''

He grew as cold and stiff as a statue, but she plunged on. "Maybe I did give up my dreams, but at least I did it for something I believed in and people I care about. I have a family that loves me. They were there for me. You might think sticking around to put my two younger sisters through college was a waste, but the day they graduated was one of the proudest I've known. I contributed to their lives in a way that will be with them forever. I made a difference. My job at the mill made all that possible.''

The tears poured down her face. She brushed them aside impatiently.

"I wasn't going to say anything about the mill,'' she continued, "but I have to. I loved you with all my heart and soul. And when you showed up here last week, all hurt and grown-up, I thought I still loved you. But the man I knew would never turn his back on these people. The man

I lo—'' she swore when her voice cracked again ''—loved would find another solution. Stop running, Chase. All your life you've taken the path of least resistance. It's time to stand and fight for what's right. If you want to fix something, fix that.''

He grabbed his shirt and slipped it on. ''You want it all,'' he said. ''Why not just cut me open and leave me here to die?''

''There has to be another way. Shutting down the mill—''

''Is the only answer.'' He rolled up his sleeves with quick, jerking movements.

''It can't be. If I ever meant anything to you, then please, reconsider.''

He stared at her. ''If I keep the mill open, will you leave with me?''

''Have you heard anything I've said?''

He walked to the stairs. ''All of it. Maybe I did run away back then. But you should take a look at why you're so damn set on staying. What are you hiding from? What are you afraid of? You claim I can't fix you because you aren't broken. Maybe you're too scared to notice the cracks showing around the edges.''

Chapter Eleven

The mill changed shifts about the time Chase pulled onto the main highway. The slow traffic, the stares from the other drivers, caused him to turn right at the first exit and drive through the quiet residential streets.

He wasn't familiar with this part of town. He'd never spent much time on the steel worker's side and the only street he knew was Jenny's. Bicycles and skateboards littered the sidewalks. A dozen or so kids played football on two adjoining front lawns.

He made another turn and realized he *had* been here recently. Anne lived nearby. He'd delivered the fishbowl and food to her house. Without stopping to think why, he followed the road and pulled in front of a modest white clapboard house. A little girl played with several dolls on the wide porch. The setting sun caught the gold in the blonde's hair and he smiled as he recognized Tammy.

The five-year-old looked up at the truck as he pulled it up to the curb. A grin split her face and she raced across the grass.

"Chase, Chase, did you bring me another fish?"

"Not this time, kiddo," he said as he stepped onto the lawn.

She held out her arms. He stared at her a second, then picked her up. Instantly, she snuggled close to his chest and wrapped her legs around his waist. Her weight, slighter than he would have thought, felt warm and secure. The trust in her smile, the sweet smell of grape juice and dirt and sticky fingers she was brushing against his neck, the roughness of her denim pants against his forearm, spoke of life and renewal.

"I told all my friends about you," she said, with a grin. "They all love my fish. But Mommy says I mustn't read too much into the gift." She leaned forward and whispered into his ear. "Sometimes Mommy forgets I can't read at all."

He chuckled. "Does Mommy tell you that you're cute as a button?"

Tammy wrinkled her nose. "Sometimes. But mostly she says I'm a born troublemaker."

"Tammy! Come inside. Now!"

Chase looked up and saw Anne standing behind the screen door. Her daughter sighed. "I gotta go."

"Okay." He set her on the ground.

"I'll be six on Halloween. We're having a party. You wanna come?"

"I'm not sure. I may not be around."

"If you are, we have cake and presents and stuff. I'd even let you play games."

"Young lady—"

Tammy offered him a wave, then ran toward the house. "That was Chase, Mommy. Remember, he gave me the fish. I invited him to my party next month, but he's not sure..." She slipped inside the screen door and was lost from view.

He watched as Anne turned away and shut the wooden door firmly. From the look on her face, he knew she'd already heard from her father.

Next door, a man pulled into his driveway. He glanced at Chase, then did a double take. Animosity and fear filled the stranger's eyes. Word was spreading fast.

Chase stepped into the Bronco and started the engine. He'd worn out his welcome in Harrisville, that was for sure. After putting the truck into gear, he started to ease out the clutch, then paused.

Where the hell was he supposed to go? He didn't want to see the mill ever again. Jenny? He shook his head. He couldn't go there. Not after what had just happened. He had no friends in town. For a second he thought of Mark Anders, then pushed the idea away. After what had been said after the funeral, it was unlikely his old high school friend would be pleased to see him. There was nowhere to go but that big house on the other side of town. Jenny's father had cursed him, saying he was just like his old man. Maybe Davidson was right. William Jackson hadn't had any friends in Harrisville, either.

As the daylight faded, he crossed the invisible dividing line of town. The haves lived on one side, the have nots on the other. If he had his way, no one would be living on either much longer.

Despite his playing the radio loud and his attempt to concentrate on driving, he couldn't stop thinking about Jenny. Even now, her words filled him, her painful accusations cutting deep into places he'd long thought past pain. And what hurt the most was that she was right. It had always been about him.

After parking in front of the big house, he walked across the lawn and down to the river. The water flowed slowly south, the twilight making it easier to hear than see. In his head he admitted there was no way to make up for Jenny's past, no deed that could erase the trauma and resulting circumstances. Regrets were fine for dreams and children, but he didn't have any of either. Intellectually, he knew that distance would be the best thing for him. In a few weeks or months, he could think about what happened to her with a rational mind. In his head—

But in his heart— Dear God, a fist squeezed tighter and tighter until something inside had to explode. He bent down and picked up a twig, then tossed it into the river. A few birds called, a slight breeze rustled the turning leaves, but otherwise, he was alone.

Love had healed her, at least part of the way. Alec, that faceless challenger, had been there for her. He'd been the one to hold her through the bad dreams, to brush away the tears, to show her with body and soul that she was whole and clean and desirable. Alec had slain the dragons.

Chase was too late to make a difference in Jenny's life. Too late to still matter. She'd loved him once. Her loss was greater, he acknowledged, but his still hurt. And when he was gone, the town would die. He'd never wanted the legacy of steel, but he'd never expected to leave a legacy of death.

He looked across the river toward the town. Lights came on, singly and in pairs. Car headlights reflected in the night. How many thousands of people would be affected by the mill closing? Five thousand? Ten? Would he hear them from his bed in Arizona? Would he see their faces in the desert sky?

Last night, between the exhaustion and the liquor, the plan had seemed so easy and right. Everyone would get something. The employees would get money and job training. Jenny would get better. And he—he'd get out. Now that he was sober, his plan didn't look quite so appealing. He leaned against a tree. If he closed the mill, Jenny would hate him forever. And he had a bad feeling he might even start to hate himself. If he kept it open, he'd be obligated to stay; that was a sentence of death. Whose life was more important? Did the workers matter because there were more of them? Was leaving the mill alone truly the solution to wanting to "fix" Jenny?

She'd told him the truth. He'd been running so hard, he'd ended up right back where he'd started. The heaviness settling on his soul warned him that the only way out of this mess was to go through it. The test of fire; he'd be purged by the flames, or destroyed.

Two lives, he thought as he returned to the house. Entwined, he believed, but destined for each other? Events of the past had shattered any hope for the future, as they'd seen it then. Did he truly care about Jenny Davidson, or was he caught up in the should-have-beens? Was it guilt? Or was it love?

In the living room, he stacked logs in the marble fireplace. When the flames burned hot and bright, he opened the folder containing the plans to close the mill. Alone in the house, with only the shadow of the boy Jenny had once loved to sustain him, he burned the pages one by one. He'd find a way to make it work. For all of them.

It was almost midnight when he parked in front of the Davidson family home. The familiar house looked exactly as it had eleven years before. If he closed his eyes, he could see Frank Davidson putting up storm shutters, Jenny hunched in the passenger seat of his car, his own blood on his shirt after the older man had belted him one.

Despite the late hour, lights glowed behind pale curtains. A figure crossed in front of the living-room window. He'd gambled on the fact that Davidson, like Chase himself, wouldn't be able to sleep tonight.

Walking up the path toward the front door was like moving into the past. How many times had he trod this exact path? How many times had he wiped sweaty palms against the leg of his jeans, cleared his throat to lessen the pressure of the lump in his throat, taken a deep breath to dissipate the nerves? The only difference was that tonight Jenny wasn't going to be waiting on the other side of that door, her gentle presence a buffer against all the world's hurts and her father's animosity. This time he'd be facing Davidson alone. Man to man.

He knocked twice, then waited. There was murmured conversation, then Frank Davidson flung open the front door. For a second, he just stared.

"You've got some nerve coming here, boy."

"Yeah, that's what I thought, too. I want to talk." Chase shifted his weight. "Can I come in?"

"You can state your business right there on the porch."

Mrs. Davidson appeared behind her husband. "Let him in, Frank. The news can't get any worse." The concern she had shown at the hospital was gone and in its place stood a tigress ready to protect her family. She studied him. Her green eyes, so like those of her daughter's, searched for a sign of hope.

Davidson stepped back and held open the door. Chase entered the living room and stood awkwardly beside the floral sofa.

"You might as well sit down," the older man said curtly.

"Thanks." He perched on the edge of a cushion.

Davidson settled in the recliner opposite and his wife discreetly disappeared down the hall.

"It's late for social calls. Say what you have to say and get out."

Chase wiped his palms against his jeans and nodded. "I've decided to sell the mill."

"Won't do any good." Davidson stared at the ground. "I took another look at those financial statements. The company's only value is in the investments. Anyone fool enough to buy Jackson Steel will shut it down, same as you, then cash out the investments and sell off the pieces for scrap. We're back where we started." He glanced up. "Not that I don't appreciate the gesture, but it won't work."

Chase smiled. "Not so fast, old man. There's one buyer who's foolish enough *not* to shut the company down. Someone who'd use the investments to buy new equipment and try to make a go of it."

"Who?"

"You."

"What?"

"Not you specifically, but the union. The workers. I'm talking about an employee buyout. I sell to you and then you're responsible for the success or failure of Jackson Steel."

Frank leaned back in his chair and whistled. "Well, I'll be. We've got no cash."

"I'd be generous with my terms. I'm not looking to make any money off this deal. I wasn't when I talked about closing it down. That hasn't changed. I'm setting up a trust for the union using my father's personal portfolio. I don't need the money and I don't want—" He rubbed his temples. "Let's just say it's my way of fixing everything that's gone wrong."

Frank narrowed his gaze. "This have anything to do with my daughter?"

"No."

"What happened between the two of you?"

"She wasn't keen on relocating at this time."

"She told you to take a hike."

"Her phrasing wasn't that polite."

For the first time since Chase had shown up at his door, Frank grinned. "That's my girl." He sobered quickly. "You serious about this, son?"

Chase noticed that he went from "boy" to "son" rather quickly, depending on which way the older man's temper was blowing. "I've got the projections in my car. As I said, I'm not looking to get rich. I just want out."

Frank followed him to the door. "While you get those figures, I'll call the union's accountant and have him join us."

"It's after midnight."

"Son, there isn't a mill worker in this town who's sleeping tonight. Let's get this finished so we can spread the news come morning."

Chase stepped outside. Davidson called him back. "What changed your mind?"

"Good question. Jenny. Your granddaughter Tammy. The river." He thought for a second. "And the fact that I didn't want to end up just like my old man."

Crow was a dish best eaten—Jenny frowned. Was it hot or cold? She could never remember. The call from her father had come shortly after five in the morning. Chase had changed his mind; the mill wouldn't be closing. He'd granted her request. And the price was losing him forever.

She walked the floor of the mill. A hard hat, ear plugs and safety glasses provided protection, but the roar of the machinery was still deafening. Furnaces heated iron ore red, then white. The sheets came out flat and thin, still hot enough to burn. She glanced down at the slender scar across her fingers. Chase had one that matched.

Up on the catwalk, someone called her name. When she looked, Mark Anders gave her the thumbs-up sign. She returned the gesture. There was an energy in the mill this morning, a sense of pride in the work done. With a single generous gesture, Chase had crushed the wall between them and given the town of Harrisville a future. Success or failure lay in their own hands. The blame or the accolades would belong to the workers. She grinned. The owners.

When she saw the tall, burly man in a familiar plaid shirt, she hurried over.

"How does it feel to be management?" she shouted over the din.

Her father shook his head. "Strange. Of course it's not official yet. We'll be having a vote today to make sure the membership agrees with the proposed plan, then another one to approve the slate of officers and the final contract."

"Daddy, you're going to be the president of Jackson Steel."

"Just make sure you tell me if I start to act like old man Jackson. I think there's something about his office that gets a man to thinking he's more important than he really is. First thing I'm going to do is get rid of that fancy furniture."

"Don't you dare," she said, leading him from the mill. "You'll need a place to impress potential clients."

"I hadn't thought of that." Her father smiled. "Never thought I'd see the day when I'd say this, but I've been wrong about Chase."

"About time." She slipped off her hard hat and goggles, then pulled out the ear plugs. "You might like to tell him that to his face."

"And who says I haven't already?"

"Me."

Her father made a fist and gently tapped her chin. "You think you're so smart. Okay. So I haven't told him yet, but I just might."

Leaving him to speak to the workers, she returned to the office building.

"He's here," one of the secretaries told her when they passed on the stairs. "Arrived about a half hour ago. He's in the old man's office, but the door's closed."

"Thanks, Millie."

The corridor had never seemed so long. Jenny hurried the first half of the way, then moved slowly until she was practically dawdling. The dark wood door, carved and imported from Europe, stood shut as her colleague had warned. The imposing barrier made her bite her lower lip before gathering the courage to knock.

"In," he called.

She turned the knob and stepped inside.

Chase looked up. "Jenny!" After tossing his pen on the desk, he motioned for her to take the seat opposite.

"That's okay. I'd rather stand."

A blush stole across her cheek, heating her skin as it traveled. She tried to tell herself it was from having been inside the fiery mill, but the lie didn't sit well. She was uncomfortable with most of what she'd said the day before. His desire to take her away might have sprung from his need to fix her, but the intentions had been in her best interests. She hadn't seen that until last night.

He watched her, waiting for her to make the first move, set the tone for the encounter. She saw from his eyes that he would follow whatever lead she chose, that what happened now was up to her.

"I heard about the mill," she said, picking the easiest of topics. "I know you didn't change your mind because of me, but thank you anyway."

"You had a part in it," he admitted. "You made me see I'd spent a lot of time running. It didn't help much." He motioned to the desk, then the room. "Look where I ended up."

She smiled and moved a step closer. "It's not so bad. Besides, you'll be leaving soon."

"Yeah. Once the negotiations are completed and the contracts drawn up, there's nothing to keep me here."

His brown eyes caressed her face. The touch, as gentle yet tangible as the kiss of a breeze, sent a shudder through her. She knew he was asking her something, but what? To go with him? To forgive him? To release him to go alone? She twisted her fingers together.

"I heard you'd been given a promotion," he said, leaning back in the big leather chair.

How different he looked from his father, she thought. William Jackson had never worn anything but a suit and tie. While Chase wore a long-sleeved shirt, he'd rolled up the cuffs to his elbows and she knew without looking that his lower half was covered by well-worn jeans and cowboy boots.

"They've offered me the job of treasurer. It's a fancy title that comes with a cut in pay." She moved another step closer. The empty chair stood directly in front of her and she clutched the back.

"About yesterday," she began.

"Don't." He smiled. "You were right."

"Not about everything. I was in shock and—"

"I needed to hear the truth. Then and now." He picked up a paper clip and toyed with it, then glanced up at her. "I know this is an odd question, and the timing is off, but did you love me in high school? Not just because we went together or that we'd been friends, but the I-would-have-married-you-and-stayed-forever kind of love?"

She gulped a mouthful of air. "I don't know what to say."

"The truth." His mouth straightened into a thin line. "I need to know."

"Did you love me?"

"I asked first."

Jenny finally sank into the chair. "Geez, Chase, you don't believe in making it easy on a girl, do you? When I gave you that damn watch, you made me admit it before you would. I thought guys were supposed to be the brave ones."

"That's a myth. On the outside we're tough as nails, but inside, about this kind of stuff, we're—" He smiled sheepishly.

The truth, she thought. Easy enough. So why was her heart pounding against her ribs? "Yes, Chase, I loved you with my heart and my soul. I never got over loving you. Not time, or Alec, or knowing you hated me allowed me to forget."

He held her gaze. "I loved you, too, but I never knew what that meant. Not until yesterday."

After rising from his chair, he walked around the desk and stopped in front of her. He leaned one hip against the corner. "Would you go out with me?"

"What?"

"Would you go out with me? On a date. Like it was eleven years ago. Just once, for old times' sake."

"I don't understand."

He smiled slowly, the lethal grin sending hot ribbons coiling around her stomach—and lower. "I'm talking burgers and fries at the diner, you wearing my letterman's jacket, if you still have it."

"I do."

"Then a movie."

And parking? she wondered. Did he mean to recreate that part, as well?

"Chase—"

"Don't you want to go out with me?"

"Yes." More than he could know.

Time was short. Her father had told her the contract would be wrapped up in less than a week. Chase would sign over the company and go back to his other life. That hadn't changed. He was still leaving and she had even more responsibilities. It was only one date. A few hours out of her lifetime. A chance to experience the "what if" she'd longed for her whole life.

"Tomorrow?" he asked.

Oh, God. What was she getting into. She smiled and nodded. "What time?"

"Six-thirty."

"Okay." She walked over to the door.

"Jenny?"

"Yeah?"

"I'll be the guy in the Camaro."

"I don't remember clothes like that in high school," Chase said, staring at Jenny.

She glanced down and blushed. "I wore jeans all the time."

"I wasn't talking about the jeans."

His gaze lingered on the lacy white strapless top that hugged her breasts and ribs, then disappeared into the waistband of her stone-washed jeans. A slight tan added a touch of gold to her skin. Bare shoulders whispered for his touch, the pulse fluttering at the base of her throat cried out for his kiss.

"These bustiers are very popular now," she said.

"God bless the fashion industry."

When she turned to grab her purse, he raised one eyebrow. Rows of elastic held the top in place, while the thin line of a zipper showed him the road home. Anticipation slammed into his gut. It was going to be a hell of a night.

"I, ah, dug out the jacket. Did you really want me to bring it?"

Jenny held up his letterman's jacket. Chase reached for the garment. White leather sleeves set off the dark blue wool front and back. He traced the letter, the football-shaped decal, the three Vs for the years played on the varsity team and the stars indicating he'd been team captain.

The wool smelled of cedar and age, but underneath lingered the scents of youth—turf and male sweat, rain and Jenny's sweet perfume. Their last year of high school, she'd worn the jacket more than he had. It had been their outward symbol. Even on warm days she'd sweltered under the heavy fabric, refusing to relinquish the prize. She'd been *his* girl.

"Maybe you should keep it," she said. Her smile didn't reach her eyes. "I planned on returning it to you, after that last day. But . . ."

But they'd never seen each other again, he thought. She'd been alone and pregnant and scared, and he'd run away.

"No." Chase slipped the jacket over her shoulders. "I want you to have it. For tonight, it's high school again."

"And in the morning?"

He covered her mouth with his finger. "Only good things, Jenny. No past, no future. Just now."

She'd brushed her hair away from her face. One blond strand drifted across her cheek, and he leaned over to tuck it behind her ear. Subtle makeup shadowed her eyes making them dark and mysterious. Porcelain skin glowed in the twilight.

"You're beautiful," he said, then brushed his lips against hers.

Soft, he thought, drawing back, then sampling again. Soft and sweet and—he plunged inside her mouth—warm and moist. He stroked and searched, discovering the textures and flavors. When her tongue flicked against his, fire erupted in his groin and spread outward. His hands squeezed her shoulders, feeling her delicate structure under the covering of his jacket.

She brushed her fingers across his chest; those capable hands danced and circled in an erotic pattern. One nail slid across his nipple. The arrow of need drove down hard. He dropped his hands to her derriere and pulled her tight against him.

Hips slightly rounded by the bearing of a child, cradled his. Her flat stomach pressed against his arousal. Denim on denim provided the friction; their bodies provided the heat.

He wanted her. In eleven years, that hadn't changed. But somehow, in the last couple of weeks, it had come to be about a lot more than sex.

He raised his head and watched while she slowly opened her eyes. Passion flared in the green depths.

"Why'd you stop?" she asked.

"This is supposed to be like high school."

"We kissed back then." She licked her lower lip.

He swallowed. "Not when I first picked you up. Your father would have had my hide."

"If I'd known you were going for authenticity, I would have invited him by to greet you at the door."

"No, thanks. Are you ready?"

"Sure." She picked up her purse from where it had fallen on the floor, then followed him out and closed the door behind her. "Where are we— Oh, my. Chase! I thought you were kidding. Where did you get it?"

He placed his hand on the small of her back and guided her toward the gleaming black Camaro sitting in the driveway. "I rented it from some kid across town. The color's wrong."

"I don't mind." She ran her hand over the long, sleek hood. "It's the same year as yours was."

"Yeah, but it should be red." He held open the door.

"I'm surprised you didn't ask the owner if you could paint it."

"I did."

She leaned over and unlocked his door. "You're kidding," she said, when he slid in next to her.

"Nope. He wanted too much money. I figured once it got dark, we wouldn't notice."

The powerful car rumbled to life. Chase pressed on the accelerator and grinned at the smooth sounds from the engine. "Listen to that baby. The kid's taken good care of this car. He told me it had belonged to his dad." He saw Jenny grinning at him. "What's so funny?"

"You."

"Go ahead and laugh, but I'll ply you with wine and your tune will change."

She buckled her seat belt. "Where are we going?"

"The diner. Where else?"

"I don't think they serve wine there."

"We'll pretend."

He backed out onto the road, then dropped the car into drive and hit the gas. Beside him, Jenny rolled down her window and leaned her head back against the seat.

"Just like old times," he said.

"All of it," she agreed.

He glanced at her. The humor in her expression had faded, leaving behind an emotion he was afraid to identify. He looked back at the road.

"Are you my best girl?" Years ago, the question had been their secret code. A way to express feelings without having to say all the words.

"Always."

She slid her hand onto his thigh. Instinctively, he covered it with his own, then laced his fingers through hers.

Yesterday she'd admitted that she had loved him with her heart and her soul. A forever kind of love. But so much had happened between them: The tragedy that led to their separation. Jenny's loss of the baby and her recovery. The distance they had been apart had created its own problems. Yet so many of the wounds had been taken care of by the passing years. Did she still care about him?

He frowned slightly. That wasn't the right question. He knew that she cared; it was obvious in everything she did. What he wanted to know was if she still loved him, or had time taken care of that, as well?

Chapter Twelve

"It's not a complicated decision," Chase teased. "Or are you trying to decide between the milk shake and the ice-cream float?"

Jenny folded the menu in half and hit him on the shoulder. "Leave me alone. I'll order when I'm ready."

"You always did take forever."

"And you always ate what I left on my plate. The human garbage disposal."

"Hey, I was a jock. I needed the energy."

"You were a pig."

He leaned across the Formica table separating them in the booth. "Are you complaining about the way I turned out?"

She glanced at the crisp white cotton shirt covering his upper body. The long sleeves had been rolled up to the elbow, exposing tanned forearms and wide wrists. In her mind's eye, she saw the way he'd looked when he'd last worked on her roof, his naked torso gleaming with a sheen of perspiration, the sprinkling of dark hair forming an upside-down triangle across his chest.

"Definitely not."

She raised her gaze to his and watched fire consume the laughter. Electricity charged the air around them and the rest of the room faded away.

How far would he take the game? "Just like it used to be" could mean anything. The reason she was having trouble deciding what to order was that her stomach was a giant mass of knots. There wasn't any room for food. Eleven years ago an evening like this would have ended on the banks of the river. If the night was nice, they would have sat on the grass. They usually chose a spot on the edge of the Jackson property line. No one bothered them there. If the weather grew cold, they retreated to the Camaro, where heated kisses and passionate whispers quickly steamed the windows.

"What are you kids going to have?" The gum-snapping waitress pulled a pad out of her apron pocket and clicked her pen.

"A small chef's salad," Jenny said, ignoring Chase's raised eyebrow.

He ordered a burger "with the works, minus onions," and fries.

"They haven't changed this place at all," he said when the waitress left. "Maybe replaced the floor and the tables, but those fixtures—" He pointed to the ceiling lights and the old jukebox in the corner. "Hard to believe places like this still exist."

"What's it like in Phoenix?" Jenny asked. "Do you live in the city?"

He shook his head. "The outskirts. Our construction business has taken us all over. I gave up trying to live close to the job and settled down in an area I liked. The house sits on a double lot. There's a big backyard. Sunsets last for hours." He smiled. "Or so it seems."

"Sounds like you enjoy the desert."

"It took some getting used to. The cactus don't change colors in the fall."

He leaned back in the booth. She jumped when she felt his foot press into the vinyl next to her. His long legs allowed him to rest the heel of his boots on her side of the bench. Her left hand moved from her lap to his leg. Chase offered a lazy smile of approval.

"Is the house big?" she asked.

"Big enough. Four bedrooms and a den. Kitchen. Family room, all the usual things."

"That's a lot of space." For one person, she wanted to add.

"I always thought—" He turned and looked out the window. "I remodeled the bedroom. Put in a big fireplace and a Jacuzzi in the bathroom. In the winter, it gets cold, but there's no snow."

"Why Arizona?"

He shrugged. "I left Harrisville with only three hundred dollars and I knew it wouldn't last long. There was a construction project on the side of the highway and a help-wanted sign. I didn't know a damn thing about building houses, but when I didn't fall off the roof of a two-story house the first day, the boss kept me on. Eventually a couple of buddies and I bought him out." He straightened and placed his foot back on the floor. Leaning forward, he captured her hand in his. "And that's the life story of Chase Jackson."

"I'm impressed."

"Good."

With callused fingertips, he stroked from the top of her fingers down, across her palm to the base of her hand, then back up. The motion tickled as much as it aroused. She'd shrugged out of the jacket when she'd taken her seat. His gaze lingered on her bare skin, dipping slightly to search the hollow between her breasts. Her breathing grew more rapid, forcing her chest against the lacy top. The thin lining, soft enough when she first zipped the bustier on, rubbed her puckering nipples. A quick glance told her their outline was becoming visible. Chase stared, as if willing her to show proof of her desire. And still his hand moved up and down against hers.

"Head's up," the waitress said.

Jenny drew back her arm and tried to smile as the older woman slid a salad in front of her. Chase nodded his thanks, then took a french fry and bit it in half. His thick dark hair fell over the top of his collar. The wavy curls would be silken to the touch. The merging of the boy she'd loved and the man she wanted created an ache inside that only he could soothe. There had been no discussion of if or when. In a week, he'd be gone forever. Once the mill was sold, Chase would leave Harrisville without looking back. Be it for a week, or a night, she would have her answers to all the "what ifs."

As they left the diner, Chase looped his arm around her shoulders. "That was great," he said. "I haven't had a burger like that in—" He paused.

"Eleven years?" she offered helpfully.

"Cute." He cupped her chin and planted a kiss on her nose. "Did you get enough to eat? You only picked at your salad."

Jenny pressed her hand against her stomach. The butterflies were soft-shoeing again. "I'm overwhelmed by your masculine charm," she said, only half kidding. "I've been swept off my feet and can't think of anything so mundane as food."

"Then how about a movie?" he asked, stopping to read the marquee across the street.

Was he kidding? What about the way he'd looked at her in the restaurant? Had that been an act? Something left over from before? Didn't he know how much she wanted, no, needed to be with him?

"I'd rather not," she said at last.

"A drive?"

"Fine. Whatever you'd like."

He unlocked the car and opened the passenger door. After settling her in and slipping into his own seat, he turned to look at her.

"I sense a resistance to my plans," he said. "What do you want to do?"

That was putting it out there. Did she have the courage to tell him the truth?

"It's not that I don't want to see a movie, it's just I'd hoped for something more—" her voice dropped "—intimate."

"Like tag-team wrestling?"

"Chase!" She glared at him. "I'm being serious."

His smile faded. "Me, too. I always make you say it first, but this time, I'll take the risk. I want you. More than I've ever wanted any woman. I didn't know it was possible to feel this much desire and still sit in a public place and not say a word. It took every ounce of strength not to take you right there in the booth."

She swallowed a moan of desire. "I—I think the waitress might have wanted a bigger tip if you had."

He touched her cheek with the back of his hand. "Come home with me, Jenny. Spend the night in my arms."

She didn't have to think about it. There had only ever been one answer she could give.

"Yes."

They drove in silence. When they reached the house, Chase led the way up to the double-wide front door, then pushed her inside.

"Where are you going?" she asked softly when he walked past the stairs and toward the back of the house.

"To the kitchen." His voice was quiet also. "There's some champagne in the refrigerator."

"Oh."

"Why are we whispering?" he asked.

"I don't know."

"There's no one here. The housekeeper only works days."

"Good."

She giggled nervously. He took her hand and laced their fingers together. After collecting the chilled bottle and a couple of glasses, he led them to the second floor.

At the entrance to his room, Jenny came to a halt.

"What?" he asked, looking down at her.

"I'm scared."

"Of me?"

She saw the panic flare and tried to smile. "It's not about what happened. I'm not afraid of making love." She covered her eyes. "Okay, I am a little, but it's you rather than the act itself."

"Are you trying to make me feel better?" he asked. "Because so far, it's not working."

"I'm nervous. Feel." She took his free hand and placed it above her left breast. "My heart is pounding and my palms are sweaty. I'm afraid you'll be disappointed, that we've waited eleven years to do this only to find out we aren't good together. My stomach's all tied up in knots and I feel like I'm going to throw up.''

"That's disgusting," he said, taking a step back. "We'll have to forget the whole thing."

"Chase!" She placed her hands on her hips.

"Aw, Jenny, don't give up on us now." Wrapping his arm around her waist, he urged her into his room.

"Stand right there," he said, positioning her beside the bed. "And don't move or speak for the next thirty seconds."

She did as she was told. While she watched, he put the champagne and glasses on the empty nightstand. Short, fat candles in glass holders had been scattered around the room. One by one, he held a long match to their wicks and lit them. Then he put a tape into the cassette player.

The opening strains of a familiar ballad filled the room. She knew the words as well as she knew her name. Lost love, found memories, a world filled with hope because of what had once been. Her favorite song. Their song.

"Dance with me," he said, reaching for her.

In the small bedroom, with the flickering candles casting broken shadows on the wall, they swayed together. Their feet barely moved, as their bodies pressed together. Her head fit perfectly in the hollow created by his shoulder. She inhaled against his neck, savoring the scent of his body and the familiar after-shave he'd always worn. The freshly shaved skin invited her touch, and she pressed a kiss above his collar.

The song ended. The tape continued silently, then the music began again.

"How did you find it?" she asked, her words muffled against him.

"It was in the desk drawer. I didn't think it would still work. I played it all last night."

The cassette contained only one song, recorded over and over. He'd made it their senior year. On the nights they'd parked down by the river, the car stereo had provided the music.

The curtain of time that separated today from the past rippled then tore, and once again she was seventeen. He was Chase Jackson, the only boy she'd ever loved, and she belonged to him heart and soul.

His hands spanned her waist, then began to move higher. She raised her head slightly and pressed her mouth against his. He pulled back.

"Why are you crying?" he asked.

"I'm not." She touched her cheek. It was wet. She tried to smile. "Don't worry. I think it's just too much emotion. I want you, Chase. Make love to me."

He reached over and flipped a switch on the tape machine. "So it'll automatically change sides," he said, then bent down and pulled off his cowboy boots and socks. She slipped out of her flats.

They came together again, but this time there was no hesitation in his touch. Sure hands pulled her close, while his mouth descended to hers.

Somewhere outside the room, life went on for other people. But for her, there was only the man and the fire he created. His tongue plunged and retreated. When she dared to follow, he challenged her with deep thrusts. She matched his movements, feeling the tension build within her body.

Her hands clutched at his shoulders, then drifted lower, to the first button on his shirt. As she undid it, she felt the zipper of her bustier pulled down an inch. She moved to the next button. The zipper slipped farther. Impatiently, she pulled the shirttails out of his jeans and crushed the warm fabric in her hands.

He lowered his head to kiss and nibble along her jaw, then leisurely flicked his tongue inside her ear. She moaned as white-hot shivers zigzagged along her spine. And still they danced.

Three more buttons remained. She worked them quickly, trying to ignore the zipper sliding soundlessly down. When she pushed his shirt over his shoulder, he released the tab and the bustier fell to the floor.

"So beautiful," he whispered, raising his head to stare at her. "Perfect."

His praise, the husky quality of his voice and the hard arousal pressing against her stomach erased the last of her shyness. She was proud to be female, proud to please him.

He shifted until one of his legs settled between hers. He bent his knee and brought up his thigh to rub against her moist heat. As the tempo of the song slowed to the finale, he held her shoulder blades and urged her to arch back. The position forced her sensitive center against the thick seam of her jeans and hard muscle of his thigh, while exposing her breasts to his gaze. His slow back-and-forth movement had her clutching his arms and fighting a whimper of pleasure.

Slowly, he drew her upright. His hands cupped her breasts, tenderly supporting the full curves in his palms. He stepped closer until the hair of his chest grazed her nipples. The silky mat, feather-soft and warm, forced the rose-colored tips to harden. And still they danced.

His tongue traced her mouth, circling round and round, ignoring her parted lips and the invitation to enter. She waited, but he only teased. At last, she cupped his head and forced him to be still, then gently captured his tongue in her teeth.

"That'll teach me," he murmured when she set him free.

His hands moved to her waistband. After undoing the button and zipper, he knelt and pulled her jeans and panties to the floor. At his urging, she stepped out of the pile of clothing, but when she would have moved to the bed, he held her in place.

He kneaded her derriere and nipped the soft skin on the inside of her knee. Slowly, agonizingly, he inched up. She placed her hands on his shoulders for support. When he'd almost reached the top of her inner thigh, he retreated and began with the other leg. Her breathing came in ragged gasps. In the background, the tape machine clicked as it switched to the other side of the tape. Their song began again.

This time, when he had nibbled his way to the top of her leg, he leaned closer and kissed her stomach just above the triangle of pale hair. One hand slipped between her legs. A single finger unerringly found the core of her desire and began to circle—slowly. Touching, then not touching. And always slow and steady.

Her grip tightened as her knees began to buckle. He caught her as she fell, then he settled her on the bed. The bedspread had been pulled back exposing pale sheets. Before she'd even rested her head on the pillow, his hand moved against her, creating unbearable tension and a long lasting heat.

"This time," he murmured as he lowered his head toward her breast. "You're not going to stop at the last minute."

"If you insist," she breathed, then bit down on her lip when his tongue stroked across her nipple.

He braced himself on one arm, the teasing at her breasts matching the languid pace below. Her muscles tensed and released in a rhythm she could not control. She wanted to make him go faster, no—slower. Her head rolled from side to side. It didn't matter, she realized.

"Just don't stop," she whispered.

There had been pleasure before, she thought as her knees spread to allow him greater freedom. Soaring releases and sizzling falls. But never had she been forced to surrender so completely.

She felt herself rising quickly to the peak. Instantly he stopped, forcing her back into an agonized state of waiting. The tension dissipated; her muscles relaxed. Only when her breathing returned to something close to normal did he start again. Slower this time, barely moving. Yet the touch—perfect in its pressure—sent her spiraling higher, closer. She passed the place that would have released her before. Now she needed more. He took her where she'd never been.

Twice more she saw her ecstacy; twice more he stopped. A fine sheen of perspiration covered her body. All had ceased to exist, save this moment and the glory of his embrace. Every inch, every pore vibrated. She shook with need. The pleasure swept over her, even as she climbed higher toward a destination she no longer recognized. And still they danced.

Then the tempo changed. His fingers moved faster. He leaned over and suckled her breasts, drawing her nipple in and gently sawing the tip with his teeth. Heat raced over her, starting at her toes and sweeping up.

"This time," she whispered with her last coherent breath. He couldn't stop again. Any more would send her into another dimension.

It began quietly. She almost didn't notice the subtle shifting in her body, the tiny flame that glowed. Small nerve endings quivered, then a few more until her whole being gave itself to the release. She heard words and knew they were hers, but couldn't understand the meaning. She spoke Chase's name, felt him urging her to plunge into the fire. She felt tears on her face. With a last flare, the heat consumed her.

In the aftermath, he held her close. His warmth and power gave her strength. When his lips sought hers, she gave back with a passion that surprised her. His exquisite pleasuring of her body had left her sated, yet now that she had experienced being loved by him, she wanted more.

Shifting slightly, until she was on her side and he was on his back, she sought to give back his gift. Her hands traced patterns across his broad chest. The crisp hairs tickled her sensitized skin.

"You feel great," he said, as her breasts teased his abdomen.

"So do you."

As her tongue followed a path down his chest, he leaned forward and kissed her neck. Her fingers slid across his flat belly and circled around his navel. After moistening her pinkie, she delicately plunged it inside.

He swore softly and stiffened, then continued his exploration of her jaw.

She moved her hand lower until she cupped his hardness. Moving slightly, she felt for the closure of his jeans. She giggled.

He bit down on her earlobe. "It's not a good idea to laugh when you first touch a man's, ah, the, ah, evidence of his desire."

"What?" She glanced up at him. "Oh, no. It's lovely."

"Yeah. Right."

"Chase." She chuckled again. "I mean I'm impressed with the size of your—"

He bit down again. "I believe this is what we call a matter of too little, too late."

She sat up, but left her hand on his crotch. "The reason I laughed is because you're wearing button-fly jeans."

"So?"

"Back in high school you used to wear them sometimes."

"And?"

"I always worried." She glanced down, then realized she was sitting naked in his bed after having had the most incredible experience of her life. Embarrassment wasn't possible. "I used to hope that you'd be wearing zip-up jeans if we ever made love."

He raised up onto his elbows. "Why would it matter?"

"With a zipper, I could pull it down by the tab. With a button-fly, I didn't know how I'd get it undone without touching... it."

He grinned and tugged on her arms until she was stretched out next to him. "I thought touching 'it' was the purpose of the exercise."

"Not for a seventeen-year-old virgin."

"I see." He kissed her. "And have you recovered from your reticence?"

"Oh, yes."

She proved her point by undoing the jeans and pulling them off his legs. His briefs followed. Then she touched him. Slowly, thoroughly, her hands stroked the thick length, readying him, teasing as she had been teased.

And when his voice grew rough and his arousal throbbed, she took the protection he handed her and slipped it onto him. He rose over her, his knees pressing against her thighs, his hands clasping hers. Inch by inch, heartbeat by heartbeat, he filled her. The rocking of his hips started her on the path she had recently taken. The tape machine clicked, reversing the cassette again. The song began. She grew closer, hotter, wetter, more ready, more aroused. Her eyelids threatened to drift shut, but she forced them open—forced herself to stare into his soul, knowing hers was equally exposed. Her body trembled, matched the movements of his. The song played on and with one final thrust they clung in mutual release.

And still they danced.

Jenny stirred against him, her long legs shifting and tangling with his.

"I'm hungry," she said, then bit his shoulder. "Feed me or lose me forever."

He glanced down at her. "I told you to eat more at the diner."

"I couldn't. I was nervous."

"And now?"

Her slow smile made him feel as if he'd been awarded first prize. "Now I'm not."

"I happen to know there's food downstairs," he said, sitting up and reaching for his jeans.

"I don't know," she teased. "I understand that this is a pretty formal place. Would it be all right to just invite ourselves?"

He tossed her his shirt. "I have an in with the owner."

At the top of the stairs, Jenny gazed longingly at the banister. "Did you ever slide down when you were a kid?"

"Lots of times. My father only caught me once, but there sure was hell to pay." He frowned at the memory, then pushed it away. "Want to try?"

She shook her head.

"Come on," he urged. "It's easy. I'll even go down to the bottom and catch you."

"I can't." She half turned away, then raised the tail of his shirt to expose her bare derriere. "No bottoms. I'd stick."

The sight of her long, shapely leg, curvy hips and rear had an instant reaction.

"Come here," he growled, reaching for her.

"Chase. What about food?"

"In a minute." He lowered his mouth to hers. His hands cupped her warm flesh and pressed her against his sudden hardness. Her whimper of surrender had him smiling.

"I'll give you a break this once," he said, stepping back. "Last one to the kitchen has to cook *and* clean up."

"What? Oh, you—"

She raced after him, but with his head start, she didn't have a chance. He was already sitting at the table when she ran in.

"You cheated!" she said as she came to a halt beside him. The white shirt covered her from neck to midthigh, but her full breasts moved freely under the fabric.

"I learned that from you. Besides, I'm faster."

"What do you want?" she asked, moving toward the refrigerator.

"Anything that's easy."

Chase joined her and reviewed the contents.

While she made sandwiches, he served up cold salads the housekeeper had made. Somehow, they'd never made time for the champagne, so he opened a bottle of white wine. After they'd settled across from each other, he poured them each a glass, and proposed a toast.

"To us," he said.

She smiled. "To us." She sipped, then glanced around. "I think this kitchen is the same size as my house."

He shook his head. "I've been in your place. The kitchen is definitely bigger." He chewed a bite of sandwich. "When I was a kid, I used to eat in here a lot. My father didn't come home for dinner much after my mom passed on. Except on Sundays."

"I remember. You used to have to leave for home early and put on a suit."

"Yeah. It was his way of making sure I'd be comfortable in the business world. I used to pray for simple meals. After about three forks, I always got lost on which one to use."

Jenny leaned her elbow on the table and propped her head on her hand. "You miss him."

"No." Her green eyes held him. Lingering passion left the pupils wide and dark, and he found himself forced to speak the truth. "Okay, yeah, I do. I didn't expect to." He took a sip of wine. "I thought once he was gone, I'd forget all about him. But I can't. I don't think I ever will."

"He *did* love you. As much as William Jackson could love anyone. I know he was pleased you were with him at the end."

"Maybe." He remembered the old man's harsh words, his assumption of Chase's failure. "I'm glad I was there, that I could hold his hand as he died. I told him—" He shrugged and looked down at his plate. "Right before he died, I felt him squeezing my fingers. I don't know if he could hear me, but I told him that I cared. That I was proud to be his son. At the time, I think I believed it."

Jenny rose from her seat and came around the table. She cupped his jaw and forced him to look at her, then she kissed him gently on the lips and settled on his lap.

"Hold me," she whispered. "Hold me."

She was asking for comfort, but he was the one being healed. Her body curved into his. The sound of her breathing, the steady beat of her heart, grounded him in the world, while her arms gave him the support to let go.

He felt the burning behind his eyes. He couldn't cry today, but soon he'd be able to mourn. Then he'd move on.

"I love you, Chase," she whispered, raising her head so their eyes met. "I'll love you forever."

The conviction in her gaze and voice humbled him.

"Come with me," he said.

"What?"

"Come back to Phoenix with me. Not because I want to fix you or make up for the past, but because you want to. We belong together."

She started to stand up, but he held her fast. "Jenny, please."

"Don't," she said, trying to pull away.

"I need you," he said. "I can't give you up now, not after all this time." Her body stiffened, but still he didn't release her.

"I can't," she said at last. "I'm tempted, but—"

"Then give in. For once in your life, do what you want, rather than what you should."

"That's easy for you to say."

She pressed against him again and he let her go. The tails of his white shirt flapped against her bare legs as she paced from one end of the kitchen to the other.

"You want to say yes."

"Of course." She paused by the counter and glared at him. "Imagine. Your house in the desert, the chance to fulfill a dream I've had to ignore for eleven years. Being with you. Why wouldn't I want to?"

"Then—"

"No! It's not that simple. Look at you. Even now you're still playing the powerful man around town. You've come back and you've won. You faced everyone down, flaunted your success, saved the mill and been declared a hero. I'm the only loose end."

"You're a hell of a lot more than that and you know it."
He rose to his feet. "Dammit, Jenny. Didn't tonight mean
anything to you?"

She folded her arms across her chest. "Of course. I love
you. But—" She stared at the ground, then looked back
up at him. "Can you say the same?"

"I—"

"Stop!" She held up one hand. "I didn't mean to back
you into a corner. I was just trying to show you that we
want different things. You still want to make it right. I
know you care, but you can't let go of the past."

She walked toward the hallway. Before she stepped out
of the kitchen, she paused. "The bottom line is I have obligations here. People who depend on me. A life that is
important and fulfilling. You've never once acknowledged that, or tried to understand it."

Chapter Thirteen

Jenny stood in the doorway and waited for the explosion. He would hate her now, ask her to leave, never see her again. The silence grew and grew until it breathed down her back like a great beast.

"Don't do this," he said quietly. "Don't tear us apart."

"I'm not."

"Yes, you are. Come with me."

She shook her head. "I can't."

"You won't."

"What?" She turned to face him. "What is that supposed to mean?"

He moved closer, stopping when he was standing directly in front of her. "I'll admit I've spent the last eleven years running. But at least I was moving. You've stagnated here. At one time, your family and the town provided you with a safe haven. You've taken that security and turned it into a prison. You've allowed your obligations to bury you. I don't think your family is interested in a living sacrifice."

"How dare you?" Her hands clenched into fists. "How dare you come back and judge me? You don't know anything about me or my life."

"I know that I love you."

It was like taking a sucker punch to the stomach. All the air rushed from her lungs. The blood drained from her head leaving her dizzy and unsure of her balance.

"Chase?"

"What did you expect?" He hauled her against him and held her in a bear hug. "My God, after all we've been through together, how could I not? I came here expecting to lay a few ghosts to rest and see the old man. I didn't know I'd find the piece of myself that's been missing." He kissed her forehead. "I didn't know I'd find you."

He took her hands in his and kissed her knuckles. The dark brown of his eyes flared with fire and an emotion she allowed herself to believe was love.

"Marry me, Jenny."

She blinked. No way he'd said what she thought he'd said. She must have misunderstood.

"Marry me," he repeated. "Take a chance on us. On life. Come back with me. Love me." His gaze dropped to her midsection, then raised. "Bear our children. Grow old with me."

Third time's the charm, she thought as the tears collected and rolled down her cheeks. The strength of his feelings overwhelmed her.

"Stay," she whispered, holding tightly onto his fingers. "Stay with me. It will be different now. You can change things here. Make a fresh start."

The fire faded, leaving a hopeless expression on his face. His mouth tightened. "I can't stay. My life is in Phoenix."

She released his hands. "I can't go. My life is here. I have—"

"Obligations. I know." He swallowed and nodded. "I'll take you home."

"Please don't."

He looked questioning.

It wasn't fair, she thought. They had come so far only to lose everything. She had been right; this love had been a mistake and now fate or circumstances or something was trying to set it right. She would concede her defeat later—alone. But not yet.

"You have a few more days," she said. "Can't we be together, share what's left?"

"It won't make up for a lifetime."

"I know. But it's better than the alternative."

"Being apart?" He studied her, considering, weighing her offer. "You're right. We will be soon enough."

"If we'd only listened to our families' objections we would have spared each other a whole lot of pain."

"Do you regret loving me?" He asked the question so calmly, as if determined not to let her know how much the answer might hurt.

"Never. You are my life." She reached for the first button of the shirt she wore and undid it. Then the next. When she was finished, she slipped the garment from her shoulders and let it slide to the floor. "I have only ever belonged to you."

He groaned out her name, then swept her up in his arms and carried her back to their bed. Back to the magic that kept the world at bay, back to a moment of forever stolen from a love that could never be.

"Signed, sealed and delivered." Frank Davidson capped the pen, then grinned. "Son, you've just walked away from a multi million-dollar corporation. Any regrets?"

Chase looked past the older man toward the circle of people watching the ceremony. His gaze moved over their faces, cataloging features, acknowledging their hopes and expectations. Until he reached Jenny. She stood in the back of his father's office, poised by the door. He hadn't heard her come in, but had sensed it, feeling her presence as surely as he felt the floor beneath his feet.

The makeup couldn't hide her pale skin and the pain. He knew he looked worse. They'd had four days—four nights. For once, the lawyers had worked at a breakneck pace. A week ago he would have been grateful, now he wanted to turn back the clock and relive those short hours in Jenny's arms.

"Regrets?" He looked back at Frank. "Only one."

"Too late." The older man motioned to the bottles of champagne waiting on the desk. "It's time to celebrate. Where are the glasses?"

By the time the drinks had been poured and the success of the new company toasted, Jenny was gone. Chase thought about following her, but held back. He'd used up all the words he had. In the hours before dawn, he'd let his body plead one last time. She heard the request and her answer had been the same.

She wouldn't leave.

He forced himself to smile at the well-wishers and slowly made his way to the door. The long hallway was empty. Party sounds rose up through the floorboards. The office staff were celebrating in the lunchroom. Outside, the mill workers gathered by the picnic tables.

He walked down the stairs, then circled around the crowd outdoors. At the entrance to the mill, he picked up a hard hat, protective goggles and ear plugs. Despite the good news, the furnaces burned hot and bright. Machinery clattered with a deafening roar. Steel production stopped for no one.

Within seconds, sweat poured down his back. The smell and ash filled his nose and coated his tongue. The familiar sensation made him long for the clean desert air. He could see his house standing on the rise, the red orange sun drifting over the western horizon, feel the warmth from the ground, hear the calling of the birds, the barking of a neighbor's dog. But this time, the vision was different. This time Jenny waited at the door, a towheaded child balanced on her hip, her rounded belly declaring the presence of their soon-to-be youngest. Her smile caught his eye, drawing him closer. Her love wrapped around him, soothing away his troubles, easing his spirit.

For eleven years he'd tried to forget, had told himself it didn't matter. He'd come home to prove them all wrong, but the lesson had been his.

He heard his name and turned. Mark Anders waved from the catwalk overhead.

"What?" Chase asked, pulling out one earplug.

"I said, thanks buddy," Mark called. "I owe you."

He shook his head and replaced the plug. "No. Now we're even."

The cooling steel lay in thin sheets. Chase reached out to touch one, then remembered the burn scars on his fingers. He'd given the mill everything he had. Eleven years ago, he'd run away with nothing but a few hundred dollars and the clothes on his back. Tomorrow morning, he'd take a plane instead of driving, but little else had changed. He'd come with nothing, he'd leave with nothing.

Not true, he thought as he stepped outside. He'd been given Jenny's love and had offered his own in return. That it hadn't been enough was something he'd think about later.

When he reached the front of the office building, he turned and looked back at the mill. Smoke and steam belched toward the sky. Workers moved around like pygmies feeding a hungry god.

Stay, she had asked him. Stay and make a difference.

He shook his head. He'd been to hell and the devil lived inside a steel mill. He'd offer his life for her, but he wouldn't—no, *couldn't*—stay.

Glancing up at the windows, he saw her standing, staring down at him. They'd said their goodbyes that morning. A tangle of sheets and bodies and tears. One last time, he'd asked her to come with him. One last time, she'd asked him to stay.

They'd never see each other again.

"Chase!" Frank Davidson stepped out onto the pavement. "I've been looking for you, son. Got those signed contracts here. You won't want to forget your copy."

Chase took the offered papers, then looked back up at the window. Jenny was gone.

"Are you going to eat that piece of chicken, girl, or are you going to chase it around your plate all night?"

Jenny shrugged. "I'm not very hungry."

Her father frowned. "There something you want to tell me?"

"Leave her alone, Frank," Jenny's mother ordered. "She doesn't have to eat dinner if she doesn't want to."

"Does your tummy hurt, Aunt Jenny?" Tammy asked from the chair next to hers. The five-year-old leaned over and whispered, "If it does, can I have your dessert?"

For the first time that day, Jenny smiled. "Sure, honey. Grandmother made chocolate pudding, just for you."

Tammy giggled. "I like celebrating. Can we do this tomorrow?"

Frank took a long swallow from his bottle of beer. "This is a once-in-a-lifetime event, Tammy. We own the mill and we're going to make a go of it."

"Goody!" Tammy offered her grandfather a grin, then turned back to Jenny. "What's a mill?"

The rest of the family laughed. Jenny wondered if they all knew she was dying inside and were pretending not to notice, or if she was somehow keeping her pain to herself.

Two extra leaves had been inserted in the big dining-room table. Even so, they had to squeeze to fit in all the family. Anne and her husband sat opposite. Except for Tammy, the other children had been fed and put to bed. Mary and her fiancé sat next to Tammy, while Randi had driven down from Pittsburgh to share in the celebration. Her mother's brother and his wife sat on either side of her father, and her mother took the last seat on the opposite end of the table.

These people were her salvation, she thought, remembering the troubled times after the rape. They had stood by her. Anne had cooked special meals to tempt her appetite. Randi and Mary had kept her company every day after school. Her mother had been a rock, even when the older woman had found her crying over a baby blanket she'd kept tucked in the corner of her dresser drawer. Her mother had never said anything, had just held her close and promised it would get easier.

And her father. Jenny glanced at the older man as he laughed and told jokes. He'd taught her about strength and family and the value of standing up for what you believe in. He'd shown her that loyalty was a trait without price; it couldn't be bought, it had to be earned. There might be gray in his hair and a few more wrinkles around his eyes, but he was as vital and commanding as ever. He'd outlive them all.

Her mother rose from the table and picked up the empty plates. Jenny stood up and began to help, as well. In the kitchen, she bent to load the dishwasher.

"Mom, could I stay here tonight?"

"I thought you'd be with Chase."

Jenny flushed and straightened. "I didn't think you knew about that."

Her mother chuckled. "Honey, your father tried to call you a few nights ago. There wasn't any answer. It took all my powers of persuasion to keep him from driving over to the big house and hunting Chase with a shotgun."

"I'm glad you were successful."

"Me, too." The other woman smiled. "So, why aren't you there, where you belong?"

Jenny rinsed a glass. "We said our goodbyes this morning."

"Did he ask you to go with him?"

She nodded.

"And you said no."

"I couldn't leave. There's too much here."

"I understand."

She glanced at her mother. The green eyes, so much like her own, flickered with what could have been disappointment.

"What?" Jenny asked. "You can't *want* me to go."

"I want you to be happy." She opened a cupboard and brought down a stack of dessert plates. "Don't you think you deserve that?"

"I guess."

Her mother pulled the bowl of pudding from the fridge and placed it on the counter. There were already two cakes and a pie cut up and ready to be served.

"Look at all these calories," her mother said. "I'll have to walk an extra mile tomorrow. Randi's spending the night in her old room. You can take the guest room. As for the rest, if staying in Harrisville makes you happy, then stay. And if leaving— Well, you're a bright girl. You figure it out."

The next morning, Jenny rose to watch the dawn. From the enclosed back porch, she could see across the river. The Jackson house wasn't visible, but she knew where it stood amidst the groves of trees. How much longer would it stand there, a lone sentinel of a bygone era? Chase had donated the house and the land to the town. Already committees were being formed to decide the fate of the steel baron's estate.

Had he slept at all? Had he sensed that the night lasted forever, yet passed too quickly? As long as it remained dark, as long as the sun didn't rise over the horizon, it wasn't really tomorrow. He wasn't really leaving. She'd stayed awake, begging time to slow. But even now, the first golden rays began to chase away the shadows. It was tomorrow. Once again, time had betrayed her.

Sipping on the steaming cup of coffee, she waited for the day. She would keep busy enough. There were reports to prepare, financial statements for the bank, schedules, a hundred tasks to keep her from thinking about him, wondering if his plane had left yet, if he'd arrived safely, if he was thinking of her.

She closed her eyes and willed her love to travel the distance between them, to wake him if he slumbered, to let him know that she would remember him with every pore of her being.

"You're up early." Her father stepped onto the porch behind her. "I used to have to drag you out of bed."

"That was a long time ago."

"True enough. Things change. Not all of them, though."

She glanced at him, but his face was expressionless. "What do you mean?"

"You and that Jackson boy. I told myself it wouldn't last. I was wrong."

"Don't worry, Daddy. I'm not leaving you and the mill."

"Hmmph. I could hire five different people in a second who could do your job."

"Thanks for the vote of confidence."

"You know what I mean."

"Yes, but it's more than just working."

"Guess you get that from me," he admitted. "The mill's always been important to this family. Sometimes it was my whole life. Your mother put up with a lot."

"We all did," she teased.

"It's been my dream."

She'd had dreams once, she thought. Of a future with Chase, somewhere beyond the confines of Harrisville. Of freedom and hope, the ability to choose.

Her father walked into the kitchen and poured himself a cup of coffee, then returned to her side. "Your mother told you I know where you've been spending your nights."

"Yes."

"You probably think I'm going to yell at you."

"It doesn't matter, Daddy. I'm all grown-up. I spend the night where I like."

"Is that so?"

She chuckled, then turned back to watch the sunrise. Eleven years ago, he would have had her hide for sleeping with Chase, now he could only complain.

A squirrel ran across the backyard, its mouth bulging with food.

"Winter's coming," her father said. "I need to get the storm windows up."

But instead of snow, she saw a warm desert scene, cactus and sagebrush and a man who had sworn to love her forever. How long would he wait? she wondered. How long before some other woman looked into those eyes and saw the loyalty and devotion and love she was throwing away? The picture hurt, but she had no choice.

Or did she?

Was she hiding, as Chase had suggested, using her family as an excuse to put her dreams aside?

"Did you think you'd lose the mill, Daddy?" she asked.

"When he first came and told me he was shutting it down—" he sighed heavily "—I damn near died. I knew then I'd lost everything. But I was wrong. He came around. And we all have a second chance. Don't get many of those these days."

A second chance? Was it too late?

"I can't stay here," she said suddenly.

"What?"

"I've got to get going. What time is it?"

"Hold on, young lady." He grabbed her arm. "What are you talking about?"

"Oh, Daddy." She raised herself on her toes and kissed him. "I love you and Mom and the family, but I can't stay here anymore. You're right. We don't get many second chances. I hope you weren't kidding about finding five people to do my job, because as of now, I quit."

"About time," her father said gruffly. "I was starting to wonder if I was going to have to kick your butt to make you see sense. Now before you run off half-cocked, your mother and I have a present for you."

"Here, darling." Her mother walked onto the porch and held out an envelope. "It's an airline ticket to Phoenix. Same flight as Chase's. If you hurry, you can make it."

Jenny set her coffee on the table and held out her arms. Both her parents embraced her. "I love you," she murmured.

"Now don't forget to call when you get to Phoenix," her mother said, brushing away tears. "Mary's looking for her own place, so she'll move into your house for the rest of the lease. I'll pack up your clothes and mail them to you. I understand that you'll want to get married right away, and I'll forgive you that, but you'd better invite me down when you have my grandchild."

"Oh, Mama." Jenny smiled. "I've got to run. I promise I'll keep in touch."

Her father sniffed.

She looked at him in surprise.

"Hay fever," he said. "Besides, I never thought we'd have a Jackson in this family. The whole town will be talking."

"Let them," she said. "Let them say whatever they want."

Chase rested his ankle on the opposite knee and tried to read the paper. The words didn't make any sense, and he tossed it into the empty seat next to him.

Damn. He hadn't even left yet and already he was losing it.

The loudspeaker hummed and a disembodied voice announced the next flight. There was more crackling, then a request for a departing passenger to pick up the white courtesy phone.

"What?"

He sat up. They'd called *his* name.

Grabbing his carry-on bag, he rose and walked to the desk. The clerk motioned to the bank of phones on the wall.

"I'm Chase Jackson," he said into the receiver.

"One moment, please."

He heard a click, then, "Chase?"

His heart stopped, then began to thunder against his ribs. "Jenny? Are you okay?"

"I'm fine."

"Where are you? Why are you calling? I thought we'd agreed—"

"I love you, Chase Jackson," she interrupted. "Will you marry me and take me away with you?"

His mind ground to a halt. It wasn't possible, was it? "You've changed your mind?"

"Only if that was a yes."

"What? Oh, hell, yes, of course I want to marry you." A thousand thoughts swept through him at once. He glanced at his watch. "My flight's leaving in about a half hour. Let me make reservations for later and I'll be back in Harrisville as soon as I can."

She giggled softly. The sound rippled up and down his spine.

"God, I love you," he said.

"Good. Turn around."

He did as she asked. Across the crowded airport lobby stood a slender blond woman with a tentative smile and eyes a man could live in forever. He dropped the receiver.

"Jenny?" he said softly. "Jenny?"

She ran toward him. He met her in the middle of the room and pulled her into his arms. She was warm and sweet and alive. But most of all, she was *here*. "I love you," he murmured between kisses.

"And I love you."

"I thought I'd lost you."

"Never that. It just took me a while to figure out what was right."

They kissed, oblivious of the people moving around them, the amused glances. Finally, he released her. "I wonder if this airport has sleeping facilities."

"Chase!"

"I'm kidding. Come on." He picked up her bag and headed toward the counter. "We've got to get you a ticket. Now that you're here, I'm not leaving without you."

"I have one." She showed him. "My parents bought it as a going-away present."

"I'll tell them thanks the next time I see them. Where's your luggage?"

"I've already checked in."

"What would you have done if I'd turned down your proposal?"

She smiled. "Followed you anyway. I brought this old trunk with me. There's a dress inside I want to wear for you."

The loudspeaker crackled again and announced their flight. Hands joined, bodies pressed close together, they moved to the boarding gate. He took her ticket and offered it with his, then paused.

His eyes searched hers. "Are you sure? I don't want to rush you if you have doubts."

"No doubts," she promised. "Not many people get a second chance. We've been lucky. I've only ever loved you, Chase Jackson. Forever."

"Forever," he agreed. "For always."

* * * * *

INTIMATE MOMENTS®

10TH

Anniversary

TM

Celebrate our anniversary with a fabulous collection of firsts....

The first Intimate Moments titles written by three of your favorite authors:

NIGHT MOVES	Heather Graham Pozzessere
LADY OF THE NIGHT	Emilie Richards
A STRANGER'S SMILE	Kathleen Korbel

Silhouette Intimate Moments is proud to present a FREE hardbound collection of our authors' firsts—titles that you will treasure in the years to come from some of the line's founding members.

This collection will not be sold in retail stores and is available only through this exclusive offer. Look for details in Silhouette Intimate Moments titles available in retail stores in May, June and July.

SIMANN

Take 4 bestselling love stories FREE

Plus get a FREE surprise gift!

Silhouette®

SPECIAL EDITION®

COMING NEXT MONTH

#805 TRUE BLUE HEARTS—Curtiss Ann Matlock
Rough-and-tumble cowboy Rory Breen and mother of two
Zoe Yarberry knew that getting together was unwise. But
though their heads were telling them no, their hearts . . .

#806 HARDWORKING MAN—Gina Ferris
Family Found
The first time private investigator Cassie Browning met
Jared Walker, he was in jail. Cassie soon discovered that
clearing Jared's name and reuniting him with his family
were easier tasks than fighting her feelings for him!

#807 YOUR CHILD, MY CHILD—Jennifer Mikels
When confirmed bachelor Pete Hogan opened his door to
Anne LeClare and her child, he thought he was saving them
from a snowstorm. But the forecast quickly changed to sunny
skies when they offered him the chance for love.

#808 LIVE, LAUGH, LOVE—Ada Steward
Jesse Carder had traveled far to rekindle the flames of an old
love—until she met sexy Dillon Ruiz. Dillon brought Jesse's
thoughts back to the present, but was their future possible?

#809 MAN OF THE FAMILY—Andrea Edwards
Tough cop Mike Minelli had seen Angie Hartman on the screen as
a former horror movie queen! Now he sensed vulnerable Angie
was hiding more than bad acting in her past!

#810 FALLING FOR RACHEL—Nora Roberts
That Special Woman!
Career-minded Rachel Stanislaski had little time for matters of the
heart. But when handsome Zackary Muldoon entered her life,
Rachel's pulse went into overtime!